THE
DEVIL
IN
DISGUISE
A BAD THINGS NOVEL

New York Times and *USA Today* Bestselling Author

CYNTHIA EDEN

This book is a work of fiction. Any similarities to real people, places, or events are not intentional and are purely the result of coincidence. The characters, places, and events in this story are fictional.

Published by Cynthia Eden.

Cover art and design by: Sweet 'N Spicy Designs

Proof-reading by: J. R. T. Editing

PROLOGUE

The Way It All Began…Maybe…

Once upon a time, twin boys were born. One was predicted to be a bearer of light, the destined ruler who would protect all humans. He would fly through the skies and guard from above. He would be on the side of good. The righteous.

The other twin…his fate was to be much darker. No goodness was seen in his future. Witches feared him on first sight. Seers turned away, shuddering at the visions they saw.

Because he was born for darkness. Every creature that hid in the night would bow to him. He would rule them. The world would fear him.

He would do very, very bad things.

Time passed. The boys grew up. They lost their humanity and became something far, far more.

One was good…wings spread from his back. Angels bowed to him.

And his brother…

He had a really fucking good time as he did his very, very bad things.

CHAPTER ONE

The whiskey burned as it slid down his throat. Luke Thorne loved that little sting. He'd always thought pain could be enjoyable, and the burn that came from a twenty-three-year-old whiskey? Damn good.

He rolled back his shoulders as his gaze swept over the bar. More of a dive really, one right at the tip of Key West. Music was blaring and laughter filled the air, but he could still hear the thunder of the waves right outside. The scent of salt air teased his nose, a scent he liked far better than the bitter odors of sweat and cheap perfume that lingered in the air around him.

Humans were in the bar. Gyrating. Seducing. Boring the ever-loving-hell out of him. He'd thought a visit to the human nightspot would take his mind off his troubles. He'd been wrong.

They're so clueless. They have no idea of the danger that is sitting right in front of them all. One wave of his hand, one whispered order, and everyone in that bar would be dead.

"You want another?" the bartender asked him.

Luke wasn't sure how many he'd had so far. But, hey, why not? He tapped the bar top and tossed down more money. One good thing about this dive…

It was the only place in Florida that had his drink of choice. Because he *paid* the bartender to keep his whiskey in stock.

His finger drummed against the bar. The whiskey wasn't calming his mind. He was still too torn up over the recent battle. The vampires and the werewolves were pissing him off. Soon enough, he'd have to put a stop to their little wars.

And that meant he'd be killing someone.

I need more than a drink. His gaze slid to the women dancing near the small stage. Women in barely-there skirts and too tiny tops. *Maybe I could use a fuck.*

As if sensing his gaze, one of the women looked his way. A redhead. Her green eyes widened as their stares locked. She seemed helpless to look away.

Because she was.

That was just part of his power. His appeal. What he wanted…he got.

Someone stepped in front of him, blocking his gaze so that he couldn't see the redhead any longer. Annoyance flashed through him and a growl built in his throat. How the fuck dare anyone—

"Trust me, you'll like me better."

Her voice was like sin. Husky and soft. Tempting and sexy.

She was small, delicate, and wearing the best-looking fuck-me high heeled shoes that he'd seen in ages. Red shoes. Devil red. His favorite color.

Nice.

His gaze drifted up her legs—long legs wonderfully bared by the skirt she wore, one that was even tinier than the redhead's had been. Her hips flared and her breasts—oh, he liked what he saw. Full and firm.

"Want to look all the way up?" she asked.

His gaze rose to her face.

And he found he couldn't look away.

She had the bluest eyes that he'd ever seen. Bright, bright blue. Framed by dark lashes. Lashes that were as dark as the curtain of black hair that surrounded her face. Her lips were red and plump, her forehead high, her nose long and straight.

She wasn't perfect—he told himself that twice, but he'd never liked perfect. This woman…she was better than boring perfection.

Sexy. Alluring.

Stunning. Her features just came together in a way that made him think of sex appeal. Pouty lips, bedroom eyes, sharp cheekbones…

Not pretty.

So much better.

"Buy me a drink?" she prompted him.

He'd buy her anything she wanted, as long as she kept talking. The sound of her voice seemed to slide right through him, igniting a hunger, a dark need that heated his body. His cock was hard and eager, and the night—oh, yes, it was definitely looking up. He motioned to the bartender. "Get this lovely lady anything she wants."

The lovely lady in question smiled at him and…dimples winked in her cheeks. He blinked at the sight, a bit bemused. The dimples were an odd touch of…innocence…when the rest of her was so seductive.

"The lady just wants a beer," she said as she glanced at the bartender. The bartender—Eli Nabb—was staring at her with the same sort of bemused fascination on his face that Luke felt.

Interesting.

Eli popped open a beer bottle and pushed it across the bar.

The woman came closer to Luke, and when she reached for the beer bottle, her body brushed against his.

The need he felt for her spiked even more.

She nodded her thanks to Eli, then said, "Nice tat." Her gaze was on the dark spider tattoo that marked the side of Eli's throat. Eli was tall and thin, and his shoulders usually hunched forward as if he were expecting a blow. Luke knew about the secrets that the guy carried — secrets like that dark tattoo — and he understood exactly why the fellow had decided to hide out in Key West.

You thought I'd keep you safe…if you kept my favorite whiskey coming. An interesting arrangement. One that had, so far, worked out for both men.

"You need anything else?" Eli asked Luke, his voice gravelly.

Luke glanced back at the woman. Actually, he thought he had everything he needed, right there. Luke pushed some cash toward the other man. "I'm good." Then he focused on his new prize.

"What's your name?" she asked. She brought the bottle up to that sexy red mouth of hers. Took a long sip. Then licked her lips.

He could have helped her out with that licking. He *would* help her. "Luke." The name came out as a growl. "Luke Thorne."

She took another long sip.

"And who are you?" he asked her.

She put the bottle back on the bar. Her hand curled around Luke's neck as she leaned in toward him. He was sitting on a bar stool and she'd slid between his legs. A dangerous place to be.

Staring him straight in the eye, she said, "I'm the woman you're taking back to your place tonight."

Direct as hell. No games. He *loved* that.

The werewolves and the vampires and their dumb ass battles could wait. He was about to have fun with the gorgeous creature before him.

His hand rose. His fingers curled around her chin and she — she gave a quick, nervous jerk. Luke frowned. "Are you all right?"

Her breath whispered out. "Let's get out of here. Take me to your place."

The words seemed to hum through him and Luke found himself nodding. Getting her out of there, getting her alone — best idea *ever* to him. But first...

His fingers were still on her chin. He tilted her head back, leaned in even closer as he brought his mouth near hers. He'd take a taste first because he had a feeling she was going to be —

"Not yet." Her finger pressed to his lips. "Once we're alone, then I'll give you that kiss. I'm not exactly the public display type."

Luke blinked.

She pulled her hand away from him and stepped back. "Are you ready?"

"No."

Surprise flashed on her face.

He picked up the whiskey glass near him. "This is the kind of drink that should be savored."

Her hair—so thick and dark—slid over her shoulders. "I'm the kind of woman who should be savored."

He believed that. He drained his glass, loving that burn, loving that little flash of pain. Sometimes, he needed that pain to remind him that he was still alive. After all of the long years he'd spent walking the earth—fucking centuries—sometimes a fog surrounded him and it was hard to *feel*.

But he suspected he'd be feeling that night, with her.

He caught her hand in his and led her to the door. People moved out of his way as if by instinct—and because of the little psychic push he gave them. He wasn't in the mood to be slowed down. Not while she was with him.

The bouncer held the door open for him and Luke stepped into the night. Hot and dark, perfect for him. He kept his grip on her and walked to the side of the building—and when he was sure no one was close, he caged her against that wooden wall.

"Wh-what are you doing?"

His eyes narrowed. In the dark, he could see her perfectly. One of his many gifts. His hand rose and his fingers curled around her neck.

She gave a quick gasp and he felt the frantic flutter of her pulse beneath his touch. Only he was willing to bet that wild beat wasn't due to arousal.

Fear.

Why the hell would she approach him if she was scared? "You knew who I was before you even came across that bar."

She stared at him.

"Why?" Luke demanded. "Why come to me?"

"Maybe I'm one of those women that likes a man with a dark edge."

Oh, he knew plenty about darkness.

"But the why doesn't really matter," she added, staring up at him. And as he looked into her eyes — that incredible blue — he swore that her words seemed to echo in his mind and…

Her eyes took on a faint glow in the dark.

Luke shook his head. His thumb caressed her throat, sliding in small circles against her skin.

And that glow got even brighter.

She isn't human. No human had eyes that could do that. And since she wasn't human…

I don't have to play the nice guy. "If you like a dark edge, sweetheart, then you had better prepare for one fun night."

Again, her pulse kicked beneath his touch. Standing so close to her — without all of the other cloying scents that had been in the bar — he smelled a sweet, light fragrance. Strawberries. She smelled just like strawberries.

"I want a taste," he whispered and Luke bent toward her. Right before his lips touched hers, her hands flew up and pressed to his chest. But she didn't push him back. Didn't shove him away.

Her lips were closed when his mouth touched hers. Soft and silky, plump and perfect…he pressed his mouth to hers, then he licked the crease of her lips.

She gave that little gasp again, a sound that he was coming to find quite sexy, and her lips parted. His tongue thrust into her mouth, going after that sweetness. Exploring, seducing, and claiming as he kissed her against the side of that building. His body pushed against hers. He trapped her against the wooden wall.

And he enjoyed the hell out of her mouth. Tasting—taking. She kissed him back with a sensual hunger that was a damn beautiful thing, a soft glide of her tongue against his, a lick, the press of her lips to his, the faint moan she gave in the back of her throat and then—

"No." She'd pulled her mouth from his. Her breath came out in little pants. "Not here. I told you…" She stared up at him with those too bright blue eyes. "I told you that I want to go to your home. Take me there."

He backed away. His dick shoved against the front of his jeans and the need he felt for her was clawing his insides apart. But she'd said not there…

Luke offered his hand to her. "I live on an island nearby. There's a boat waiting for me — it can take us over."

"G-good." The faintest stutter. She put her hand in his. A soft hand. Delicate.

His fingers tightened around hers and he led her toward the dock. Luckily for him — and his growing hard-on, the dock was just a few yards from the bar. As a general rule, Luke didn't normally bring a guest back to his island. Having a guest wasn't the safest of plans considering the friends who made a habit of staying at his place but…

One night wouldn't hurt.

"Devil's Prize," she murmured, reading the name of his sports yacht when they stopped at the edge of the wooden dock. The yacht was a real beauty. Forty feet of pure fun.

She turned, studying him with her head cocked. "Are you the devil?"

"Only if hell's on earth." He jumped onto the boat and then turned back for her. His hands curled around her waist. She stared at him, and he saw the surprise on her face.

Luke smiled. He kept his hands on her, but didn't lift his mystery woman onto the boat, not yet.

Footsteps rushed behind him. "Boss?" Marcos Mantez called. Marcos was his driver for the night. A retired Navy man who'd wanted to vanish in the Florida Keys, Marcos didn't ask any unnecessary questions and the guy could captain any boat with ease. Two important requirements for any captain Luke hired. "You going back early tonight?"

Luke didn't look away from his prey. "Indeed, I am." He lifted her onto the boat. His strength was enhanced, far greater than a normal man could ever imagine. Even though the delectable woman with him wasn't human, he'd still have to be careful with her.

He had to be careful with all of his lovers.

"I'll get us underway." Marcos hurried toward the dock, moving to untie the ropes that kept them in place.

"I think I should get your name now," Luke said, giving her a brief smile. "Otherwise, things will get awkward later."

"Why?" The wind caught her hair, teasing it, blowing it around her face. "It's not like we're planning to see each other past the night. Why can't we just be two strangers coming together? Isn't that the way these things work?"

These things. She'd done it again. Slipped up just the slightest bit. She looked like a femme fatale, pure sex in motion, but little tells kept giving her away.

She wasn't what she was pretending to be.

His jaw set. "Tell me your name or I'll leave you on this dock."

Her eyes narrowed. "No, you won't." Her voice, if possible, had gone even huskier. It was like a sensual stroke right over him.

She was right, he wasn't about to leave her. But he wanted her name.

Marcos brushed past him and headed to take the wheel.

"Mina," she said, glancing away from him. "My friends call me Mina."

He caught her hand in his, brought it to his lips, and pressed a kiss to her knuckles. Because he was watching her so closely, Luke saw the little shiver that slid over her skin. "We aren't going to be friends." Just so there would be no confusion.

Her gaze skittered back toward him.

He held that blue stare a moment, then smiled. "We're going to be fucking insane lovers."

CHAPTER TWO

Minalynn James — truly "Mina" to the few friends she possessed — tried to take deep breaths — a whole lot of them. Her stomach was in knots, her hands were sweating, and she could *not* let the walking sex god beside her realize just how terrified she really was.

Lucien Thorne. She'd found him. Finally. She'd only been searching for the guy…oh, for the last *five* years. For a while, she hadn't even been certain he was real. Most folks thought he was just the stuff of legend, a nightmare character used to terrify and control those who would threaten the paranormal status quo.

Mina knew all about paranormals. A lot of humans didn't. They were blissfully ignorant. She didn't have that luxury. Mostly because she wasn't human.

The boat was rushing across the water, Lucien — Luke — was staring at her as if he wanted to devour her, and she was trying to figure out how *not* to get herself killed. Because if she made the wrong move with him…

Well, she knew what happened to his enemies.

But I've got this. I can control him. I've proven that already.

"We're almost there," he murmured.

Her eyes squeezed closed. His voice — sure, it didn't have the power that hers did, but that deep, hard rumble was sexy. She hadn't expected that. She hadn't expected to find *anything* about the guy to be sexy.

After all, Luke was the big bad monster that the paranormal world feared. Immortal, incredibly powerful, capable of controlling all the dark magic out there...he was rumored to be *pure* evil.

Evil wasn't sexy to her.

But...

Lucien was.

Tall, probably around six foot two or six foot three, the guy totally dwarfed her. And he was strong — not in a bursting-at-the-seams body builder kind of way, but...with wide shoulders. A broad chest. And, the way that shirt was sticking to him as the wind battered against them...*looks like a twelve pack going on there.*

His hair was thick and black. And his eyes — they were so dark and deep. When she'd first looked into them, she'd almost forgotten to breathe. He had a little cleft in his chin, a slightly hawkish nose, and lips that should have looked a little cruel but…

Sexy. He just comes across as sexy. His appeal seemed to fill the very air around him.

Yes, so she'd seriously miscalculated when it came to that part of the equation. The plan had been for him to want her. For him to be putty in her hands, but when Luke had kissed her…

She'd wanted to jump his bones.

Mina cleared her throat and tried to *focus.* She'd come too far to screw this up now. "Not many men have their own islands."

"I'm not many men."

Well, technically, she didn't think he *was* a man. He was a whole lot more.

"How big is the island?" But she already knew. The place was—

"Just over a hundred acres. It's the biggest private island off the coast of the Keys."

It was a freaking *billion* dollar island and she could see it—right up ahead. A massive house was illuminated on the island, full of glass windows that shined out light. Gorgeous. Like something right out of a magazine.

Who would have thought hell would be so pretty?

The captain hurriedly secured the vessel and then Luke was walking her toward the dock. She scrambled out of the boat quickly, mostly because she didn't want him putting his hands on her again, not yet, anyway. She needed to think.

Step one…a very, very big step one had been getting to the island.

Step two…that would be getting him alone. Convincing him that he had to give her a very special prize that she knew he kept inside his home.

A treasure, of sorts. Though some said it was supposed to be more of a curse.

"What's the rush?" Luke asked as he moved behind her. The guy's steps were perfectly steady on the dock. "We have all night."

No, they didn't have all night. Because if he found out that she was working him, the guy would—well, she didn't know what he'd do. But it wouldn't be good.

"I just want to be alone with you," she said, turning to look at him from beneath her lashes. She made sure to inject power into her voice. No one had ever been able to resist her before, and he was showing signs of being just as susceptible as other men. So much for the all-powerful Luke Thorne. "Take me into your home."

"Of course." He offered his arm to her. Very gentlemanly-like, but she didn't think there was anything at all of the gentleman in him. It was his eyes that gave him away. They stared at her with a predatory intensity.

He slowed his steps to match hers. A good thing considering the heels she wore should have been lethal weapons. She'd been focusing with all her might on not wobbling in them. Men liked sexy shoes, right? So she'd upped the sexy ante in order to catch Luke's attention. But, since that first glance at the bar, he really hadn't looked at the high heels again.

But he did keep staring into her eyes, and...

He opened the door to the house. *Mansion. It is more of a mansion than anything else.*

"You don't keep it locked?" she blurted. Seriously, what in the hell?

He laughed. "I own the island." And, with his left hand, he gestured around him. "I know every person who comes and goes."

Right. Got it. "You have security cameras in place."

He leaned toward her. His scent—masculine, crisp, and with the faintest hint of the ocean—teased her. "Even better. I've got the best guard dogs on earth."

Guard dogs? She tensed. Her voice wasn't going to do anything to help charm guard dogs. Her power didn't work on animals. "They're locked up right now, aren't they?" She wasn't able to control the nervous hitch that broke through her words.

He pushed open the door. "Um."

Um wasn't an answer. She hurried in after him, nearly tripping, dammit, in her shoes. Ridiculous heels. "*Tell me…are the dogs chained up?*"

His dark head angled back toward her. He had the most gorgeous, golden hued skin. "Of course not. If they're locked up, how would they protect my island? Besides, beasts like to roam free."

A shudder worked along her body. She hadn't come prepared for the dogs.

Immediately, Luke wrapped his arm around her and drew her closer to his body. "You're cold."

No, she was terrified. Big difference.

"I can warm you up." His voice was low and seductive and she had no doubt that the guy could probably warm every woman on the planet. Luke Thorne was pure sex appeal, and she was not immune to him at all. When he'd been kissing her, Mina was pretty sure that her toes had been curling. Unacceptable. *Wrong*. Because he was wrong.

They were in the foyer of his home. A glittering chandelier was overhead, and she was standing on gleaming white marble. The place even smelled expensive.

"How about I take you up to my bedroom?" Luke offered. "I'm sure you will be plenty warm there."

His touch was pretty much already singing her. As close as she was to his body, there was no way for Mina to miss Luke's arousal. And if she went up that curving staircase with him…She swallowed. "A tour," Mina blurted.

His brows rose.

So she tried again, injecting as much power into her voice as she could. *"Take me on a tour of your house. Show me everything. All your secrets."* Because she had to find one secret item in particular, and she figured it was probably hidden in a very sturdy safe some place.

He blinked at her. For a moment, Luke looked confused. She figured the confusion was probably due to two reasons. Reason one…

No woman had ever turned down an invitation to his bedroom.

Reason two…

Is this the first time you've ever been under someone else's control?

She was willing to bet it was. After all, Luke was a very, very powerful being. He was rumored to control the darkness in the world. To control all the creatures that used that dark…

Vampires. Werewolves. Demons.

And even people like me. Because despite her efforts—all her life—Mina knew the truth about herself. She wasn't good. No, she was far, far from good. That was why she was there…about to literally rob the Lord of the Dark.

She just hoped her plan didn't go to shit.

He was still staring at her. She smiled at him and let her body lean into his. Mina ran her index finger over his chest. "I'd love to know everything about you...please show me your home."

His jaw locked. "I know just where we can start."

If he said the bedroom again...

He backed away. Offered her his hand. "Did you know the back wing of the house used to be a prison?"

A what now? Her fingers linked with his. "N-no, I didn't."

"Dry Tortugas isn't far from here." He looked back at her. "Ever been there?"

"No." This was her first trip to the Keys. But she knew about Dry Tortugas. "That's the National Park, right?" She tried not to gawk as he led her through the house. She could practically smell the money in the air. Giant pieces of artwork were perfectly hung, expensive vases gleamed, thick rugs cradled her heels...apparently, it paid very, very well to rule the dark.

"Dry Tortugas is a National Park now, yes, but during the Civil War, the fort on Dry Tortugas was used as a prison." His fingers tightened around hers. "What most people don't know is that a prison was also built on *this* island, too. But the prison here wasn't for Union deserters. It was for people who committed much, much darker crimes."

There was a door up ahead. Only it wasn't fancy like the others in the house. It seemed to be a big, heavy metal door. A keypad was near the doorknob. Luke paused a moment and typed in a code. There was a little beep and then the door opened.

He waved her forward.

She didn't move. Mina gave a nervous laugh. "I'm not like...walking through the doorway to hell or anything, am I?" She asked the question just to be safe.

His head cocked as he studied her. "This is the second time you've mentioned hell to me." He paused a beat. "Any particular reason why?"

Mina swallowed. "No. Sorry." And she squared her shoulders and walked through that doorway. Immediately, the world grew darker. There were no more fancy rugs. No more glittering chandeliers or beautiful artwork. She was in a rough, carved stone tunnel. Old, so old...the air itself felt stale. The door clanged shut behind her and Mina jumped.

"Hope I didn't scare you," Luke murmured.

You do. You scare me a whole lot. I just can't let that fear stop me. "Don't be silly," she said, tossing her hair over her shoulder — Mina thought that was a rather nice touch. "What's frightening about you?" *Only everything.*

His body slid past hers in that narrow tunnel. There were lights on the stone floor — faint lights that seemed to just come out from the stone itself. Because those lights were down so low, shadows filled the area. It felt tight, too compacted and —

He was leaving her. Never, *ever* let it be said that Luke Thorne was a gentleman. Behind him, she glowered, then Mina's heels clicked as she double-timed it to keep up with him.

Soon the tunnel was ending. Another door waited, with another keypad. Only this door was thicker than the one before. Once more, she gave a nervous laugh when he typed in the code. "Just what kind of criminals needed to be kept here, exactly?" And *why* was there a modern key code set up at an old prison?

Because, obviously, he still uses this place.

She'd been looking for a safe that hid his most valuable possessions. She'd used her power to compel Luke to show her his *secrets.* So maybe he used the old prison as his safe now. Excitement had her heart racing.

The door swung inward but Luke had turned to face her. His gaze — hooded — swept over her. "Very, very bad criminals." His voice was even rougher now. "The kind of criminals that needed to be locked away from the rest of the world."

Her goosebumps were huge. Every instinct she had screamed for Mina to run. She felt as if she were in the scary movies she'd watched so much as a teen. She was the heroine, about to make a seriously stupid move. She should run away. Run, run but…

I can't leave. I need that treasure too badly. More than just her life was at stake.

So she pasted a broad smile on her face and stepped right up to him. Her breasts pressed to his chest and her fingers skimmed down his arm. "What do you know about being bad?" She injected just the right note of flirtation in her voice. Just the right hint of sly seduction that would whisper through his mind and control him.

He leaned toward her and she felt his body tense. "Everything," he told her, his voice so dark and sinister.

And she believed him.

Her heart stuttered in her chest for a moment, but she rose onto her toes. Mina pressed a light, teasing kiss to his lips. "Then maybe you can show me."

His eyes — they seemed to change. To shine. His stare hardened with promise. "I will."

She licked her lips, a quick, nervous swipe of her tongue, and he gave a little growl.

I am so out of my depth.

She had to keep her control, for just a little bit longer. He was blocking that doorway. She needed him to move. "Take me inside," she said.

His head inclined. "Only if you promise the same for me."

He had *not* just said that to her – she barely stopped her jaw from dropping but he was…laughing now. A rough, almost sinister chuckle and he'd turned to step through that doorway. His fingers had locked around her wrist, and he pulled her after him. Her eyes widened, straining to see in the darker room. Only…it wasn't just a room.

It was a massive space. Big, wide and *not* filled with the treasures that she'd hoped. *Dammit.*

There were cells in that room. Prison cells. The bars were thick and heavy, gleaming as if they were made of silver. Her frantic gaze swung around but, luckily, no one was *in* those cells.

They were empty, as if they were just waiting.

And, quite suddenly, she had an idea. A wicked one, for a wicked man.

"Your turn," Luke said.

Her turn? She looked over her shoulder at him, and the desire on his face told her exactly what he wanted.

Only if you promise to do the same for me. His words rang through her head once more.

Tricky devil. But Mina had her town tricks. She thrust back her shoulders and walked inside the nearest cell. The door was wide open. No furniture was inside the cell — it was empty and yawning and being inside was creepier than all hell but she walked right to the middle of the cell. She turned to face Luke. She smiled at him and then she crooked her finger.

He raised one dark brow.

"Oh, come on...surely you have a...dark side," Mina said.

Luke didn't smile. "You have no idea."

Oh, she had plenty of ideas. But he wasn't coming forward. She needed him to get his ass in there. "Come kiss me," Mina invited. No, an invitation wouldn't work. "*Come and kiss me*," she ordered him.

He stalked toward her, moving with a slow, dangerous grace. His gaze never left hers, and there was no missing the hunger in his stare, a wild desire that would have terrified her, if she hadn't thought that she could keep controlling him. But she *could* keep up that control. For just a little while longer, anyway.

His hand lifted and sank into her hair, tipping her head back. His other arm curled around her waist, pulling her forward.

And he kissed her.

He nearly *devoured* her.

In all of Mina's twenty-eight years, she'd never been kissed quite that way. With a passion that burned through her whole body. With a need that made her ache. He wasn't careful or gentle. Luke was rough and domineering and the guy could just use his tongue so, so well.

Her fingers curled around his shoulders. The plan had been to distract him but…surely, kissing him just a little longer wouldn't hurt.

Just a little…longer…

He knew how to kiss. How to use his tongue. How to lick. How to make her body ignite. He pulled her closer and she barely felt it when his fingers trailed down to the hem of her shirt. She was just—lost to that kiss. Enjoying him, letting herself go when she *shouldn't*.

Then she felt the quick touch of air on her skin. He'd lifted up her shirt. His fingers—warm and slightly callused at the tips—were on her bare skin and she—she liked his touch. She wanted his fingers to keep rising. She wanted his fingers on her breasts, wanted her whole body naked while he touched her and—

Naked.

She pushed against his chest. Stared into his eyes. In that gleaming stare, she saw her own desire staring back at her, and Mina wondered just what sort of powers Luke truly possessed. Because he was certainly making her lose her reason.

All for a kiss.

She had to stop him. No, she had to stop *herself*. "Strip," she said, and there was more than seduction and power in her voice. There was desperation because she was losing herself. So very fast. "Strip for me, Luke."

He smiled. Oh, that smile was trouble. Slow and seductive, it stretched his lips. Then he said, "Only if you promise to do the same for me."

The same words he'd given her before. She didn't speak, mostly because she didn't trust herself to lie right then. She did manage a stumbling nod.

He moved away from her, circling around her body, putting himself in just the position that she'd wanted.

Now she stood between him and the cell door. So close...

His hands went to the buttons on his shirt. Staring at her, he slowly began to unbutton them.

She took a step back.

More golden skin was revealed. Strong muscles. That definite twelve pack she'd suspected. Her mouth got very, very dry.

The shirt hit the floor.

And his hands went to his pants.

"*Keep going.*" The order was for him and for herself. Because this was her chance. His head tilted down as he started to unhook his belt.

She bolted for the cell door.

"Mina?" Her name was a question.

She slammed the door shut. The key was still in the lock — she'd seen that when she first walked into the cell. A shiny new key and lock on a cell that *shouldn't* have even been there. But it was — it was a prison in a modern-day paradise and she was going to use that cell to her advantage. *Cell. Cage. Same thing right now.*

"*Mina!*" Now her name was a roar — an infuriated bellow. He ran for the door.

She yanked the key to the side, locking the cell and she jerked that key back, tumbling away even as his hand shot through the bars. He came inches away from grabbing her shirt-front. She fell, landing hard on her ass as she stared up at him.

Rage poured from his eyes. Hot and scorching. "Unlock the cell."

She shook her head, honestly too terrified to speak in that moment. Power seemed to crackle in the air around him.

His hand slid back through the bars. He stared at her, his rage just deepening.

"Sweetheart," the word was a growl, not an endearment. "You don't want me for an enemy."

Too late, she was pretty sure he already was her enemy. She backed away from him, moving like a crab until she hit the wall. Then she started hauling herself up, hoping her trembling knees would straighten up. Her hand slammed into some kind of — of button on the wall. A button she hadn't even seen but she felt the depression beneath her fingers.

A slow stream of gas spread into the cell that caged Luke. He looked up at the gas. "Fucking hell."

Uh, oh. She started to choke on the gas. It was burning her eyes, her mouth, her —

"Get out, sweetheart. Get the fuck out now," he ordered her. His eyes still gleamed. "When I wake up…I'm coming for you."

She stumbled toward the heavy door, that gas was still burning her, and when she looked back at him —

Luke had sunk to his knees in that cell. "Get out," he gritted at her.

She frowned. He was…protecting her? No, no, that didn't make any sense. She covered her mouth and ran to the doorway. She entered that little tunnel and felt the rush of cool air around her body. Air was being pumped into the tunnel — she could feel it. Not stale air, not any longer. Fresh and clear. She gulped it greedily.

Then she thought about Luke.

And she wondered just what she'd done to him. Careful now, Mina tip-toed back into the area that held all of those cells. She didn't hear the hiss of the gas any longer. But her eyes started to burn and…

Luke was in his cell. On the floor. Not moving.

Did I just kill the Lord of the Dark?

She raced toward him, only realizing right then that her left hand still clutched the key to his cell. She shoved the key in the lock, she started to open that cell.

And his body began to jerk.

Mina froze.

CHAPTER THREE

"Are you okay?" The voice floated to Luke. Worried, scared.

Most people were scared when they talked to him. If they were sane, anyway.

He wasn't so sure *she* was sane.

"Please don't be dead. I mean, I know you're not dead, I can see your body moving but...don't *die*. That's what I meant. Please don't die on me. I need you."

Did she? How very interesting. He put his hands down on the stone floor. Hands that still belonged to a man, not a beast. For the moment.

"You're moving again," she said, relief thickening the words. "That's good."

Good for him. Not so good for her. Luke opened his eyes and stared at her through the bars. He was on his hands and knees, crouched like an animal. And she stood there, so dangerously close to the cell, her eyes wide and worried. Her face was still as beautiful as before, a face made for seduction, and her body was the

best fucking temptation he'd seen in ages but…
"Your voice is different."

She blinked at him. Her eyes weren't shining
with power right then. *Because I'd been
unconscious? Because she hadn't needed to work her
magic on me when I was out fucking cold?*

Her lips parted. She was about to speak — and
he strongly suspected the woman was about to
try and control him again. *Sorry, sweetheart. Not
happening.*

In an instant, he'd sprung across the cell. She
cried out in surprise — the only sound she was
able to make — before his hands shot through the
cell. One hand locked around her waist. *That's
what happens when you stand too close.* And the
other slapped over her mouth, smothering her
cries.

She stared at him in absolute horror, her eyes
wide and desperate. "I had two options," he told
her. "I could have locked my fingers around your
throat and just squeezed…that would have
stopped you from talking, too."

At those words, her gaze wasn't just
desperate, it was horrified.

His jaw locked. He…didn't like that look of
horror, not from her. Despite the shit the woman
had pulled, he didn't want her looking at him as
if he were the monster. Even if he was. "I didn't
go with that option," he muttered. "Obviously."

She twisted in his grip. He laughed. He had enhanced strength. Even the strongest shifters in the world couldn't beat him when it came to raw power. She wasn't getting away.

But, because of the way he held her, Mina's left hand was free — and just out of his reach. That left hand held the key. A key he needed.

His strength was great but the cell he was currently trapped inside of had been built — by fucking him — to hold all sorts of paranormal predators in check. He couldn't break the bars. He needed… "The key," he snapped. "Give it to me, now."

Over his hand, her wide eyes jerked to the left, as if she'd just remembered the key. Her fingers twitched when her hand moved.

"Good girl," he said, "that wasn't — "

She threw the key — threw it far out of his reach.

"Bad girl," he snarled. His hold on her tightened. "Very, very bad."

She was trying to mutter behind his hand. He shook his head. "You think I don't get it? The power is in your voice. Despite what you think, I'm not the type normally led around by my dick." Though she'd sure done that to him, *before* the gas. "So to fix this…I can just make sure you don't speak again."

That horror deepened in her stare. He growled again. She needed to stop looking at him that way. His gaze raked her. "Maybe it was the drinks...I'm not normally susceptible, not to any damn one, but you caught me on an off night." And he needed to test himself...that was why he was easing his grip on her. That was why he was moving his fingers away from her mouth. Just that reason and *not* because he wanted to ease the horror and fear in her stare.

Her breath heaved out. She stared at him, and...she didn't make a sound.

Now she gets quiet?

"Who are you?" Luke demanded.

"I-I told you...I'm Mina. Mina James."

So he'd asked the wrong question. "*What* are you?"

She stumbled away from the cell. If he went by her expression, he would have thought the question *hurt* her. He rubbed his chest. His naked chest. Luke glanced around. Right. She'd told him to strip and he'd just tossed off his shirt for her.

"What do you think I am?" Her voice was husky, sexy, but it didn't ring with the note of power he remembered. The power that had been there *before* he'd gotten knocked out by the gas.

The gas had been another one of his inventions. A bit of magic and science. Only he'd never expected to be on the receiving end of that dosage.

"Luke," she bit off his name. "What am I?"

Curious, he looked back at her. Maybe she didn't know. He wasn't one hundred percent sure himself, but he still guessed, "A siren?"

Her lips parted but no denial burst from her.

He nodded. "Makes sense. Sexy face, sexy body. Built to tempt." Once more, his gaze swept over her. *Damn.* "Every single part of you. Especially the voice." But if that were the case, then she would be under his dominion. Sirens were dark creatures. Her power *shouldn't* have worked on him. "I had too freaking much to drink," he groused. His hand rubbed over his face. And another thought struck him. "How long was I out?" Because he didn't feel even a little drunk any longer. Sure, he had an extremely fast metabolism—a nice paranormal bonus but—

"A-a while," she said. "I don't know exactly…I was afraid to leave you but…" She pulled out her phone. Stared at the screen a moment, then said, "Had to be at least two hours."

Two hours wasn't so bad. Most paranormals would have been knocked out for at least twelve. And with two hours…*I'd be able to push the alcohol out of my system.* His hands curled around the bars. "What do you want from me?"

She sucked in a sharp breath, as if gathering courage, then she looked him right in the eye again. Her eyes brightened with her power and Luke knew she was getting ready to use her magic on him. His hold tightened on the bars, his hands turning white as she said—

"I want the jewel. I need the Eye of Hell."

Silence.

She swallowed. "You *will* give me the Eye of Hell."

His right hand slowly unfurled from the bar. He lifted his hand.

She stepped toward him.

He curled his finger at her, the same way she'd done for him.

She inched closer. "You have it on you?"

"No, sweetheart, I don't."

Her shoulders fell. "But you will give it to me. You'll tell me where it is. How to use it. *You will give me the Eye—*"

Luke started laughing.

"Uh, want to share what's so funny?"

It took him a moment to quell his laughter. And, damn, but the woman was even sexy when she was mad. When she had that little furrow between her brows and her plump lips tightened and a hint of red touched her cheeks.

"Share," she blasted at him.

"You're what's funny."

The red in her cheeks deepened.

"I'm not drunk anymore."

"Yes, so?"

"So…" Luke drew out the word. "Your sexy little power doesn't work on me any longer. Not when I'm sober."

She backed up a step. A quick back-up.

"It worked when I was drunk because I'd let down my guard." Luke shook his head. "I'll make sure not to make that mistake around you again."

Her breath was coming faster. He could see the frantic jerk of her chest. "Yes," he said, considering. "You probably should be afraid. After all, if you *are* a siren, well, then that means you're *mine*." Part of the dark world that he commanded.

"I'm not yours," she whispered.

We'll see about that.

"Just give me the Eye," Mina said, almost pleading. "And you don't ever have to see me again. I'll leave you alone, I promise."

"Who said I wanted that?" Now his gaze dipped over her. "I believe there were…promises exchanged." He smiled at her, and he knew his grin would be evil. "Besides, do you truly think I'll just let you walk away from me now? You *imprisoned* me. You drugged me —"

"The gassing was an accident! I didn't mean to hit the button!"

"Like you didn't mean to lock me in this fucking cage?"

She bit her lower lip. A waste. He could do that for her.

After a moment, she gave a long exhale. "That part wasn't an accident," Mina admitted. "The whole locking-you-in thing was deliberate."

He would *not* let her charm him. But…most others would have been cowering before him in that moment. She was scared, he could smell her fear, but she was still standing up to him.

Sexy.

Dangerous.

His head cocked. "Why do you want the Eye?"

She didn't speak. *Always a bad sign when a siren doesn't speak.*

"Did I ask the wrong question?" He rolled back his shoulders. "Fine, let's try again…who is it that you want to destroy? Because that's what the Eye does. I don't know what stories you've heard, but the Eye doesn't *give* power. It takes it away." Mostly true.

Mostly.

He'd always been good at bending the truth. One of his specialties.

"I know that," she said, but she backed up another step.

"Then you're bloodthirsty." Luke nodded. "I find that trait very attractive in a woman."

Her eyes narrowed on him. "I'm pretty sure you find every trait attractive in a woman," she fired back.

He laughed. Dammit, she was fun. If he weren't currently caged…

"Why are you looking at me that way?" Mina asked, nervously tucking a lock of hair behind her ear.

"Because I want to fuck you."

Another quick back step. "That isn't happening."

It so will.

"This is what's going to happen." Her chin notched up. "You're going to tell me where I can find the Eye or I am going to leave you in that cage."

He shrugged. "Leave me here."

The furrow between her brows deepened.

"You think I don't have help coming?" He winked at her. "I do. We aren't the only ones on this island. Back-up will be here by dawn." Since he'd already been unconscious a few hours, dawn wouldn't be far away. "Then I'll be free and you…you will be *mine*."

She hurried toward the wall and her hand hovered over the button that would dispense that drugging gas once more.

He tensed.

"Tell me where the Eye is," Mina ordered him, her voice shaking just a bit. "Or you will go down."

He didn't relish another face slam into the stone. "Another dosing will kill me."

Her fingers trembled, a small, but telling movement. *Interesting.*

"Is that what you want?" Luke pushed her. "To kill me? If I'm dead, then I guess you can search my whole house for the Eye." *But you won't find it.*

"I don't want to hurt you." Her fingers hovered over the button. "I just need that Eye. Please, give it to me. *Give it to me.*"

The power was back in her voice and this time, he could feel the push against him. But…*Sorry, sweetheart. I'm in control now.* "That Eye is mine. I don't give up what's mine." *You're mine, too. You just don't realize it yet.*

I do.

She stared at him and he could have sworn tears gleamed in her eyes. Odd, most of the Dark Ones didn't cry, at least…not until after they'd suffered a whole lot of pain. "Who hurt you?" Luke asked and his own voice had gone cold and hard.

"They'll keep hurting me," she said, her voice soft now. "Unless I have the Eye. Give it to me. Please."

He couldn't. It was far more dangerous than she realized. And only he could control it. "Get me out of here. *Now.*" Because he didn't like her tears.

She glanced at the button.

"Mina…" he growled.

Her hand jerked back. "It was my last hope. I-I was desperate." Her hand raked through her hair. "I didn't want to hurt you. I don't want to hurt anyone! That's the problem—don't you see?"

He saw that she was on the edge. "Open the cell."

But Mina shook her head. "When you get free, I know you'll want your pound of flesh, but I can't give it to you." She turned away from him. "Forget me."

Impossible.

She was heading for the tunnel.

"Stop!" Luke roared and yes, that was fear inside of him. Unusual. Unwanted.

She looked back.

"You can't escape the island. Marcos left with the boat right after we walked away from the dock. He'll only come back when I call him." And he wasn't planning to make that call. "There's nowhere for you to run. I'll be out of here soon and you—"

"I'm one hell of a swimmer," she told him, even giving him a weak smile. One that made his chest ache. "I'll take my chances with the water."

His body tensed. "Going for the deep blue sea instead of the devil, huh? *Bad* choice." A choice that might just kill her.

She wasn't looking at him any longer. She was heading through the tunnel.

"You won't make it if you swim! The water's too rough! It's too far from shore!"

She wasn't stopping.

"Mina!" Luke roared her name. "*Mina!*" But she didn't look back. And soon, the sound of her footsteps had faded.

Fucking hell.

He grabbed the bars — bars that were made of silver so they'd burn werewolves, bars that had been reinforced so that even a vampire's strength couldn't break them. He grabbed those bars and he bellowed as he fought to pull them apart. *Caught in my own trap. An inescapable hell.*

Or at least…it *should* have been inescapable.

He pulled up more power and his roars echoed around him.

CHAPTER FOUR

Luke's roars and bellows followed Mina as she ran through the tunnel. She ditched her shoes because those heels were just slowing her down. She needed to run and she needed to run fast.

He said there were guard dogs on the island. The last thing she wanted was for one of those beasts to tear into her. No, actually, the *last* thing she wanted was for Luke to get her. She didn't even want to imagine what sort of punishment the Lord of the Dark would hand down to her. Probably the killing kind.

She staggered to a stop before the second metal door, the one that blocked her frantic exit from the tunnel. It was locked and the keypad blinked at her. It must have locked automatically when it had shut after her and Luke. Good thing she'd been paying attention to the code when he typed it in…

Her fingers flew over the keypad. A moment later, the lock disengaged and she was racing through the mansion. Her bare feet slipped on the marble floor, and she hurriedly steadied herself by grabbing for a big, nearby vase.

Only that vase staggered and toppled beneath her clumsy grip. It fell, shattering into a hundred pieces. Her eyes squeezed shut. *Oh, please, don't be as expensive as I think you are.* Another reason for Luke to be pissed at her.

She hopped over those broken chunks. Mina rushed to the foyer and her hand curled around the banister. Maybe she should run upstairs and search through the rooms up there for the Eye. Maybe she should search the whole house.

"*Mina!*"

That roar was louder — loud enough to reach her as she stood in the foyer.

Maybe I should cut my losses for the moment and get the hell out of here while I still can. She'd come up with another plan once she was safe. Once she was far out of Luke's range.

She yanked open the front door. It was still dark outside, but she could see the faintest edge of red in the sky. The sun would rise soon. Luke had said his back-up was coming at dawn, so she didn't have much time left.

She knew just one destination on that island — the dock. She knew how to get there and she wasn't about to leave the well-lit path. Thick vegetation was on the island, and she feared the *guard dogs* might be lurking in there.

Besides, there was always the chance that Luke had been trying to trick her. The boat could still be docked. She could hop on it and get away. Easy.

Hopefully. Maybe.

She—

A sudden growl reached her. Low and rough, and sounding way, way too close.

Mina immediately froze.

The growl came again.

This is not my night.

Her head turned, just a few inches, and she found herself staring into a pair of green eyes. *Glowing* green eyes. Those eyes stared at her from the dark vegetation.

"G-good boy?" Mina stuttered, lifting a hand in what she hoped was a let's-be-friends-doggy type of way.

But then the beast came from the dark and she saw that she wasn't dealing with a dog. Her breath heaved out.

It's a wolf. A giant, white wolf with massive fangs, saliva dripping from those fangs—and powerful muscles that were bunched and ready to attack.

"You're not a guard dog," she said, her voice barely a whisper.

Another rumble came...only this time, the sound was from behind her. *Another wolf?* Slowly, because she sure didn't want to make any fast movements that might lead to an attack, her head turned to the left.

Golden eyes. Bright, predatory.

She tried to swallow her fear. It didn't go down. It was hard for her to clearly see this threat—all she could discern were those golden eyes. Such a deep gold, with big, black pupils. "Nice wolf?"

The beast moved forward, a low, graceful movement. Power flowed from him and as he stalked closer to her, coming a bit into the light of the path, she saw that she wasn't dealing with another wolf.

Instead, a massive black panther was coming toward her. His mouth opened and when she saw his mouthful of sharp teeth…

"Oh, shit." Mina didn't try to stay still any longer. If she remained frozen, they'd just both jump her. Rip her apart right then and there.

That's what happens when you cross Luke Thorne.

She ran. As fast as she could. The panther gave a high, rumbling cry and the wolf snarled. She kept running. She could hear them behind her, the heavy pad of their paws and the scrape of their claws on the stone walkway.

She could almost feel their breath on her, but they weren't attacking. Not yet. *They're playing with me.*

The dock was up ahead. And the boat was gone.

They're playing because they think I don't have anywhere to go.

They were wrong.

Her feet pounded over the wood of the dock. She breathed fast, sucking in the air for energy.

"*Mina!*"

At the fierce cry, she staggered and looked back. Luke was there, standing about thirty feet away, his bare chest heaving and his hands clenched. He'd gotten out of his cell.

His *guards* were closing in.

There was about to be serious hell for her to pay.

As she stared at him—it just *had* to be a trick from the dim light—but she could have sworn she saw shadowy wings behind his body. Big and black, stretching out.

"Don't, Mina!" Luke yelled at her. "Don't you even think about—"

She whirled toward the churning waves. She'd already told him before. If she had a choice between the devil and the deep blue sea...

The sea would always win.

Mina jumped into the water, flying off the dock and sinking beneath those rough waves.

***

She'd jumped into the water. Water that was far too rough and vicious. Water that would pull her under and take her from him.

"No!" Luke bellowed. The wolf and panther were just fucking standing there, staring at the water. Not doing a thing to help him out.

Wolves couldn't swim for shit, so the fact that Rayce didn't jump in wasn't exactly surprising but Julian? Cats could damn well swim.

He shoved them out of his way and started to leap into the waves after her.

The panther slammed into Luke, pushing him away from the edge of the dock.

"Get your paws off me!" Luke yelled. "What the hell kind of guards are you two? The woman is going to die!"

The panther blinked its eerie golden eyes and backed up.

Luke dove into the water. He sank deep, then shoved back up—not to take in air because he could have stayed down much, much longer—but he popped to the surface so he could call for her again. "Mina!"

He didn't see her. Just saw the churning waves. They slapped against him. *Maybe she didn't come back up. Mina is still below. The water has her.* He'd warned her not to try escaping.

Luke sank beneath the waves again. It was nearly pitch black down there, but he could still see—he could always see in the dark. He looked to the left, looked to the right, searched *under* the dock in case the battering water had pushed Mina's slight body under there and she'd become trapped. He didn't see her, but he had to keep searching, had to—

Hard hands grabbed him. He spun around, and found himself staring into a pair of angry golden eyes.

Cat's eyes.

Cats can swim so well.

Only a panther hadn't grabbed him in the water. The beast had shifted back into human form. Julian pointed upward and kicked away from Luke. Then the guy's naked-ass body was flying upward. Luke followed him, breaking the surface. "She's down there!" Luke blasted as he drew in a breath. "We have to—"

"Your woman can swim," Julian Craig's rumbling voice cut through his words. He lifted his hand and pointed in the distance. "Thought you'd want to know that she was hauling ass that way."

Luke spun around, slapping the waves, and, sure enough, in the growing red glow of dawn, he saw Mina's dark head just above the waves. The woman was definitely hauling ass.

"Looks like an Olympic contender to me," said a deep, amused voice. A voice that came from the dock—Rayce Lovel's voice. "Or someone who is really, really motivated to get the hell away from you."

Luke swam back to the dock. He hauled himself up, and the water poured down his body. He was soaking wet and completely furious.

"Didn't charm her, huh?" Rayce asked, nodding his head. He wore a pair of jeans, nothing else. Like Julian, he must have shifted back to human form while Luke had been frantically searching the water. "Had to happen sooner or later, you know. Every woman you meet won't just drop her panties for you and —"

Luke grabbed him. It was an instinctual, animal attack. He locked his hand around Rayce's neck and lifted the guy up into the air, holding him easily even though Rayce was roughly his same height and shared his muscular build.

"Don't," Luke gritted out, "ever fucking talk about Mina that way to me. Not if you want to keep living. I can skin you in an instant, wolf or man."

Rayce's green eyes had widened.

The dock trembled as Julian pulled himself up. "Hey, guys…let's all take a breath here."

Luke wasn't in the mood for a breath.

Julian closed in, his steps soundless, the way they always were. "This is classic displacement," he said, his voice hinting just a bit at the British accent he couldn't ever seem to fully shake, despite the fact that he hadn't been in his homeland in years. "You aren't mad at Rayce. You're mad because that gorgeous lady just gave you the slip—"

Luke's left hand flew out and locked around Julian's neck. "I'm furious at both of you assholes because you *let her go.*"

Julian wasn't fighting him. Neither was Rayce. If they weren't fighting, then where was the fun in an attack? Snarling, he shoved them both back. "Get some clothes on."

"Hey!" Now Rayce was insulted. "Not like we can wear clothes when the beasts take over. You of all people should know that. And I *did* stop to put on jeans."

Luke just glared.

"Right, getting clothes," Julian said quickly.

"And get Marcos out here." Luke turned to stare at the reddening sky. He could still see Mina, swimming so strongly. But she wouldn't be able to keep up that pace, not for long. Good thing that Marcos just had the Devil's Prize in the dock house, right around the side of the island. He'd be there in moments. "I need to hunt."

Mina wasn't getting away. There was going to be a price for her crimes that night. He hoped she was ready to pay.

She paused in her swimming right then and glanced back at him. She bobbed in the water. The waves pounded against her, and he found himself tensing. She was too delicate to be out there. Too small. She was going to drown —

She lifted her hand. And, at first, he thought she was waving good-bye to him.

Then he realized…

She was only waving with one finger.

His lips curled. *You've got to stop doing that, sweetheart. You're just making me want you more.*

She spun away and dove beneath the waves.

***

Garrick McAdams shoved open the door at the dive bar. The scent of ocean air mixed with stale booze as he marched inside.

"We're closed!" A voice yelled, a grumpy drawl that came from behind the bar.

Eyes narrowing, Garrick headed in the direction of that voice, and as he approached, an older guy — balding, with big, bushy brows and a tattoo of a spider crawling up the side of his neck — poked his head from behind the bar.

"Didn't you hear me?" the guy groused. He was thin and tall, but he hunched over, losing a few inches. "The bar's closed. Dawn's nearly here. This shit is shut down."

Garrick tossed his ID down on the scarred bar top. "I'm looking for a woman."

The bartender laughed and the spider on his neck seemed to move — a trick of the poor light, surely. "Son, ain't we all?"

Garrick leaned toward the guy. "A specific woman. Black hair, the bluest eyes you've ever seen, about five foot four — "

"Yeah, yeah…" The bartender waved his hand and turned away. "Like I don't get hundreds of broads in this place every single day — "

He grabbed the bartender's shoulder. "You wouldn't forget her. Not after you heard her voice." After all, Mina James had a very, very unique voice.

The bartender stiffened. "Get your hand off me, buddy."

"I'm not your buddy." But he moved his hand back. His fingers tapped near his ID. "If you'd bothered to look, you'd see that I'm Special Agent Garrick Mc — "

"Big fucking deal." The bartender rubbed his hand over his neck. "You can be Special Agent Fuck Off for all I care. My bar is closed and you need to leave."

The bartender's hand fell away.

And the spider tattoo on his neck…it was about two inches away from the spot it had been in before.

Garrick smiled at the guy. "What's your name?"

The bartender was sweating. A little moisture above his upper lip. A little on his high forehead. "My name's Screw Off."

Garrick lifted his brows. "Okay, Screw Off…let me tell you how this is going to work…" He rolled back his shoulders. "You're going to tell me where Mina James is—"

"I don't know any fucking Mina James—"

"Or the agents I have waiting outside are going to storm in here." His voice lowered, heavy with a threat that he completely meant. "And they're going to take your paranormal freak-ass into custody."

The bartender blinked.

"They'll throw you into a cell, and they'll keep you there until they find out exactly what kind of secrets you're keeping. They'll lock you in tight and you won't—" He broke off, swearing, because a big, black spider had just scuttled across the bar top and headed for him.

The bartender shot back, running toward the rear of the place.

"Got a runner," Garrick snarled. He was wearing a very small ear piece, one that would have picked up and transmitted his whole conversation with the fleeing man. He knew the other agents outside would take immediate action. "Seal the back exit." He leapt over the bar top. His feet slammed into the floor and he gave chase, ducking through a small storage room and then flying to tackle the bartender before the guy could grab for the back door.

"Not ditching me, not until I get *what* I want," Garrick snapped. He hauled the bartender to his feet. The spider that had been on the guy's neck?

It was gone.

Because that damn thing came across the bar at me. Nervous now, Garrick looked around the dimly lit storage room.

"You need to let me go," the guy huffed. "You don't even want to mess with the friend I've got."

Friend? As in…singular? Like one friend was supposed to intimidate him?

"My *friends* are all waiting just behind that door." Garrick inclined his head toward the rear exit. "And one word from me and they'll throw you into that pit I mentioned. And soon enough, you *will* be talking." *They always talked.*

The guy's eyes were bulging from his head.

"Your name," Garrick demanded.

"Eli."

They were making progress. "Where's the woman, Eli? Because I know she came here." He'd already tracked her movements *to* the dive bar. He just didn't know where Mina had gone once she left the place. "Let me tell you more about Mina. She's a woman who sounded like every wet dream you've ever had. She would have looked like pure sin and when you heard her talk…you would have been ready to do anything for her."

He'd fallen into her trap a time or two himself.

Paranormals. They *couldn't* be trusted.

Eli was shaking. "H-he'll kill me…"

"Death is easy." Garrick's voice was hard and he made sure his face showed no emotion. In his line of work, emotion just got in the way. "What you'll have with us won't be easy." The words sounded like a promise. They were. "I have to find Mina James. Tell me where she is, *now.*"

"I-I don't know!"

He yanked the guy closer. *Shit…was that another spider tattoo on the back of the guy's hand?* It had better not start moving toward him. "Mina was here tonight."

And…Eli gave a grim nod. "But she left! I swear! She left!"

The spider had moved just a little, a bare inch.

Garrick shoved the bartender away from him. "Did she leave alone?"

Eli hesitated.

And we have a winner. "Mina left with a man." Figured. Probably some dumb ass that she mistakenly believed would help her. The woman had already led him on a chase all the way down to the tip of the U.S. What had she thought? That she'd get on some boat and —

"They rode off on his boat," Eli admitted.

Yeah, she'd definitely thought she could ride off into the night. She needed to think again. She was too important to his agency. The woman didn't get to vanish.

She had a job to do.

"Tell me the guy's name," Garrick ordered.

But Eli started shaking his head. Back and forth, again and again and…

More spiders were appearing on his skin. At least a dozen of them. On his hands and neck. "What are you?" Garrick asked.

But he saw the answer in Eli's wide and desperate eyes.

The guy is terrified.

And suddenly, Garrick understood. "The man she left with…you think he's the one who'll kill you?"

Eli rubbed at his hands, at the marks that appeared to be tattoos of spiders. "Y-you don't piss him off…"

"Give me his name. His name, and you walk away." A total lie, but…

Eli looked up. "You don't scare me. You're *nothing* compared to him."

The back door burst open. Other agents — two men and a woman dressed in black and wearing bullet proof vests — stood with guns drawn.

Garrick nodded to them and then glanced over at Eli. "We'll see about that." Then he pulled out his gun.

And he shot Eli, slamming the bullet right into the guy's chest. Eli went down, not making a sound as the drug pumped into his system. It was a real sweet little blend, one designed to knock out even powerful paranormals.

"The spider trick is interesting," Garrick said as he approached the fallen man. He toed the guy's leg, but Eli didn't stir. "I think my bosses would like to learn more about that." He motioned to the agents. "Take him into custody."

"Yes, sir," Timothy Lang said immediately. That was Timothy, always eager.

Garrick pointed to Madeline Slate. "Our girl disappeared with a man. Knowing Mina's taste, he'll be rich." Mina had grown up with nothing, and she was always like a little girl with her nose shoved up against a fancy window, looking inside at the world others possessed. "The guy has a boat, so we need to start checking the properties near here. Maybe a private house or…" He tapped his chin. "An island?" That would certainly mesh with a rich man's lifestyle. The mystery man had to be rich *and* powerful…because Eli had feared the guy. Garrick nodded as he considered the options. "Yeah, let's pull up a listing of the private islands around here." He knew they dotted the area. "Mina's close by, and we're going to find her."

She was far too fucking valuable to lose.

He stepped over Eli and headed for the back door. "Oh…" Garrick looked over his shoulder.

Timothy was crouched near the fallen man. He was reaching for Eli's hands, getting ready to cuff the guy.

"Mind the spiders," Garrick advised him. "I'm pretty sure they bite."

Timothy's eyes widened in horror as he looked down at their perp.

Paranormals. Just when he thought he had them figured out…

Something new lands in my path.

Something new…once upon a time, Mina had been his something new. Mina had been *his.*

Then she'd fled.

He walked outside and saw the red sky. *Red sky in the morning…sailors take warning.* The old saying slipped through his mind and he smiled. It wasn't the sailors out there who needed to take warning. Mina needed to be on guard. Because he was coming for her.

She wouldn't get away from him. Not ever again.

CHAPTER FIVE

"How long has she been in the water?" Marcos yelled as he raised his voice over the roar of the wind and the waves.

Too long. Luke's jaw was clenched tightly. He stood near the search light, moving it back and forth across the waves. She'd been dipping beneath the water a lot, and he'd lost sight of her again. Mina needed to pop her head back up, right the hell then.

"She can sure hold her breath a long time," Rayce muttered. He sounded nervous. Rare for the wolf shifter.

She'd better be holding her breath. Luke's hands shoved the spotlight to the left and — "There!" he bellowed. "Port side!"

She was bobbing in the water, caught now in the bright light. Her dark hair was slicked back and her hands circled gently at her sides. She should have looked terrified. Should have looked like a damn drowned rat after that frantic swim in those rough waves.

But…

She didn't.

With the light on her, her eyes shined, hinting at her paranormal powers. Her skin seemed to glow. In that water, she was even more beautiful than she'd been on land. Not struggling, not desperate to stay afloat…

She just drifted there, ever so easily, as if she'd just been waiting for him.

"Uh…Luke?" The worry was deeper in Rayce's voice. "Just what are we dealing with here?"

He wasn't touching that one, not yet. He let go of the light. The sky was a red right then, deep like blood, and soon, more of the sun would be falling onto them. He probably would have found her without the search light, but Marcos had insisted they use it. Marcos…a by-the-book human if Luke had ever met one.

"How long has she been in the water?" Marcos asked again. Everyone on the damn boat was worried about Mina, that was obvious.

"She's been in there long enough." It was time for her to come back to him. Luke took a deep breath and leapt over the side of that boat. He sliced into the water, powerful, deep strokes.

He thought she'd run from him. But…

She waited.

This time, anyway. Maybe she was more tired than she looked.

Luke closed in on her. She stayed right there, swimming so easily. But...

The closer he got to her, he realized that her body was tense. And her gaze darted nervously around her, as if searching those dark depths below her.

"Stay the fuck there," he growled. He was so close to her.

"G-get back on your boat," she told him and there was fear quaking in her voice. Yes, she needed to be afraid of him. She needed — "Sh-shark." Her stutter came again. "It brushed against me. You need to get out of the water and get back on the boat."

He paused, just the smallest of hesitations. *A shark wouldn't dare take a bite out of me.* Most creatures — those on land and on sea — recognized him for what he was. A primitive awareness of danger.

Humans, though, they were the exception. They always foolishly ignored their primal instincts. They chose to ignore the warning signs that went off in their heads when he was near. They didn't acknowledge the danger he presented to them, not until it was too late.

But Mina...she wasn't afraid of him in that moment. The woman actually seemed afraid *for* him. What an unusual twist.

His hand grabbed her shoulder. He pulled her closer to him. Their bodies brushed beneath the water.

"Shark," she said again, and her whole body was shaking. "I-I saw its fin…it came right up to me. *Bumped* me. That's what they do right? Just before they bite, they *bump* their prey—"

"Nothing is going to bite you." Well, he might. But that would be for later. And lots of fun. "Hold on to me."

Her hands came up and curled around his neck. She held him tightly. And he…liked it. He bent his head closer to her, pulled, compelled to get—

Something came whizzing by his face, missing his head by about a foot.

"Life preserver!" Rayce yelled as the object splashed into the water. "Grab it and I'll pull you both back."

He didn't need to be pulled back. And Mina was still treading water just fine, but to shut up the wolf—Rayce always had a tendency to worry—Luke put an arm around the life preserver and held it. Rayce immediately started hauling them back toward the boat.

"I-I think I felt it bump me again," Mina said, voice sharp. "You have to get away!"

And again…she was trying to protect him. Needless, but cute. "I don't feel anything." Nothing but her. "It's okay. Relax. I've got you."

She'd been looking down at the water, but at his words, her gaze jerked up and locked with his. "But...I thought you wanted to hurt me."

He wasn't sure what he wanted from her yet, but her pain? No, despite the stories circulating about him, *her* pain wasn't on his agenda. Others? Well, of course, but...not her.

They were at the back of the boat now. Rayce stood near the ladder.

"Give her to me!" Rayce called.

Luke curled his hands around Mina's waist and he started to lift her up. Rayce was hanging over the back of the vessel, his arms outstretched to her. "Be careful, wolf," he said, the warning slipping from him without thought. *Handle her with care.*

Luke lifted Mina as if she weighed nothing. Water poured down her body and Rayce locked his hands with hers, pulling her up.

Luke followed, dragging his body up the ladder. He swiped a hand over his face, wiping away the water. Then he paced forward. Mina stood there, her arms around her waist, and her clothes were soaking wet. Her shirt clung to her like a second skin and her skirt had hiked up her incredible legs even more. She was shivering and he could see the tight outline of her hard nipples against the front of her top and—

Rayce was staring, too.

Luke walked past him and shoved the guy in the gut. "Look away."

Rayce spun on his heel, immediately turning his back to Mina. He started whistling. Off-key, terrible whistling.

Marcos hurried toward Luke. "Here's a blanket, boss."

Mina jerked at the sound of his voice. Her eyes were so big and she seemed so…helpless standing there, soaking wet. Though he knew someone with her particular skill set would never truly be helpless.

Unless she couldn't speak.

He took the blanket from Marcos, and Luke wrapped it around Mina's shoulders, being extra sure to pull the ends forward so that the front of her shirt — and her breasts — were covered. "Are you okay?"

Her hands had flown up to clutch the blanket. "No, I am *not* okay."

She sounded furious. Her fear seemed to have vanished now that they were on the boat and away from any potential shark attacks. He nodded toward Marcos. "The lady's all right. Get us back to the island, would you?"

After a quick inclination of his head, Marcos rushed back to the wheel. A moment later, Luke heard the whir of the anchor rising. When he'd jumped overboard, Marcos must have lowered that anchor really quick. Luke made a mental note to give the guy a bonus for his work.

"Is it okay to turn around?" Rayce asked, voice amused.

Since he wasn't feeling a bit of amusement, Luke shot the wolf a glare. "Yes, but watch yourself."

Moving slowly, Rayce turned toward him. Rayce met Luke's stare first — a sign of respect — and then the wolf shifter's gaze darted to a still shivering Mina. "You sure swim fast."

"If it hadn't been for the shark, I would have kept swimming." Her focus was on the water. She swallowed. "It was circling me. I could feel it in the water. Just going around and around me. Like it was holding me in place." Suddenly, her stare jerked toward Luke. "Did *you* do that?"

He let his brows climb. "Did I convince a shark to hold you prisoner? Interesting idea...and I'm flattered that you think I can control everything and everyone around me...but sharks don't exactly fall in my dominion." They weren't evil. They were just...

Fish. Swimming. Eating. Surviving. No matter what Hollywood and their movies wanted to say, sharks weren't some sort of predatory killing beasts. And, to date, he'd never encountered a shark shifter. Not to say there weren't any out there but...

"What is your dominion?" Mina asked as the boat turned and she stumbled just a bit.

Automatically, his hand reached out to steady her. His fingers curled around her waist and he pulled her against his body. *Much better.* Her shivers seemed to ease when he touched her.

"She doesn't look particularly afraid," Rayce mused. "Shouldn't she *look* afraid?"

Probably.

Mina's head turned toward the wolf. "Same eyes," she said. "I guess they don't change, whether you're man or beast?"

Rayce blinked the green eyes in question.

"White wolf," Mina continued. The lights from the boat shined down on them. "That would explain the blond hair."

Rayce's blond hair was thick and unruly, curving over his forehead.

The guy was wearing jeans and a t-shirt. Luke was glad the shifter wasn't bounding around naked any longer. When you had shifters as friends, you learned fast that they let their animal sides out...a lot.

"Uh...did you just call me a wolf?" Rayce laughed. "Lady, you must've had one hell of a lot to drink to—"

"She knows the score, Rayce." Luke kept his hold on her. He liked having Mina close. "So don't bother with the bullshit. I'm not." Most humans didn't know about the monsters who lurked in the dark. Most didn't want to know.

Mina was different.

Because she was one of the monsters?

Rayce's features tightened as he took a step toward Mina. He suddenly didn't look quite so easy going. His gaze raked over Mina and his nostrils flared. "She doesn't smell like a shifter. She smells like—"

"The ocean," Mina muttered. "Considering my swim, I—"

"Strawberries," Rayce said, nodding. "Sin."

Mina's body inched closer to Luke's.

The boat hit a hard wave and shuddered. Considering how fast Marcos was driving, Luke was surprised they didn't all stumble. To be on the safe side, he tightened his hold on Mina. He also glared a bit more at Rayce.

Rayce stared back at him. "What is she?"

Mina stiffened in Luke's arms. "Um, excuse me, *she* is right here, wolfie."

Rayce growled.

"Don't." Luke gave the order flatly. "You don't want to threaten her."

Now the wolf shifter's jaw just dropped. "Are you kidding me, man? The woman was running from your house, fleeing like a thief who'd stolen you blind. She jumps into the water—swims because she's so desperate to get away from you—and now you're treating her like she's some delicate piece of glass that's going to shatter if *I growl at her?*"

He shrugged. "I'm dealing with her. Your job—and Julian's—is to make sure there aren't any other unplanned exits from the island." Because he'd decided something important. Luke caught Mina's chin in his left hand and turned her face toward him. "Guess what, sweetheart?"

"What?" The one word came out worried, fearful.

He grinned. "I'm keeping you."

***

Mina was in Luke Thorne's bedroom, and she was wearing a silk robe that he'd given to her. Just that silk robe and nothing else.

She was scared. She was pissed. And she was way, way out of her league.

"You can't just...keep me," Mina said for what had to the twentieth time. "You don't get to keep people. That's not legal."

He was standing in front of the big, gleaming French doors that led out onto the balcony. "Who cares about legal? You know human laws don't work in our world." He threw open one of the doors and walked out onto the balcony. "Come enjoy the view. It's killer."

She didn't want to enjoy anything with him. She wanted to get the Eye and get the hell away from Luke and his crazy self.

Luke. The wolf. The panther. I want away from them all.

Her hands fumbled with the robe's belt, just to make sure it was good and tight. "I want to leave. I want to get on the boat and go back to Key West."

He was outside, seemingly not even hearing her. Such a lie—Mina was willing to bet he had super hearing. *Supernatural* hearing. She hurried out onto the balcony. "Luke!"

Lazily, he turned toward her, propping one elbow on the balcony.

"Take me to the mainland, take—" Her robe blew up and her words stopped on a gasp. Oh, hell. She was pretty sure she'd just flashed the Lord of the Dark. She shoved down the robe, holding the silk against her thighs.

"Absolutely beautiful."

Her heart was about to burst out of her chest.

"Feel free," Luke invited with a lazy grin, "to flash me anytime."

"Not funny," she snapped back at him.

He kept leaning against that balcony, looking as if he didn't have a care in the world. Probably because he didn't. How wonderful it must be to just…be him.

His head cocked as his gaze slowly rose to her face. Her rather flaming face. "I wasn't being funny," Luke told her, his voice almost…tender. "I was being dead serious. When I first saw you, I thought you were sexy. A wet dream walking right up to me."

Her mouth had gone dry and her heart beat raced even faster.

"Now I realize I was wrong. You *are* absolutely beautiful."

She wasn't. Her nose was too long. Her lips too wide. Her eyes —

"Beautiful," he said again, utter conviction in his voice.

Her fingers had fisted around her robe. "I need to get back to Key West."

He just stared at her.

She had to get this conversation back on track, ASAP. "Get Marcos to come back and take me to the mainland."

"Are you trying to use that tricky little power of yours on me?" He lifted his index finger and actually shook it at her as if she were some naughty school kid. "Didn't we agree that only works when I'm drunk?"

Then I need to get him drunk.

"And I don't plan on drinking," he added, as if he'd just read her mind. "When you're near."

"*Luke!*" He was about to drive her insane.

His smile stretched at her. "Yes?"

"I'm sorry I tricked you." Maybe that was what he wanted. An apology. Her groveling. Fine. She could handle that. "So sorry." She hoped she sounded sincere. She wasn't. "I won't do it again. I won't bother you again. I just want to leave and—"

"But I don't want you to leave." He turned away from her and went back to staring at the sun. "So you aren't."

He couldn't do that. She took two fast steps forward.

"You know about the Eye of Hell. You know about monsters. You know about me. Or at least, you *think* you do." He didn't look back at her.

So he missed seeing her freeze.

"What, exactly, do you *think* you know about me?" Now he just seemed vaguely curious.

She licked her lips and tried to figure out what to say. And what *not* to say. "You rule the dark."

He waved his hand vaguely in the air. "Go on..."

Mina glanced over her shoulder. Oh, but the temptation to run again was strong. She could get down to the dock, dive into the water...

"And find yourself surrounded by sharks."

She gasped. "You can read my thoughts!"

He laughed again. A low, rumbling laugh that she shouldn't have found sexy, but she did. Dammit, she did.

"No, Mina." He glanced over his shoulder at her. "But I am starting to figure out the way that you think. You might fear me, but I learned you fear the sharks even more."

"They have a lot of teeth," she mumbled. "Sharp teeth."

"So do I."

She frowned at him.

"Come take a look at the view. You'll enjoy it."

Well, okay, fine. She took her time sidling up to the balcony. The wind hit her again, coming strong off the ocean, but she still had her death grip on the robe, so she didn't flash anymore skin. Her breath eased out as she looked at the sun. At the waves. At the beauty all around her. "Incredible," the word slipped from her, but it was true. The view, the scene—it was as if they were thousands of miles away from everyone else. The water just stretched. The waves rolled. She'd never seen anything so gorgeous.

"I agree," he said, his voice a rasp.

Her head turned and she found Luke staring at her, not the view. He wasn't smiling. Just…watching her.

Her heart stuttered. "You're still angry."

"Because you lied to me, manipulated me with your power, locked me in a cell and gassed me?"

Mina nodded.

He leaned toward her. His fingers slid under her jaw. A delicate touch, one she didn't expect from him. "No, sweetheart, I'm not angry. I'm impressed. There's a difference."

He was—Mina frowned. "What now?"

"How many people…" His fingers slid down her throat, pausing over her frantically beating pulse. "Do you think have ever managed to get the drop on me like that?"

"Probably not many."

"Only two. You and…" He stopped, clearing his throat. "Well, my asshole of a twin, but we won't talk about him right now."

Oh, no. He had a *twin?* "That part of the story is true, too?"

His fingers stopped their gentle caress. "You've heard about him?"

His touch made her feel funny. Hot. Shivery. Weird. "Could you move your hand?"

His brows lifted.

"Please?"

"Am I hurting you?" His fingers were still around her throat.

"No."

"Then why move?"

Her eyes closed. "Because I think you're turning me on. And it's weird…wanting you when I'm scared. Wanting you when all you're doing is touching me on my throat."

He'd gone silent.

"I think you're using your power against me now." It was easier to speak when she didn't have to look him in the eye. "Payback, huh? To see what it's like to be vulnerable? To need someone else, to want someone, against your instincts. To—"

He laughed again. Only the sound was richer. Darker.

Her eyes opened. For just an instant, she could have sworn that she saw the flash of gold in his dark gaze. Gold...like the panther shifter's stare. But then the flash was gone.

"I'm not making you want me. I'm not using any power against you." His lips brushed lightly against hers. "What you feel is real desire. No tricks. You want me, Mina. You want to strip off that robe and have sex with me right here, right now."

He was wrong. "That isn't me. I'm not like that." Despite what everyone thought. Despite what she'd *made* others think. "I'm not supposed to want you."

He kissed her again. His tongue slid past her lips, pushed into her mouth. Tasted her.

A moan broke from Mina.

"Why not?" he rasped against her mouth. "I want you."

She had to stop this. Stop him. Stop herself. Her hands flew up and pressed to his chest. "Don't do this to me! Stop punishing me!"

But he shook his head. "Desire isn't a punishment, especially not between us."

She realized that he was telling the truth. "You...aren't doing anything to me?"

"No."

Her heartbeat seemed to echo in her ears.

"You just want me." He shrugged. "Most women do, so don't beat yourself up over that."

Jerk.

"Only I don't want them..." Luke continued in the next moment. "Not the way I want you. You're...something different. Something special."

She'd spent most of her life thinking she was a freak, and any "special" talk had always been an insult. But this was different. His voice, the way he looked at her...

"I think you're something extraordinary."

She swallowed twice. "I'm a siren. My voice makes humans lose their control. I'm...evil."

"Then that just makes you mine, if the stories are true."

Ah, right. The stories. They were back to that. And she found that she had the courage to push him a bit. "I know one of those stories. According to it, two twin boys were born, a very, very long time ago. One was predicted to rule the dark and all of the creatures that found solace in the shadows."

He didn't even blink. "And one was supposed to reign in the light. To have an army at his call, to defend the weak, to protect the innocent…and blah fucking blah." He exhaled. "An old tale. Good twin, bad twin. Only we went to some pretty big extremes in my family."

Yes, they had.

"Leo," Luke said. "That's my brother, older than me by all of two minutes and the biggest pain in the ass you can imagine."

"I doubt that." Her gaze was on his mouth. She needed to stop staring at his lips. "I've got my own pain that I'm dealing with right now."

As soon as the words left her, Mina knew she'd said the wrong thing. The very air around her seemed to thicken. Tension rolled through her — tension that came from him.

"Someone scares you, sweetheart?"

"You scare me," Mina said quickly. "That whole 'I'm keeping you' thing isn't normal, you know. People don't just — "

"I'm not people."

No, she supposed he wasn't.

"Who scares you?"

"I scare myself." Another truth she had always kept hidden from others. But for some reason, out there, with him, she was finding that her secrets wouldn't stay silent. "I don't like being this way. I don't like having the ability to control others. I don't like having to watch every single thing I say for fear of hurting someone, killing someone."

He nodded, seeming to understand. "Words can be powerful weapons. Especially, I imagine, *your* words."

He had no idea. But that was exactly what she'd become. A weapon. One that some very deadly people were determined to use, whether she was willing or not. "I really wish you'd just give me the Eye," she muttered. "It would make everything so much easier."

His hand slid away from her throat and she immediately missed the warmth of his touch. "The Eye…the precious token you came to steal from me."

She didn't deny it.

His gaze swept over her. "You can't get the Eye by theft."

Now he was staring at her legs.

Her chin kicked up. "Do I get it if I fuck you? Is that the price?"

And his eyes — they flashed pure, bright gold again. An angry flash. "Do you fuck to get the things that you want?" Anger, no, rage burned in his voice.

"No," her immediate denial. She wasn't holding down her robe any longer. Her hands had clenched into fists at her sides. "I thought you were saying the only way I'd get it was to fu—"

His fingers curled around her shoulders and he brought his face in close to hers. "You will fuck me because you want me. Because you want the wild, rough pleasure we're going to give each other. I don't trade sex for favors. And I sure wouldn't trade it for the Eye."

You will fuck me because you want me. Her breath rushed out. "And *I* don't trade sex for anything," she threw at him. "Just to be clear. I have sex when I want someone. I don't care what anyone else says…I don't care—"

He pulled her even closer. "Tell me the name of the bastard who dared to say anything like that about you, and I'll have him in the ground by dusk."

Her mouth dropped open. He wasn't serious. He…wasn't?

Luke stared back at her.

He is dead serious.

"Y-you can't kill people like that."

"Who said anything about killing? I was just going to make the bastard's worst nightmares come true. In this world, death is the easy way out. Pain is the gift that lasts much longer."

Okay, he was everything the stories had said and more. "You…you are the Lord of the Dark, aren't you?" And she'd been kissing him. She still wanted to kiss him.

She still wanted him.

That was wrong.

But then again, *she* was wrong. Or so everyone had always said. Mina cleared her throat. "You control all the monsters." That was why he had a panther and a werewolf on his island. Why he had prison cells in his home.

"Someone has to keep them in check. Can't just have vampires draining every human in sight. Can't have shifters ripping apart their prey and leaving the bodies in the streets. I'm the one they all fear because I'm the one who can hurt them all. I'm the one they must answer to when their reckonings come."

Her mouth had gone desert dry. "I really need that boat." Because she had the terrible feeling that she'd jumped from one fire...

Straight into hell.

"Too bad, sweetheart. You're not getting it because I'm not done with you."

That sounded so bad. And his eyes — they weren't dark any longer. She could definitely see the glow of gold. "Why do your eyes do that?" Mina whispered. "What does it mean when the color changes that way?"

His smile was wicked. "Means a few things...mostly a power surge."

Oh, damn.

"Happens when I'm angry. It's not exactly safe to be around me when I'm enraged."

Right. She already had a mental note going for that one.

"And it happens when I'm aroused." If possible, his gaze heated even more. "Just so you know, dear Mina, turns out…you arouse me one hell of a lot."

Before she could speak, there was a fierce pounding from inside — a pounding at her door. Or rather, at Luke's bedroom door. He whirled away from her and ran back inside.

She followed on his heels, wondering what was happening — and also feeling real grateful for her reprieve.

"Luke!" A man's voice called. "Get decent and open the door! We have a situation!" A slightly clipped, accented voice. British?

Luke yanked open the door.

A tall, dark-haired man stood there, faint stubble covering his square jaw. "Sorry to interrupt…" His golden stare cut to her.

Gold. Like the panther. It wasn't the same shade of gold that glowed in Luke's eyes. Luke's stare was nearly a yellow-gold, very bright when his power surged. But that British guy's stare — it was softer, deeper. Not nearly as intense. Or scary.

"But I thought you'd want to know something is happening at Eli's place," he added.

"Fuck me, *not my whiskey.*" Luke said immediately. "He just got in the new shipment!"

She padded to his side. "The whiskey?"

"Eli orders it special for me. You have no idea how hard that shit is to find." He exhaled.

"Whatever. What's going on? Drunk tourists? Or did one of his exes find him again and —"

"The bar is on fire. Smoke is billowing up. You can see the dark clouds for miles."

Luke's whole body tensed. "And Eli?"

"I don't know…" The man's gaze jerked back to Luke. "He could…still be in the flames."

Luke snarled then, a deep, inhuman sound that made chill bumps rise on her arms. She wanted to step back. Wanted to run and hide but…

She reached out to him. "Eli was the bartender, wasn't he?" *Because he'd given Luke whiskey.* "He's your friend?"

Luke turned to look at her — not her eyes, but at the hand she'd curled around his upper arm. "Not a friend, not exactly." His gaze lifted and she saw the flare of gold once more. *Power.* "But he's one of mine."

A dark paranormal?

"Keep her here," Luke bit off.

It took a moment too long for those words to sink in for Mina. By the time they did, Luke was already out the door, and the dark-haired, British guy was in her path. "Luke! Wait!"

He did wait, for a moment, long enough to warn, "Her voice is magic, so you'll probably need to gag her."

"*Luke!*" Her voice was a scream then, definitely nothing magical about it. She lunged after him, but the other man grabbed her around the waist, holding her tightly.

Then...the air itself seemed to still. Luke turned toward them and his face had gone hard. Cold. "You will not hurt her, is that clear, Julian? You will not so much as bruise her skin."

Immediately, the hold on her eased.

"She isn't to leave the island," Luke said. "So don't let her compel you. If she tries her tricks, you can always put her in a cell."

Oh, the hell, *no*. Her glare should have burned him. "Luke, you and I are going to have issues over this."

He smiled at her, but the smile didn't reach his eyes. "You wanted payback, sweetheart. This can be step one."

"I didn't want—"

He'd walked away. The jerk had just walked down the hallway and left her. "I want to help you!" Mina yelled the words without thinking. "You're hurting! I see it! I just want to *help* —"

The man who'd been holding her turned Mina carefully in his arms, making an obvious effort to 'not so much as bruise' her. "Trust me, lady," he said, the British definitely creeping through in his upper crust accent. "Luke isn't the type to need help."

"Everyone needs help." She understood that fact all too well. "Everyone."

Even the man that the monsters feared.

CHAPTER SIX

The bar was gone. A total loss. The fire truck was still at the scene when Luke arrived and the dark, heavy clouds of smoke hung in the air. When he took a breath, he could taste the fire. The ash burned his mouth.

Cops were at the scene. The local guys who thought they ran the show but didn't really do jack. A crowd of tourists were staring at the scene with shock evident on their faces.

And there was no sign of Eli.

Had he died in the wreckage? Luke marched toward one of the cops, a guy he'd crossed paths with more than a few times. A guy who had the sense to tense when Luke approached and for fear to flash in his eyes.

"M-Mr. Thorne," the cop gasped. A decent enough sort, for a human. Wesley Strauss. Once upon a time, Wesley had worked as a homicide detective in Atlanta. But when the bodies had just kept piling up, the guy had fled down to the Keys, probably thinking he'd be doing nothing more strenuous than throwing drunk college kids in jail for some hard sobering up. He'd been wrong.

"Where is the bar owner? Where is Eli Nabb?"

Wesley's brown stare jerked toward the charred remains of the bar. "Because of all the alcohol, it looks like the place went up fast. The bar ignited, almost like a bomb went—"

"Where. Is. Eli?"

Wesley's eyes widened. "I-I don't know."

"I can help you with that information."

At that voice—low, drawling, and coming from a few feet behind him—Luke tensed. His nostrils flared as he pulled in all of the scents around him. His shoulders straightened and he turned to see just who was being so very helpful.

A man with blond hair—sun streaked and clipped short—stood a few feet away. The guy was wearing a suit, the boring type favored by government agents. The fellow moved his arm back a bit, and Luke saw the holster just beneath the suit coat.

Interesting.

This guy wasn't local. He *was* human.

Luke's gaze assessed the man. The guy was an inch or so shorter than Luke, but muscled in that I-Work-Out way. His skin was tanned, and his hazel gaze glinted with both intelligence and cunning. Luke knew he'd have to tread carefully with this one.

"I know what happened to Eli." The man offered his hand to Luke. "I'm Agent Garrick McAdams."

Luke shook the hand. The guy had a good grip — again, for a human. Strong enough. "Luke Thorne."

Garrick nodded, as if he'd already suspected Luke's identity. "Right. I've heard that name. You're pretty famous in this area, aren't you?" He smiled, a friendly grin. "I think one of the cops even mentioned you've got your own private island — he told me it was quite the place to see."

"It is." Luke didn't smile back at him. He didn't like that this agent already knew so much about him. "Where's Eli?"

"Oh, your friend was taken to the hospital." The smile slipped. "I'm afraid he suffered second degree burns on a substantial portion of his body. With all the alcohol in there, the fire spread quickly, too quickly. The building couldn't be saved but...I happened to be close by. I was able to pull your friend to safety."

"Well, aren't you the hero."

Garrick blinked.

"What hospital?" Luke demanded.

Garrick's lips parted.

Luke waited.

"I'm afraid I can't disclose that," Garrick finally said regretfully. "Your friend is in...protective custody right now."

"Trust me," Luke said, voice low, "if Eli needs protecting, I've got him covered."

Garrick looked over at the crowd, then he put his hand on Luke's shoulder. "Can we talk a moment? Alone?"

"Aren't we already talking?" He didn't like this guy. There was something about him...

Garrick steered Luke to the side, moving them a few feet away from the crowd. His voice lowered as he revealed, "The fire wasn't an accident. It was arson."

Someone would pay.

"I believe that your friend Eli made contact with a very, very dangerous woman last night."

Luke didn't let his expression so much as flicker.

Garrick reached into his coat, flashing that holster again, and then he pulled out a small photo. Even before the guy handed it to Luke, he knew who he was going to see.

Mina.

She stared back at him in that picture, her hair longer as it slid over her shoulders, curling a bit. Her eyes were the same sharp, startling blue, but her skin was a bit darker. A faint smile curved her lips, as if she were on the verge of being happy.

Or as if she'd been smiling for the man who'd taken her picture. An intimate smile.

"She's beautiful, I know," Garrick said. "But a gorgeous face can hide a very dark soul."

"Tell me something I don't know." Luke kept staring at the photograph.

"Her name is Mina James, or at least, that's the last alias she used. She has a talent for charming men."

Yes, she does.

"You might not believe this," Garrick continued, his voice earnest, "but we believe it's almost a form of hypnotism. Mina can get anyone to do what she wants...and she wants some very dangerous things."

Oh, Mina, you are tricky.

"Her MO is that she picks her prey, usually a male because her hypnosis works better on men...and, of course, because they see a woman like her...and they immediately think of sex."

His grip was too tight on the photo. He was about to rip it.

"She manipulates the men. Gets them to do whatever she wants. They'll lie for her. Steal for her. Even kill for her."

Luke finally glanced up at the agent. "They sound like dumb asses."

Anger flashed on Garrick's face, just for an instant. "As I said, she's very talented at manipulation. Those men are her victims. Just as I believe Eli was her victim."

He inhaled, pulling in the ash and the smoke that lingered so heavily in the air. "She set the fire?"

"Eli told us that she tried to convince him she needed his car. That he had to give it to her. You see, she knew I was tracking her."

Were you now…

"When he refused, she commanded him…she gave him the order to set himself on fire. To destroy his own bar."

The agent was watching him far too closely. Luke made himself laugh. "Seriously? I'm supposed to believe some woman *told* Eli to burn himself…and he did?"

"She isn't some woman." Garrick's voice was still low, carrying only to Luke. "She's very, very dangerous." He glanced swiftly at the crowd and then back at Luke. The guy started to unbutton the top of his dress shirt.

Luke let his brows climb. "Agent, if you want to go strip, there's a club for that just down the road."

A muscle jerked in Garrick's jaw and he kept unbuttoning the shirt until…

A long, thick scar was on his chest.

A fresh scar, one that was still angry, still red.

"She told me to cut out my own heart," Garrick told him, voice and face both stark. "And I nearly did."

***

He'd put her in a cell. Gently, not so much as bruising her per Luke's orders, but Mina was in a cell. And she was gagged.

As far as days went, this one was pretty shitty.

Mina glared at the guy—Julian. He'd told her his name was Julian. *Right after he gagged me.*

"I am so sorry," Julian told her, actually looking contrite as he paced right outside of her cell. "I just can't run the risk of pissing off Luke. Trust me on this, you *don't* want to see the bugger when he's pissed. Not a pretty sight. I mean that with one hundred percent honesty."

She muttered behind her gag.

"And I know what you are, too." He inclined his head toward her. "Siren. Sirens speak, and men do really dumb ass things. Sorry, love, but I can't have you getting in my head. I already have enough damage up there as it is."

She jerked at her handcuffs because—lucky her—he'd handcuffed her, too. He'd locked her hands behind her back and put the cuffs in place.

He thought they'd stop her from getting the gag out of her mouth.

He was wrong.

After shooting him one more glare, Mina sat down on the floor.

"Yes." He nodded, all encouraging. "Do that. Just get comfortable. Before you know it, Luke will be back and he can take over your…care."

She shimmied. She rolled. She lifted up her knees and she pulled her cuffed hands under her body, looping them so that they could come in front of her once more.

"Wait!" Alarm raised his voice. "You're a limber thing, aren't you? Normally a bonus with women but—*stop! Stop that!*"

No way. The cuffs were in front of her now so she could reach up and jerk the gag right out of her mouth—exactly what she did. "Screw you," she snapped at him.

His eyes immediately…glowed. Lust flashed on his face and he grabbed for the cell door.

Oh, no! I said the wrong thing—again! That was her problem. She always said the wrong thing. She *did* the wrong thing. "You want to get away from me!" Mina yelled, hoping to stop him before this went too far. "You don't want to screw *anyone* right now. You just want to get far away from me, fast."

He immediately turned on his heel, like a puppet on a string and nearly *ran* from the area.

Her mouth dropped. "No!" She lunged forward and grabbed the bars. "I mean…*you want to get away after you let me out!*"

She could hear the thud of his fading footsteps.

"*You want to let me out first!*" Mina shouted.

But it was too late. Apparently, Julian could run very, very fast.

Her forehead pressed against a bar. "I did it again." Wrong, wrong, *wrong*.

Now she was trapped.

Unless someone else happened to come into the cell area. In that case, she'd be ready. And she'd plan her words very, very carefully.

**

Garrick buttoned up his shirt. "You think I don't know the story sounds farfetched? I thought the tales about her were bullshit, too, until I had her close and she stared into my eyes, parted those sexy lips, and told me to cut out my own heart."

Luke's heart was drumming too fast. His heart never raced that way. Not unless he was getting ready to end someone.

"When you aren't of use to her any longer, Mina eliminates you. It's the way she works. Eli didn't have a boat she could use, he didn't have a car…just his motorcycle. That wasn't going to help her. So she found someone else to get her out of this place and she planted the order to die in Eli's mind."

Had Mina been alone with Eli? He wasn't sure where she'd been when he'd first arrived at the bar. He just remembered looking up—and she'd been there. Perhaps she'd talked to Eli before he'd arrived...

"You know her, don't you?" Garrick asked him.

Luke looked back at her picture. At the faint smile there. Such a temptation. The way her eyes gleamed... "Never seen her before in my life." He handed the photo back to Garrick. "What agency did you say you were with?"

A little muscle seemed to tick near Garrick's right eye. "The FBI."

"So impressive," Luke murmured. His head cocked to the right. "May I see some ID?"

Garrick put Mina's picture back in his coat pocket and pretty much threw his ID at Luke.

Luke gave it a cursory glance. "Fascinating. The FBI has come all the way down to the tip of the Keys after a killer...one who told *you* to cut out your heart." Now he tossed the ID right back at Garrick. "Were you fucking her?"

Garrick's hand fisted as he clenched the ID. He took a surging step toward Luke. "Where is she?" His voice was low, deadly.

"I'll take that as a yes." Rage surged inside of Luke. Dark and twisting, only…this rage was different. Not the usual fire that burned him when someone had done something very, very wrong and pissed him off. This was…like nails, like claws, cutting into his insides, and he wanted to lift his fist and drive it into Garrick's bland face, breaking the guy's nose, blackening his eyes because the bastard had *known* Mina, because he'd touched her, because he'd kissed her and —

Luke stepped back. "That's what it's like, huh?"

Garrick frowned at him. "What? What in the hell are you muttering about?"

Jealousy. I just had my first taste. And he didn't particularly like it. Too bitter. "Did she…hypnotize you into fucking her?"

Garrick's face flushed bright red. "You're making this a joke. Mina James is no joke. What she did to me, what she did to Eli, what she has done to *dozens* of other victims…it's no laughing matter. The woman needs to be stopped."

"And you're just the man for that job." Luke glanced down and realized that he'd clenched his own fists. Unacceptable. Humans weren't supposed to stir that much emotion in him. He kept his control. Always. Even when fury rode him hard, he stayed in control.

Because when he lost control, well, his bad side came out.

And people died.

"I'm the man on her case. Half a dozen agents are down here. We're hunting her. We *will* find her. She'll be taken down." Garrick's gaze held Luke's. "And anyone dumb enough to be helping her will go down, too. Collateral damage."

"That almost sounds like a threat." Luke shook his head. "Not very FBI-like, is it?"

Someone called out Garrick's name. A woman with red hair who was sporting an equally boring suit. Probably another FBI agent.

Garrick pulled a small, white business card out of his pocket and handed it to Luke. "If you do see Mina, call me. I can help you."

Luke took the card. He held it between his thumb and his index finger as he watched Garrick walk away.

The card started to burn.

Mina, you have very poor taste in men.

In seconds, the card was nothing but ash, drifting in the wind. Luke stared at that drifting ash, watching as it blew toward the ground. The ground and…

A spider.

His shoulders tensed. There was a big, fat spider on the ground. One that was scuttling fast as it moved to follow Garrick McAdams. The spider ran right up to him but before it could attack, Garrick glanced down. His lips tightened in distaste as he stared at the spider, then his shoe lifted and slammed down on the arachnid, squashing it. He twisted his foot, as if making good and certain that it was dead.

Luke focused his gaze on the charred remains of the bar. He looked down, staring at the ashes and the soot and…another big, fat spider scuttled out. Unerringly, it went straight toward Garrick McAdams.

But this time, it was the female agent who squashed the spider. Stomping it quick beneath the heel of her shoe.

He waited to see if more spiders would come, but they didn't. Only two had been left. Two — because Eli was gone. They must have slipped from Eli before he'd been taken away. Those last two spiders had done their job, though. They'd shown Luke just what he needed to see.

The FBI agent couldn't be trusted.

A good thing…because the instant Luke had found out that Garrick had an intimate past with Mina, he'd wanted to kill the bastard. Now, well, he had a more legitimate reason for the fury.

Even he had standards, after all. If you were going to destroy a man…

It helped to have a few reasons for the dark deed.

***

"Does he know where she is?" Madeline Slate asked. Her red hair was bright in the afternoon sun. Her eyes—a light brown—darted over his shoulder to peer at Luke Thorne.

"I think he does." Garrick didn't look back at the guy. Luke Thorne was a dick, but the guy was also their key to finding Mina. "We're going to watch him when he leaves and follow his ass back to the island." Once there, away from the prying eyes of the crowd around them, Garrick and his team would take control.

They'd get Mina back.

And Luke? Well, they'd deal with him, too.

"Is he already under her power?" A slight furrow appeared between Madeline's eyes. "If he is, he'll fight to keep her."

"Doesn't matter how hard he fights." Garrick wasn't even a little worried. *Mina is close. I'm getting her back.* "Our orders are to bring her in. She's too valuable to the organization. We'll get her back and she *will* cooperate."

Madeline licked her lips. "If she doesn't?"

There was no choice for Mina. Not after all that she'd done. "Then she dies."

CHAPTER SEVEN

Footsteps.

Mina jumped to her feet when she heard the distinct thud of footsteps approaching her cell. She ran toward the bars, grabbed them, held tight and —

Okay, wait. This looks too desperate.

She immediately pushed back from the bars, smoothed her hair, straightened her robe — she was still wearing the damn thing — and tried to look as if she were totally and completely relaxed. When Julian had left her, he'd rushed out and left the door to the cell room open, so it only took a moment before she saw a flash of blond hair appear.

And Rayce walked into what she thought of as her new personal hell.

When he saw her, he stopped short. "Where's Julian?" Rayce demanded. He crossed his arms over his chest, frowning.

Her shoulders lifted. "I don't know. He locked me in here…" She hoped that she looked suitably pitiful as her lips curled down. "And he just left. Maybe Luke called him? Maybe something happened with Eli?"

Alarm flashed on Rayce's face. A handsome enough face. Hard jaw. Sculpted lips. But…not *dangerously* sexy. Not like Luke.

"Let me out," Mina said, pushing power into the words. "Then we can get the boat and go together to Key West. We can help Luke."

Rayce blinked, looking vaguely confused. He was also not moving to *let her out.*

So she needed to ramp up her compulsion. Unfortunately, she was feeling a bit weak. It had been one long-ass night and she couldn't exactly remember the last time she'd eaten. "Let me out," Mina said again, drawing on her reserves. She'd been waiting too long in that cell, hoping that someone would appear. It would have been ever-so-helpful if Rayce had just brought his wolfie self in earlier but…

He walked toward the cell.

Better late than never.

"Thank you." Relief made her light-headed. Or maybe that was the hunger. Didn't really matter. "Open that lock as fast as you can and get me *out.*"

He reached for the lock. Then he stopped, his brows furrowing. "I don't have the key."

He didn't have the—Her teeth snapped together. "Julian has it." Julian, who was somewhere running wild on the island. "Just—

just break the bars, okay? You're a shifter, right?"
Wolf shifter, werewolf, whatever he wanted to be
called was fine with her. "That means you're
super strong. Just rip the bars apart. Luke did it."
She pointed to the cell on her right, the cell she'd
trapped Luke in before. Two of the bars had been
heaved apart so he could slip out. "Just do what
he did." *Do it now. Now, now, now.*

Rayce curled his fingers around the bars. He
sucked in a deep breath and then he yanked on
them, straining, the muscles in his arms and chest
bulging, his face darkening, lines of strain
appearing and—

Nothing happened.

His breath panted out.

Mina narrowed her eyes. "Tell me that's not
all you've got." She'd heard whispers about wolf
shifters. They were supposed to be wild, fierce, so
far up the paranormal chain that they were *not*
fucked with by others.

And this guy couldn't break a bar for her?

"Luke did it," she said again. "You can, too."
She snatched for her own power, pumping it into
her voice. "Bend the bars. Get me out. *You can do
it.*"

Rayce nodded grimly, and he braced his
body. His muscles strained as he pulled and
pulled and she *thought* she heard a faint groan
from one of the bars.

Excitement fired her blood. "That's it! Keep going! Keep—"

Smoke began to rise from his hands. And she caught the acrid scent of...*burning flesh?* Horror had her mouth dropping open as she realized that the bars were actually burning him. *Silver and a werewolf don't mix. Oh, shit.* "Rayce, stop—"

"He isn't me, sweetheart."

Rayce's shoulders slumped as his hands fell away from the bars.

Mina's whole body went cold, then hot.

And Luke walked into her hell. He flashed her a wide smile. "Up to your usual tricks, are you?"

"Trying to be," she muttered back. What was the point in a denial?

"Um." He pointed to Rayce. "If you know she's a siren, then why would you ever let her compel you? Would putting in some ear plugs have been too much to ask?"

Rayce shoved away from the bars. "I was...looking for Julian." His hands were covered in blisters.

"Ah, yes, Julian. That panther was supposed to be keeping watch." He paced toward the bars and lifted one dark brow as he stared at Mina. "What did you do to my friend?" Anger was there, cold, deadly, staring at her from his eyes and chilling her in his voice.

"I didn't hurt him," she said quickly. But she had hurt Rayce. She hated the sight of his hands. "I'm sorry," she whispered miserably to Rayce. "You need to bandage your hands."

"His hands will heal."

Actually, they already appeared to be healing. That was good.

A muscle jerked in Luke's jaw. "Now let's talk about Julian again. Where is he?"

She backed away from the bars. A little space between her and Luke might be a good thing, especially considering the way he was looking at her. "I just sent him out, told him to get away from me, okay? That's all." She put her still cuffed hands in front of her, feeling the silk of the robe beneath her fingers. "Trust me, I needed the guy to get away. It was in everyone's best interests."

Luke's hand curled around one bar. "And why is that?"

Her gaze darted between him and Rayce. This was embarrassing. "Can we maybe talk in private, Luke?"

"What happened between you and Julian?"

Okay, jeez, that low voice was kind of terrifying. "I said the wrong thing, all right? I told you, I do that. You have no idea what it's like to have to watch every single word you say. I said the wrong thing, I messed up, and I had to send him out to—to stop him."

His gaze seemed to burn into hers. "Stop him from what?"

Her cheeks felt as if they were on fire. Her eyes jerked toward Rayce, then came back to Luke. "Can we talk about this alone?" she asked again, hating the pleading tone of her voice.

"Rayce," Luke's voice rumbled. "Go find Julian. Make sure he's not hurting himself."

Horror widened her eyes. "He's not! I didn't tell Julian to hurt himself—I wouldn't—"

"The same way you *wouldn't* tell a former lover to cut out his own heart?"

The sound of her sharply indrawn breath seemed way too loud. *Oh, crap. He met Garrick.*

Rayce gave a low whistle and his gaze raked over her with new appreciation. "Didn't expect that. Bloodthirsty, huh? Guess that definitely makes her your type, Luke."

"Go. Find. Julian."

"Right. On it." Rayce hurried out.

Luke kept that dark stare of his on her. She wanted to look away, but couldn't. "I can explain…" Mina began.

"I certainly hope so. I mean, I would hate to think you just went around from man to man, fucking them, using them, and leaving death in your wake."

The pain hit her—so sharp and unexpected that tears actually filled her eyes. She should have been used to the accusations. After all, plenty of

people hurled them at her. But for some reason—
some stupid reason—hearing those words from
Luke cut her right to the core.

He swore. "Are you *crying?*"

A tear leaked down her cheek.

"Stop it," Luke snapped. "Stop it right now!"

She swiped at the tears, lifting her cuffed
hands. "I'm not a whore, despite what you
think."

"You tried seducing me last night." Like she
needed that reminder. "And your ex just told me
that was your MO." The faint lines near his eyes
tightened. "Didn't I tell you to stop crying?"

"It's not like I can do it on command!" Mina
fired back.

He glowered.

"I made a mistake with Julian." Her voice
had dropped to a whisper. "I was mad and when
I'm mad, I don't think well enough before I
speak. I said, 'Screw you' and it was like a light
switched on inside of him. I could see it. The lust
was there, burning too hot for him to control. He
was charging for the cell, getting ready to unlock
it—"

An animalistic rumble came from him.
Deeper than a growl. Way rougher.

Goosebumps rose on her arms. Odd because
she could have sworn that it had just gotten
warmer in there. "So I told him to walk away. To

get out of here. Before something happened." She swallowed. "Before someone got hurt."

Silence.

She didn't think silence from Luke was a good thing. "How is your friend Eli?"

"Eli isn't my friend."

She rocked back on her heels. *Still very, very furious.*

"Did you talk to Eli?" Luke suddenly asked her.

"I told him that I liked his tat." She remembered the intricate spider that she'd seen on Eli's neck. "That a crime?"

"No, but using your *voice* to tell a man to kill himself, to get him to destroy his bar, to burn my *whiskey* — that is a crime."

Tell a man to kill himself. She took a step back. "I didn't." Her voice was too low and the past was suddenly all around her. Grabbing at her. Slicing into her. Hurting her. "I didn't!"

"Eli wasn't there when I arrived," Luke said, his voice curt. "He was gone, apparently sent to a hospital for treatment because of the burns that he sustained. A very helpful Agent Garrick McAdams was at the scene, though. He told me about you. About how you used Eli — you wanted a boat from him, wanted transportation —"

"The only thing I ever told the guy was that he had a nice tat!"

"When he couldn't provide that for you, Agent McAdams said you gave Eli a dark compulsion. Death. And then you went on to your next victim." His lips twisted. "That would be me."

No, no, no. She ran forward, toward the bars. Toward Luke. "That isn't how it happened! I went to the bar to find you! I waited outside until I saw you arrive, then I went in. I went straight to you. I didn't talk to anyone else. I was so nervous that I was afraid I was going to pass out before I got to you, but I had no choice."

He stared at her through those bars. "Why?"

Garrick had found her too fast. "Because I need that Eye. I told you already that I need it."

"The Eye hurts. It destroys. If you wanted it, then you had your sights set on killing someone."

She shook her head. "It isn't like that."

His jaw clenched. "Agent McAdams had your picture. He wanted to know if I'd seen you."

No, no, no. "What did you tell him?" She held her breath.

He gave her that slow smile. One that made her stomach clench. "That I'd never had the pleasure."

The dizziness was back. Maybe it was from relief again.

Or fear.

Or the damn hunger that had hollowed out her stomach. She'd been so desperate and so scared for such a long time. Running, always running and looking over her shoulder for threats. She'd barely slept. Barely ate as she closed in on Luke.

"I don't think he believed me, though," Luke added. "Can you imagine...someone thinking that I would lie?"

And she wasn't feeling relief any longer. "He would have followed you."

"Um." Luke didn't seem particularly concerned.

She was terrified. "Garrick would have followed you. Probably in the air, on a chopper. He would have tracked you back to the island. He'll...he'll come searching for me."

"No doubt. He seemed to want you very badly."

The handcuffs banged against the bars. "I have to get away! *You have to let me go.*"

And once more, the air seemed to heat around her. "I warned you about trying to use your power on me."

"I'm not!" Her voice was breaking. "I'm scared, okay? Scared and desperate and when I get scared, I can't control myself!" Her power leaked out.

"Who were you going to use the Eye on?" His demand was driving, relentless. "Your ex-lover? Were you going to try and kill him again?"

"No! It wasn't like that! I'm not the one who tried—oh, dammit, I was just fighting to survive that day! He told me that if I walked away, if I left him, it would be like cutting his heart out." She shook her head. Her breath was ragged. "You don't know what he did to me. What Garrick and his agency made me do…"

"The FBI? I thought they were the human version of good guys."

Mina blinked at him. "Garrick isn't with the FBI. If he told you that, he's lying."

"Or you are."

She slammed the handcuffs against the bars. "He's coming! We don't have time for this. Garrick could be bringing his chopper over us at any moment."

"Then tell me who you want to use the Eye on. Convince me that I should trust *you*, and not the FBI agent."

"He's not an FBI Agent!" How many times did she have to say that? "Garrick works for a different group in the government—a group that captures paranormals. That *uses* them—that uses us." Because she'd been used. "They want to fight wars with the best weapons out there, and those weapons are the paranormals."

His expression hadn't altered. He didn't believe her.

And was it her imagination? Or could she hear the whir of helicopter blades?

"Time's running out," Luke said. "Tell me the truth or I'll give you to him."

She blinked away tears.

"*Not* the tears." Luke's voice held distinct bite. "I don't like them from you."

"I don't like them either!" Mina yelled back. "I don't like being with you! I don't like being in a cage! I don't like being used as a weapon! I don't like anything that has happened to me. This isn't what I wanted!" And it was as if a dam had burst inside of her. She couldn't hold the words back any longer. "I didn't want to track you down. Every story I'd heard about you terrified me. And at first, I thought you were just a myth. A story that people tell in the dark. Then I found out you *were* the dark. I found out about the Eye and what it could do and I knew I had to have it."

"Because you wanted to punish the ones who'd used you…"

"*Because I want to use it on myself!*" The words blasted from her. Then they hung in the air, stark and terrible and she couldn't take them back. "I wanted to use it on myself," she said, her voice softer. "The Eye of Hell is supposed to take away the powers of the dark paranormals. I wanted it to take away my power."

"Stealing power is just one of its perks," he said, his eyes never leaving hers. "It can steal life, too."

She sucked in a sharp breath. "I have lived with this curse since my thirteenth birthday. I don't want this. I have to turn it off…that's all I want. To just stop it. If I don't have my power any longer, then Garrick and his team can't use me. I can't hurt anyone."

"How noble."

She banged her cuffed hands against the bars. "It's true! I'm telling you the *truth*." And she definitely heard the *whir, whir, whir* of a helicopter. "He's here." Fear knifed into her insides. "Please, help me. Don't let him take me away."

His hand shoved into his pocket. He pulled out a key. A moment later, she heard the snick of the lock as it opened.

Her eyes squeezed shut. "Thank you." She was so damn grateful that the guy had been carrying a backup key.

"Don't thank me yet." His hands had curled around her wrists. His fingers smoothed over her skin. "The cuffs bruised you."

Her eyes opened. She looked down and saw the dark circle of skin beneath the handcuffs.

"I thought I was very explicit when I talked to Julian. You *weren't* to get so much as a bruise."

"I—"

He grabbed the cuffs. Shattered them with his touch. They fell to the stone beneath their feet. *Oh, he is definitely strong.*

But then Luke lifted her wrists. First he brought her right wrist to his mouth and he pressed a soft, tender kiss there, just above her pulse point. "I'm sorry."

He'd just apologized? The Lord of the Dark?

"I will take more care with you."

He brought her left wrist to his mouth. Kissed the dark skin.

Her heart slammed into her chest. This time, that mad racing wasn't from fear or anger. It was from lust. Because when his mouth pressed to her skin, when his dark head bent and she saw his lips feather over her...

Arousal sparked in her blood. It was wrong. She was in his cell. Garrick was hunting her. "How are you doing this to me?" Her voice was husky, confused. "How can you make me want you like this?"

His lashes—dark and thick—lifted. His stare held hers. "We're only getting started." The words were a promise.

"Luke—"

He kissed her. His lips were soft, gentle, feathering over hers. She found herself leaning in toward him, wanting that softness, wanting the care that he was giving to her. Her lips parted for him and he licked her lower lip. A sensual caress. His tongue thrust into her mouth. Not taking. Not dominating this time but...seducing.

Whoop. Whoop. Whoop. The sound of the helicopter had changed because it was so close now. Not a whir, too loud for that. It sounded as if the helicopter was right above them.

He eased back and stared into her eyes. "I don't like it when you cry." His hand lifted and brushed across her cheek. She hadn't realized that another tear had escaped. "Don't do it again."

Despite everything, a little laugh broke from her. "Can't guarantee that. In case you missed it, I'm having a pretty bad day."

"It will get better."

She wished he was still kissing her. "There's a helicopter over us."

"Yes. Sounds like it."

"We're not in international waters. They'll come to search the island. They'll come to take me."

His expression was very serious. "I'd like to see them try." He started to back away from her.

She grabbed him, her fingers tightening around his arms. "I don't want you hurt."

"Watch it, sweetheart, or you'll make me think you care."

The problem was…she did. And she'd just met the guy.

His lips hitched into a half-smile. "They won't take you. Don't worry."

Easier said than done.

"I need you to stay here," Luke said. "No, wait," he added, when she started to protest. "I won't lock you in the cell. The door will stay open, but I don't want you to leave this area. I have safeguards in place. The humans can search the rest of the island, but they won't ever find this chamber. If you stay here, you'll be safe."

"Or I'll be a sitting duck." If he was lying to her, if he was setting her up, if he believed Garrick and not her...

"Guess you have to trust me."

Yes, she did. "And what will I owe you in return?"

"We'll start with a night...one night to do anything I want..."

Her hands pulled from him, as if she'd been burned. "I told you before, I'm not a whore. I get that I gave you the wrong first impression. That's on me. I wore the fuck-me-shoes, I tricked you, but I am not—"

"You won't sleep with me as payback. You'll sleep with me because you need me more than breath. That's what the one night is about. It's about my chance to show you what we'd be like together."

Seduction. He wanted to seduce her.

He was also offering to keep her safe. And right then, she was not about to refuse a safe haven. "I'll stay here."

She wouldn't promise more than that. The idea of seduction — his seduction — scared her.

"I'll come back for you when it's clear."

He stepped back. Turned away. Walked determinedly out of the cell.

"Wait!" Mina called.

He stilled.

"If he thinks you're human, you're safe from Garrick. But if he thinks you're... something else, he may try to take you into his custody."

"I'd like to see him try..."

"No, you wouldn't."

He looked back at her.

"He has special bullets. More like tranquilizers. They can take down paranormals. I've seen it happen. Strong paranormals — like vamps and shifters — go down in an instant. They're knocked out and then they wake up..." She gestured around her. "They wake up in a place pretty much like this." Which was why she *hated* that cell.

"Did they do that to you? Did they drug you?" Anger tightened his jaw.

"Yes."

"They won't do it again. I won't let them."

He sounded so certain. Her head tilted. "Luke, just how strong are you?"

"You should probably hope that you never find out." Then he turned away. She watched him leave and when he was gone, when he'd sealed up the tunnel, she bent and touched the shattered handcuffs.

Very, very strong.

CHAPTER EIGHT

Luke had a helipad on the island, but that was for his personal use, not so that some dick with the government could bring his chopper in and storm the place.

Rayce stalked to his side, with Julian trailing just a few steps behind him. "What's the plan?" Rayce asked, lifting his hand to show that claws had already sprouted from his fingertips. "Do we teach these boys that uninvited guests aren't welcome here?"

Luke didn't respond to that, mostly because he was still considering his options. He glanced over at Julian. "You okay?"

"No." His face was grim, as grim as his voice. "I messed up. You were counting on me, and I let you down. If she hadn't ordered me away…"

Luke moved to stand in front of him, ignoring the blast of wind that came from that landing chopper. "You'll be better prepared next time."

"I owe you so fucking much," Julian rasped. "I'd be dead without you. My family abandoned me, the pack turned, if it hadn't been for you—"

"How about we save the feel good moment for a time when a chopper isn't landing?" Rayce cut in. "You two can have a bromance later."

Julian glared at the wolf. "Keep pushing…"

Luke locked one hand on Julian's shoulder and he curled his other around Rayce's. "Before those agents get out of that chopper, we need to be clear on a few very important things."

Both Rayce and Julian had gone dead silent.

"One, Mina doesn't leave. They don't find out that she's here. You haven't seen her, you don't know her. Got it?"

They nodded.

"Two, they don't get near the cell chamber. I have safeguards in place, so that shouldn't be an issue. If there's a fuck-up, though, you keep them away, understand?"

"Yes." Julian exhaled slowly. "They won't get her."

They'd better not. "Three." He forced his jaw to unclench. "Neither of you ever fucking thinks about touching Mina, got it? Because friends or no friends…debts or no debts…I will *destroy* the fool who tries to come between me and her. I want her. She's going to be mine." He hadn't had anyone of his own in a very long time.

Maybe…ever.

Silence. No, not silence. That chopper's *whoop, whoop, whoop* was overwhelming. The gusts of wind beat at him, shoving his clothes against his body. Luke just locked his legs and didn't move.

"Is it…safe to want her that way? That much?" Rayce asked.

Luke laughed. "Since when have I worried about safe?"

The chopper was on the ground. Time to cover point four. "Mina said they're packing tranqs that can knock both of you out. The agents on that helicopter are *not* to know that you're paranormals. You're my human guards, nothing more, nothing less."

"*Why* aren't we attacking them?" Julian wanted to know. "We could totally take them out."

"They aren't the leaders. They're the followers. Mina said there is a government agency in place. If they're going after the paranormals the way she says…" He thrust back his shoulders. "Then you don't kill a snake by chopping off its tail. You take the beast's head." The agents would lead him back to the head.

He just had to wait. And Luke had to *not* lose his control and attack Garrick McAdams.

The chopper's blades stilled.

Luke crossed his arms over his chest and stared at the helicopter. Garrick was the first one to emerge. He was sure the bastard made a point of flashing his holster. Again.

Because I'm supposed to be scared of him?

The redhead that Luke had spotted at the crime scene exited next. Then an African American male, wearing a slightly more stylish suit than the others, climbed out. He had on dark glasses and his body was tenser than the others.

He's afraid.

Interesting.

"Three on three," Rayce murmured. "Easiest odds we've ever had. They must be freaking idiots to come this way."

Maybe. Maybe not. Luke noticed that the pilot seemed particularly watchful. He still had his headset on. Just who was he in radio contact with?

"Mr. Thorne!" Garrick called, flashing him a wide smile. "Your island is definitely —"

"You weren't invited here, and I seriously doubt that you were able to get a court order to search my home so quickly." He kept his legs braced apart. Rayce and Julian were with him, their bodies tense, but not too aggressive, not yet.

Garrick's hand went toward his holster.

Don't even think it.

"We're here for your safety, Mr. Thorne." It was the woman who spoke. Her voice was low, probably in an effort to be soothing. Only he wasn't in the mood to be soothed. "If you're under Mina's control, then you aren't responsible for your actions. You can't —"

"I can do just about anything, and I usually do."

Her eyes narrowed. Anger flashed on her face. *Ah, that agent has a temper.*

"And, trust me," Luke added, just so they were all clear. "I'm responsible for my actions. No one is controlling me." He was standing in the middle of the path that led to the house, and since Julian and Rayce were with him...*we make for one very interesting wall.*

"Agent Lang," Garrick snapped to the now sweating younger agent in the slightly more stylish suit. "Show these men our authorization."

Agent Lang stepped forward. He pulled a thick envelope from his suit pocket. The guy's forehead was covered in moisture.

"Little warm for that suit, don't you think, mate?" Julian asked.

"Something tells me it's just gonna get hotter," Rayce added, ever helpful.

Lang's fingers were trembling as he handed the envelope to Luke. Luke pulled out the folded papers inside, scanning the typed text there. "Oh, wow, signed by the governor...*and* the Director of the FBI. That is exciting." He was tempted to burn the paper right then and there. It would pretty much just take one stray thought. "I guess I'm supposed to be extra impressed? I would be except nowhere in there does it say you have the right to search my *private* property."

Garrick's glare twisted his face. "That gives me the authority to conduct *any* necessary search in the hunt for Mina James, I can enter this facility, I can search every building on this island, and any other as long as I have just cause—"

"That would be the thing," Luke interrupted silkily. "You don't have just cause. I've already told you, I don't know Mina James. Never had the pleasure." *But I will.*

Garrick marched forward, stopping only when he was toe-to-toe with Luke. Then, voice low and cutting, he said, "I know you're lying."

"He just insulted you," Rayce said. "First he arrived uninvited, then he insults you. That is ballsy."

"Wanker," Julian threw in, nodding.

Garrick's gaze cut first to Rayce, then to Julian. "Who the hell are you two?"

"They're my personal security team," Luke said, his voice perfectly smooth. "They monitor all of the activity on the island, and I assure you, if Mina James was here, they'd know it."

"Mina who?" Rayce wanted to know.

"Got a pic of her?" Julian asked at the same time.

Garrick's skin couldn't get much redder. Beside him, Agent Lang glanced around nervously while the woman — she kept glaring at them all.

"Of course, he has a picture," Luke announced, after a beat as the tension mounted. "Garrick keeps it in his inner coat pocket. Right next to the heart she wanted him to cut out."

Garrick surged forward.

Luke put his hand on the man's chest. "You don't want to do that." He didn't use any force, though he was sorely tempted to shove the man back. To toss him twenty feet. To throw the guy's ass into the ocean. "I have cameras all over this island. And I'm sure the last thing your boss at the FBI wants is for you to suddenly appear on the evening news, starring in a video as you attempt to attack me." He paused. "*Attempt* being the key word. Because that video would mostly show you getting your ass kicked."

"Get your hand off me," Garrick spat.

The female agent had circled around them, moving off the little path. Her hand went to her holster. The other agent, Lang, was still standing there, and sure looking as if he wished to be a million miles away.

Luke let his hand linger a moment longer, long enough to prove that he was moving it away from Garrick only because he wanted to do so.

"There are two ways to do this," Garrick informed him as the agent's hands went to his hips.

"Oh, tell me more..." Luke invited, sounding bored, because he was.

"You let me search your property. You and your *guards* stay out of my way. You let me get Mina James and my team will walk out of your life."

Julian leaned forward. His hands moved languidly in the air, the movement imitating wings. "I think you mean fly out. 'Cause you can't walk on the water."

Garrick sent him a killing look. "Option two," he snapped.

"I can't handle the suspense," Luke said.

Garrick's hands had fisted on his hips. "Option two is that we leave now...and we're back in the hour with a *full* force of FBI agents and local law enforcement authorities. We tear your house apart, and we still find the woman. Only we take her and all three of you..." His index finger swept over the group. "And you're charged with harboring a fugitive. All of you are locked up. No more private island. No more mansion. Just a new cell buddy and a pot to piss in as you wait for trial."

Luke couldn't help it. He tossed back his head and laughed. Oh, damn, but he hadn't realized that Garrick would be amusing. It was just...

Adorable.

"I'm not fucking kidding," Garrick snarled.

Luke couldn't contain his laughter.

Garrick shook his head. His fingers were hovering so close to his holster.

It will take more than tranqs to stop me.

Luke sucked in a deep breath, then another. "Sorry," he finally managed. "That was just...so cute. That you think I don't have a dozen of the highest priced lawyers in the world at my beck and call, just waiting to deal with any shit that comes my way. Or..." Another chuckle escaped. "That you don't think half the senators in D.C. owe me favors—that I don't have pull at the FBI or every other government agency."

For just an instant, worry flashed on Garrick's face.

Luke had no more laughter. He did have a cold promise to offer. "You're playing out of your league with me. I'm warning you about that now. Tread carefully or you will get burned."

"Did you just threaten a federal agent?" Garrick demanded.

Luke shrugged. "Take my words however you will..."

Garrick motioned toward the other two agents. "We *are* searching this island. You can't stop us, we—"

"I'll go with you on that search," Luke announced. "I'll personally escort you around my home. Then you and your friends will leave—minus this mysterious Mina James because she isn't in my home — and you will *never* show your face here again. If you do, I'll be calling my lawyers and all of those friendly senators I mentioned."

Garrick was seething. "Then get the hell on with that escort."

Luke rubbed his chin. "You know, it wouldn't kill you to use some magic words. Have you ever heard of *please*?"

Oh, if looks could kill…

"What about *thank you*?" Julian wanted to know. "That's bloody magical, too."

Disgust flashed in Garrick's eyes. "You guys think this is a joke, don't you? People are dying, and that's *no* laughing matter. Mina James is a monster. She will be stopped and anyone helping her…I will take them down, too."

Luke and Julian shared a quick look. "Well, I guess we've been warned. Good thing we aren't helping that woman, eh?" Then Luke turned his back on Garrick. "Let's get this show on the road. I have plans for the night."

Plans that involved a woman who very much *wasn't* a monster. And Luke should know. After all…

I'm the baddest monster of them all.

***

The helicopter slowly lifted into the air, sending out bursts of wind as it rose. Luke Thorne stood down there, a tight smile on his face, as he watched the chopper.

"I hate that man," Garrick announced, voice biting. He had his headset in place and a microphone was near his mouth.

Madeline shot him a quick frown. "It was a thorough search. She *wasn't* there."

"She's there." He knew it. "He just hid her." But that was okay. Because while he'd been *escorted* around by Luke, he'd given Thomas Lang a few orders, too. He turned, meeting the other agent's dark stare. "Did you plant the devices?"

Lovely little listening devices that would be ever so helpful to him. It was a good thing Uncle Sam had made some nearly microscopic tech.

"In several rooms at the main house," Lang told him. The guy had been nervous as all hell about that plan. He'd started sweating the minute they got off the chopper. "We'll be able to hear plenty."

And as soon as he heard Mina's voice...

He looked down at the island, at Luke Thorne, still standing there, appearing arrogant. Cocky.

When I hear Mina, I'll be back to take her from you.

"You think he's under her control?" Madeline asked. "Because I'm not sure I buy it...a guy like that...I don't think he'd be so easily manipulated."

Garrick's back teeth ground together. "And what? I was *easy* prey?"

Her lips parted. "I-I—"

"Mina is far more dangerous than she appears to be. She never used her powers on you or Lang, so you two don't know what she's capable of doing." His chest seemed to burn. "But I do." *And I'll have her back.* "I do."

He knew Mina far better than anyone ever could.

As for Luke Thorne...yes, he thought the bastard was under Mina's spell. *You'd better not touch her Thorne. She's for me. Only me.*

It was Mina's fault. She'd made him this way. He knew the obsession he felt was dangerous but he couldn't stop it.

She did this to me.

And he was going to make her pay.

***

"The sweaty guy left some listening devices," Rayce announced as the chopper flew away. "Want me to destroy them?"

Luke pursed his lips and considered that. "How many? And where are they?"

"Saw him drop five of them. Bastard thought he was being sly."

Luke was still staring at the chopper. "Nothing gets past a wolf." Agent Lang's mistake.

"Not much," his friend conceded. "Not usually."

But there was a note in the guy's voice…worry? Luke's brows furrowed as he turned to look at the shifter. "What is it?"

Rayce exhaled on a rough sigh. "You sure it's safe to have her here? I mean…if they're FBI, do you really want that kind of heat coming your way?"

Luke braced his legs. "You think I'm afraid?"

"No!" An immediate denial. "I've never seen you be afraid of anyone or anything. That's the problem. If this escalates…if it gets too big…the paranormals will be *out,* man. Is that what you want? No more hiding, no more secrets. Do you want the world to know that they're living with monsters?"

He would have been happy if the monsters had come out long ago, but his brother had been the one to demand the secrecy. "Leo's law," he murmured.

The law that said Luke and his dark brethren had to stay in the shadows. That humans were supposed to be left alone.

A basic peace. Delicate.

Most days.

"Are you *trying* to break that law?" Rayce asked him.

Luke considered that question. His shoulders rolled back. "Maybe I'm just sick of all the rules." So damn many. "Maybe I've decided that I'll start taking what I want."

Rayce glanced over at the waves as they battered the shore. "If that happens, a war will come."

"So it's been predicted." For thousands of years. That one day, he and his brother would battle. Only one would survive.

One brother was of the light.

One was of the dark.

Life. Death.

"I'll always be on your side." Rayce was looking at Luke as he made that pledge. "I hope you know that. You saved me from…shit, from myself. From that beast that I was meant to be."

Because Rayce wasn't like other wolf shifters. He couldn't live in a pack. His beast…it was just a little bit…wrong.

Too strong.

Too powerful.

Too dangerous.

It craves blood and death. A true beast. Rayce had been running wild, on the brink of hurting far too many innocents when Luke had found him. Rayce had been the first paranormal to stay in the cells that Luke had made on his island. The first, but far from the last.

"I have your back," Rayce added. "Know that."

Luke inclined his head. "Getting sentimental on me, are you?"

Rayce didn't smile. "I'm worried about you." That was new.

Rayce pointed toward the house. "I don't trust her. She's doing something to you."

Luke rather thought that she was. "Mina isn't to be hurt. Not by you. Not by those human fools. Not even by my brother." He wanted that understood. Luke walked past his friend, his shoulder brushing against Rayce.

"But what about you?"

He didn't understand. Luke hesitated.

"What if you're the biggest threat to her?"

Anger spiked in Luke. "I don't intend to hurt her."

Rayce put up his hands. "Easy." The wind was hitting harder and dark clouds had rushed toward the island, seemingly from nowhere. "Sometimes, we don't mean to do things. You think I *meant* to attack those people before you found me? That I *meant* to scar that human? I didn't. Sometimes, we all lose control. You're different around her. If anyone can make you lose the control I've always seen you hold so tightly, it's her."

Luke just stared back at him.

"What if that happens? What if she…sees who you really are?"

"She won't." He was just keeping her for a little while. Keeping something that he wanted. Someone.

"What if you try to hurt her?" Rayce had tensed his body, as if expecting a battle. "What then?"

It wasn't something he wanted to think about, not ever. *It won't happen.* "Then you stop me." He drew in a long breath. "By any means necessary."

Shock flashed on Rayce's face. "No, you don't mean—"

"She isn't to be hurt." He couldn't stand that thought. "Not by anyone." Then he turned and began walking toward the house.

Toward her.

"What about the listening devices?" Rayce called.

"Throw them into the fucking ocean," Luke said. Though he wished he could see the look on Garrick's face when the guy tried to listen in to a feed…

Did you think you would come to my house and trick me? Oh, the hell, no.

His steps quickened as he neared his home. As he got closer to Mina. For the first time in longer than he could recall, Luke was actually eager to see someone. He knew Mina would be afraid, and he didn't want that.

He wanted her to look at him and smile.

To feel safe.

Crazy, of course, because no one was ever truly safe when he was near. That was part of his curse.

You weren't supposed to feel safe in the dark.

***

Rayce watched as Luke disappeared into the mansion. He felt something right then...something he hadn't experienced in a long time, not since the morning he'd woken up to find blood all around him.

The morning he'd nearly killed a human.

Fear.

"He isn't thinking clearly," Julian said.

He didn't look to the right. He'd known that Julian was there. When it came to lurking, the panther was an expert.

"I think she's gotten to him," Julian added as he came closer. "When she talked to me before, I just—I had no control. I couldn't stop myself. I was like a puppet on her bloody string."

That didn't make Rayce feel any better. Like him, Julian was one of the dark paranormals who'd wound up on Luke's island because he was too dangerous to be anywhere else. For a time, they'd both been in those cells. Both been more beast than man.

Julian liked to be the panther too much. And his humanity? Sometimes, it slipped away from him. But after the hell he'd been through, well, Rayce wasn't surprised. Julian had learned — very early on in life — that both humans *and* paranormals weren't to be trusted. "So she's really a siren?"

Just when he'd thought he'd heard it all…

"So it would seem," Julian told him. They were side by side now. "And Luke is so blind with lust for her that he'll bring hell to us all."

Quite possibly but… "I'll still be on his side." Fighting, burning. Whatever came their way.

"Wolves, so fuckin' loyal." Julian's smile was bitter. "If you were smart, you'd be finding Marcos, hopping on that boat, and getting away from here as fast as you can. Those FBI agents? They're not going to give up. They'll be back. Luke *knows* they'll be back. He wants the battle. He loves shit like that. After all, chaos is his thing, right? He gets off on it."

I think he gets off with her. But he knew better than to say those words. Luke didn't like it when anyone said the wrong thing about his new pet.

Is that what we all are to him?

Sometimes, he wondered.

"I'm not getting on the boat." Because if they were gearing up for battle, his wolf would want the blood. His head cocked. "Are you?"

But Julian just laughed, a sound that was laced with sadness. "I sold my soul to Lucien Thorne long ago. Made a deal that I won't ever take back."

"And what deal was that?"

Julian's gaze turned distant. "I...hurt someone. Someone I made the mistake of caring about. She was going to die. I couldn't let that happen."

Oh, damn. "You didn't—"

"The Lord of the Dark knows how to keep just about anyone alive."

Rayce whistled.

"I owe him. So, no, there isn't a boat ride in my future. I'm in this thing to the bitter end. Blood and battle and death and then...whatever is waiting."

For a moment, Rayce considered Julian's words. "Do you have regrets?"

"Only that I never fucked her."

Surprised laughter came from Rayce, but Julian's gaze had gone distant. "She hates me now," Julian admitted. "Rightly so, I suppose, but my regret, oh hell yes, mate, it's that I never made love to her. Seems a crying shame to die without that pleasure."

Rayce clapped his hand over Julian's shoulder. "You're not dead yet."

Julian seemed to absorb that for a moment. "No, I don't suppose I am."

"From what you said, neither is she."

But Julian's jaw tightened. "*Undead,*" he muttered.

"Whatever." He wasn't touching that one. "All I'm saying is…there's time. Maybe you can get the chance to cross that little item off your to-do list."

Julian's stare raked him. "Sometimes, you're an arsehole."

"Yeah, but I'm a right arsehole." He smiled. "And I've got some bugs to take care of. See you later, cat."

Rayce was whistling as he walked away.

CHAPTER NINE

The door to the Chamber of Horrors opened — well, that was the name that Mina had given to the room of cells, anyway. It swung open and she cowered against a wall. There really wasn't any good place to hide, and she hoped that —

"What *are* you doing?" Luke demanded.

She opened her eyes. Yes, okay, fear had made her squeeze her eyes shut.

He stared at her with one raised brow. "Closing your eyes doesn't make the bad things disappear, sweetheart." He gestured toward himself. "Still here."

He was there. Just…him. Not Garrick. Not any of the other FBI goons. "Where are they?" Her voice was a whisper.

"Flying away on a chopper —"

He didn't get to say more because she'd run forward and launched herself at him. Mina threw her body into his and held on to him as tightly as she could. "Thank you." Her heart was about to burst out of her chest. "Thank you!" She hugged him even harder. "I will find a way to repay you, I swear, I will. I will give you—"

But her words broke off.

Because she'd just tilted her head back and met his stare. Such a dark, deep stare. The kind of stare that, if a woman wasn't careful, she just might get lost in.

"Don't stop now," Luke murmured. "Tell me more...just what will you give me?"

She couldn't look away from him. "What do you want?"

His smile came, slow and seductive. A smile that made her feel warm on the inside. A smile that made her nipples tighten. A smile that made her need things she shouldn't.

Her breath caught and she started to back away from him, but his hands lifted and curled around her, holding her to him. "What do I want?" His voice had deepened. "So many things."

Her body was pressed fully to his, so she could feel his heat, his strength.

"How about we start with a kiss?"

Because he thought he could seduce her. Hadn't he told her that before? That he'd be able to entice her into his bed. That she'd go, willingly, easily.

He didn't realize how many others had tried to seduce her. Tried and failed. Like she was some sort of game to be played. A pang hit her heart, but he'd just saved her ass, and denying him a kiss…there seemed no point in that. After all, it was just a kiss. "Okay." She tipped back her head. Closed her eyes. And waited.

Then she felt the faint stir of his breath over her cheek. "I told you already, sweetheart…closing your eyes doesn't make the bad things go away."

Her lashes fluttered open.

"I'm still here."

She could see that.

"Remember, Mina. Bad things don't just disappear."

Their mouths were so close. She could almost taste him.

"How about we get you out of that robe…" Luke murmured.

No, no, stripping hadn't been part of the deal. A kiss. *Just a kiss.*

"…and we put you into some real clothes."

Her eyes widened.

"I know…I'm actually getting you *into* clothing. Trust me, I have issues with this, too," he said and his expression was wry.

Her lips curved and her heart seemed to soften a bit. "You are not nearly as big and bad as people say."

His gaze was on her mouth. "Oh, I am. Never doubt that."

He sounded so certain but…Mina gave a quick shake of her head. "You've been good to me. You have every reason to rage and to hate me." They'd hardly had the best beginning. "But you aren't. You're helping me." She just didn't get that. No one ever went out of their way to help her, not without getting something big in return. "Why?"

"You interest me," Luke replied softly. The words were spoken as if he were puzzling through the reasoning himself. "I laugh with you. I…can't figure out what move you'll make next." He nodded. "You surprise me, and I find that I like that."

Her smile widened. "Careful…or you may find that you like me, too."

His stare was still on her mouth. "I may." His hand lifted. Touched her cheek. "You have a dimple, right here."

His touch made her heart jerk.

"And another to match on the other side." His eyes gleamed. "Everything else about you seems built for sin and seduction. You're a walking fantasy, and then I see the dimples…"

Her smile slipped.

His gaze rose to meet hers. "And I think of innocence. Dark creatures aren't known for their innocence."

"I don't want to be dark." Wasn't that the whole reason she'd come to him? Why she'd risked so much? "The Eye can change who I am."

"No." He seemed sad, for her. "Nothing changes who we are. The Eye will only make you weaker. You'll still be the same on the inside. We are what we were always born to be."

So...what? She was born to be an instrument of destruction? A weapon to be used and abused? "I don't believe that. Anyone can change."

He pulled away from her. "I have some clothes in my room that you can use." He turned away.

She didn't follow, not yet. "Just how long have you had the clothes? As long as you had this robe?" She was figuring another former...guest...had left it. "If so, then why am I just learning about a clothing option now?" And not hours ago?

He looked back, his lips curving. "Because I liked you in the robe. You've got killer legs."

She growled at him.

"But I don't exactly want to share the view of you this way." His eyes gleamed for a moment, power flaring. "And if your FBI ex comes around again, he won't find you this way."

Luke was almost out of her Chamber of Horrors, so Mina hurried after him. "How did he *not* find me this time?"

"I made the entrance to the tunnel vanish." He spoke so casually, as if it were the easiest thing in the world to do. *Making a whole tunnel vanish, no biggie.* "Mortal eyes couldn't see it. He walked right past it and never even knew it was there."

She was just a step behind Luke then. He was fast, but—

He whirled toward her. His face had gone cold and hard. Such a sudden change. "We should be very clear about one thing."

"Ah, what's that?" And what was up with his sudden mood change?

"I won't ever be cutting out my heart for you."

Her own heart stilled. "I wouldn't ask you to do that."

"Really?" His dark head cocked as Luke studied her. "Isn't that what you told *him* to do? The FBI ex-lover? Wicked, wicked Mina." But he sounded...admiring.

She didn't speak again. Just hurried out of that tunnel and back into the luxurious walls of his house. He thought she was bad to her core, and maybe that was why she...interested him. But if he knew the truth? If he knew that she'd been a victim, not some powerful paranormal force, would he react the same way?

Maybe she wouldn't interest him then. Maybe she'd lose her appeal.

So she'd play the role he wanted, for now. And she'd try to figure out a way to escape — escape Garrick and escape Luke.

They walked toward his curving staircase, and when she reached for the banister, she caught a glimpse of Rayce. He was smashing something in his hand.

"Got them all, Luke," Rayce called, his voice almost cheerful.

She frowned. "Got what?"

"The bugs your boyfriend left behind," Rayce told her with a quick nod. "Don't worry, they won't hear anything you two do now."

"First, Garrick is *not* my boyfriend. Not even close." She had a flash of pain. Of terror. Of herself begging. Her trembling fingers pressed to the banister. "And next...*bugs?* The guy left listening devices here?"

Luke just shrugged. "You heard Rayce. They're gone now."

"How do you know you got them all?" Then she slapped a hand over her mouth. If they *hadn't* gotten them all, then Garrick had just heard her talking. He'd know she was there. He'd come back for her. He'd lock her up. He'd —

Luke's fingers closed around hers. "You're afraid."

Rayce stepped closer. His nostrils had flared. "I can smell her fear."

She was about to hyperventilate. Garrick could be circling around in his chopper even then. She'd thought she was safe but she wasn't. She *wouldn't* be safe. Not as long as she still had her power. Not as long as Garrick still wanted her.

"We got all the bugs," Rayce told her again, voice softer, and his gaze was considering as it slid over her. "I'm a wolf remember? Not much gets past me. I watched the agent who was sweating...he was giving off as much fear as you are. It was easy to follow his movements."

"S-sweating?"

"Agent Lang," Luke said. He was caressing her hand, almost absently. "He didn't look as thrilled as Garrick and Agent Slate to be here. It was obvious he'd been given a separate mission."

To bug the place.

"Lang...he was always nice to me. Or he tried to be." Her shoulders hunched. "I'd like those clothes now, please."

"The magic word," Rayce muttered.

"What?" He'd lost her.

But Luke was already wrapping an arm around her and guiding her up the stairs. As if she needed guiding. Mina looked back at Rayce, he was still watching her with that assessing stare.

"You aren't who you seem to be," he said.

But the warning—was it for her? Or was it for Luke?

"Fuck off, wolf," Luke ordered, his hold tightening on Mina. "I have her."

For the moment, it would seem that he did.

***

She wore jeans—jeans that hugged her legs and curved over her ass. Jeans that stretched and felt pretty much like heaven on her. Her top was loose, dark red, a color that she secretly loved. It was as soft as silk and she loved it, too.

And he'd given her back the fuck-me heels. At least they matched her shirt but...she didn't love them.

Mina took a deep breath and opened the doors that would take her out onto the balcony. "I guess your last lover and I must be the same size—" she began.

But her words ended when she saw the table. A perfectly set table that even had lit candles softly glowing. Luke stood by the table, wearing...a suit. Black coat, white dress shirt, perfectly tailored pants. He looked absolutely sexy. Drop dead gorgeous.

Mouthwatering.

He frowned at her. "Why would you say that? You're not the same size as my last lover. You're nothing like my last lover."

"Uh, the clothes?" Mina cleared her throat. "I just meant, um, they fit—" Her words broke off. The wind had tousled his dark hair. He was lethal. Damn, damn, *damn* but he made that suit look good.

"They're *your* clothes. I bought them when I went to the mainland to check on Eli and no, before you get all worried...Garrick wasn't aware I'd made the purchase. I gave your sizes to a trusted friend and she picked things up for me and had them sent to Marcos. All very secretly, I assure you."

She should move. Step out of the doorway. Go to the table. Not drool at him. Do *something*. "How did you know my size?"

He pulled out the chair to his right. Very gentlemanly-like. "Because I've touched you. I held your body close. I know *you*."

Her legs were moving again. That was good. Her high heels clicked. "You may have figured out what size jeans I wear...but trust me, you don't *know* me." She sat in the chair. He pushed her forward, just a little bit.

Then he moved around the table and sat across from her.

She managed to yank her gaze off his sexy self and actually focus on the table and then— there was no help for her drooling. A feast was before her. An actual, honest-to-God feast. And her stomach was cramping she was so excited.

"Fresh seafood," he said. "Shrimp and grilled fish, some calamari, oysters if you like them…"

She liked *everything*. Mina put her hands in her lap so that she wouldn't start grabbing things and shoving them in her mouth.

"What's wrong?" Luke asked, that faint line appearing between his brows. "Aren't you hungry?"

Aren't you – She was almost crying because she was so hungry and there was just so much food there. So much.

"I can get something else," he said, voice stilted. And he reached for a little silver bell that she hadn't even noticed before. What, did he actually ring that bell to get service? Because she hadn't seen anyone else and if he was about to make someone appear —

Her hand closed around his wrist. "Stop." The word came out hoarse.

He was staring at her with the dark gaze that made her want to get lost…*in him.*

"What's wrong with the food?" Luke asked quietly.

"Nothing." Absolutely nothing. "Thank you."

His eyelashes flickered. She released him and tried to *slowly* put some food on her plate. She was going to be careful, and she was not going to act as if she were starving.

She *wasn't*.

Mina picked up her fork and knife. She cut into the fish, hoping that her shaking fingers wouldn't send the utensils flying. But she actually managed to get a little piece cut and she lifted it to her mouth.

"How long has it been since you've eaten?"

Well...

"I left you today without food. I'm sorry." His voice had thickened. "Fucking sorry...I will *never* do that again."

She ate the fish and it was so good. So incredibly good. She took another bite. Another. She squeezed her eyes shut. Tried to make herself slow down and chew.

"Longer than just a day...wasn't it?" Now there was a bite in his voice. "*Mina.*"

Her eyes flew open. "I-I ate some yesterday." And—screw it. She was not going to keep fighting her hunger and act all prim and proper. She was *starving.* She started shoving shrimp into her mouth. She ate and she *loved* it and she was so happy that she wanted to laugh, but she was afraid she'd choke on all of that delicious food if she did.

And he just...he watched her. Luke drank his whiskey—she was sure that amber liquid in the short, squat glass was whiskey—and he watched her eat.

She cleaned her plate. Since he was just sitting there, she may have helped herself to his, too. *Why waste the food?* Then she went for the wine that was waiting. The dizziness that had been filling her body all day was gone. She was back to being herself. She was—

"You will *never* go without food again."

"It's hard to stop for meals when you're running for your life." The words slipped out. She drank more wine. "That was...delicious."

"You were weak...from hunger."

"Hunger, fear, desperation—you name it." She took another sip. That wine was *incredible.* So sweet. She'd never had anything quite like it before. She drank more.

"Your ex-lover was after you."

"Because he wants to use me. Garrick knows what I can do and his little team of twisted agents—they're hunting me down because they want me to be their weapon." She poured more wine. *Don't mind if I do.* "But I'm not going to be their weapon." Another long sip. More of a gulp. That wine was *fantastic.* Never, ever had she had a drink that good. "I won't get into the heads of humans and make them do things...make them hurt each other. I don't care what Garrick has in mind. He can torture me again. He can lock me up again, but *I won't* use my power to hurt people." She lifted her wine glass, preparing for another long gulp. "I—"

"*Enough.*"

He sounded angry. Why? Oh, was it because she was drinking all the wine? Her bad. "Do you want some?" She offered the wine to him, blushing a bit.

He looked at the dark liquid. Red wine.

"Your whiskey is gone." She licked her lips, still savoring that wine. "It only seems fair to give you some of this."

"Fair." It was almost as if he were tasting the word. "I suppose that would be fair." He leaned forward. "Just a sip."

Her breath caught. *Just a sip.* "Because you're afraid that if you get drunk, I'll use my power on you again?"

But he gave a deep, rough laugh. "Ah, sweetheart. I've learned my lesson. I'll keep my guard up when I drink around you." His smile was lethal. "I'll stay in control. Don't you worry about that. When we're together, I'll always have free will. Everything I do, it will be because I want it. You have nothing to fear on that end."

A man she couldn't hurt with a careless word. Finally.

She put the glass to his lips and Mina watched, oddly fascinated, as he drank from her. His lips—why had she thought that they were cruel? They weren't. They were sexy. *He* was sexy.

"Ask me a question, Mina. I'll give you the truth now. Fair play and all that jazz."

She wasn't sure what he meant. Her mind was a little foggy. Maybe she was drunk. "Do you want me?" Mina blurted.

"I'd like nothing better than to strip you naked and take you right here."

Her lips parted. *Yes, please* was literally on the tip of her tongue. She had to *fight* to hold those words back and that was when Mina knew... "You bastard." She could only shake her head. Her heart thudded in her chest and her hands began to shake. "There was something in the wine, wasn't there?" The wine she'd been chugging.

He shrugged. "Only a little bit of truth."

She shot to her feet. "What does that even mean?"

He tilted back his dark head as he stared up at her. "It means...payback."

She was *hurt*. He'd blindsided her. "I thought you were helping me." She had to blink, quickly, because—

He grabbed the sides of the table, his hands clenching. "You are *not* crying."

She was. She dashed at her left cheek, swiping away a tear. "So what if I am? What does that do to you? Why does it *matter*?"

Luke rose to his feet. "It *hurts* me."

The wind wasn't blowing any longer. Everything was suddenly very, very still.

"Your tears *hurt* me. I can watch a thousand humans cry. I have watched that. I've watched paranormals die. I've watched them suffer in agony. None of that mattered. It's *your* tears that have my guts feeling like they're being ripped out of me." His breath was ragged. He was still gripping the table too tightly. "That's why it matters. Because for some fucking reason that I haven't fully figured out yet...*you* matter to me."

Her gaze jerked to the wine glass. The glass she'd given to him. "You...you took the truth, too." Whatever had been in that glass, whatever potion that had made her lips too loose and truth spill from her mouth...he'd taken it too.

I suppose that would be fair.

"Better hurry with your questions, sweetheart," he gritted out. "I only had a few sips. You'll be spilling secrets all night, but I only have a few moments more. Not as much brew, and..." He gave her a slow wink. "Faster metabolism, too."

She could ask him anything—and he had to tell her the truth? "Where is the Eye of Hell?"

And he lifted his right hand. On his ring finger, she saw a heavy flash of gold. Big, thick.

"The Eye is in here," he told her, gazing down at the ring. "But it won't do you any good. Only I can wield it. You want power taken away...that's something only I can do. On your hand, the Eye would be useless."

Dammit. If he had to tell the truth…

This was all for nothing. She should have kept running. She could have hopped a boat and made it to the Caribbean. Maybe Garrick wouldn't have followed her there.

"My turn," Luke said. "Did you really tell your lover to cut out his heart?"

"No." She felt almost numb. "What I said was…'Do it.'" Two such simple and terrifying words. "I'd managed to get free of the chains that he was keeping me in. I tricked him and locked him in my cell instead. He was yelling at me, screaming that if I left him, it would be like cutting out his heart." She shuddered as she remembered the feel of all the bruises on her. "So I told him to 'Do it'. I ran and didn't look back." Did that make her evil? Well, since everyone thought she'd been born evil, she wasn't sure it really mattered.

He walked around the table, coming toward her. The wind was blowing again. The ocean was pounding. And the sun had set—she hadn't even noticed what must have been one killer view. "Chains?" he rasped.

She smiled at him. "Do you think you're the first to lock me up? Not even close. Garrick and his agents were supposed to be the good guys. I went to them because I wanted to help, not hurt people. I just…I never wanted to be bad." That was the story of her life. "But once the government had me, they didn't want to let go." Her muscles tightened as she remembered that prison, buried deep underground, far from prying eyes. "Such a small cell. And the chains were tight. They usually kept me gagged, too, just like you did, because if I talked—"

His hands were on her shoulders. "Do you want them dead?"

"What?"

"Tell me everyone who hurt you. Give me the names, and I'll end them all."

She hadn't been afraid of him before…wait, okay, she had but…*in this moment, he utterly terrifies me.* Because she was sure he meant exactly what he'd just said.

"Don't look so upset," he murmured. "They have Eli. I was planning to go after them all anyway."

He was planning—"No." Now she was the one grabbing him. "They can't know what you are. If they know, they'll try to take you, too. They'll try to use you. I've already brought too much attention to you as it is." She'd put him in Garrick's sights. Dammit.

For nothing.

"Now, sweetheart, you sound as if you truly care what happens to me." His smile was temptation itself. "Is that true?"

"Yes." The single word was ripped right from her. Stupid wine. "I don't want you hurt. I don't want them hurt, either, despite what the agents did to me. I just want…I want out. I want a normal life. Is that so wrong?"

"Normal is over-rated. And boring."

"Normal is good. Normal is happy." She'd never had that, though.

His gaze narrowed. "Tell me what you want most in this world, right now. Tell me…and I'll give it to you."

Disbelief rocked her. "Why?"

"Because I can still see the tears on your cheeks. Because they still hurt me." Each word was growled. "Because *I* did this to you. I gave you the wine. I knew it would force you to tell me your secrets. I should have fucking stuck to just seducing them out of you."

"I…thought I could trust you."

"I know. That's what makes this even worse." His lips twisted in disgust. "I don't know what you're doing to me, but it *will* stop."

Yes, yes, it had to stop. She didn't know what he was doing to her either. This mad attraction, this need that rose within her — it all had to stop.

"Tell me the one thing you want — anything, and it will be yours."

What did she want? That was easy. She wanted her power gone. She'd already told him that all she wanted was to be normal. So she'd tell him again and he'd use the Eye and she'd get —

"You." Mina barely recognized her own, husky voice. "I want you."

His pupils flared. The darkness of his eyes just deepened and then—he'd yanked her toward him. His mouth was on hers. She should stop. She should say that she'd misspoken but…

She hadn't.

In that one moment, her soul laid bare, she did want him. She wanted to let herself go. To give in to the attraction that she felt for him. An attraction that seemed to burn her from the inside. A need too powerful to be real.

Too strong to ignore.

Later, she'd blame that damn wine. She'd curse it. But for the moment, her mouth opened beneath his. She kissed him, her desire blazing inside of her.

The sun had gone down. Stars glittered. So many damn stars. Thousands of them. And his hands were tight around her. His mouth claimed hers, seduced. She tasted that sweet wine on his tongue and maybe it was making her even drunker, but she didn't care. Mina grabbed his fancy coat and shoved it off him. She reached for the buttons of his shirt and yanked—

The buttons popped and he laughed.

Why did that sound make her feel so warm on the inside?

His hands curled around her hips, he lifted her up, holding her so easily, and he walked back, pinning her against the exterior wall of his home, holding her against the stone with his muscled body in front of her. Mina's legs wrapped around his hips. She could feel the hard thrust of his cock, shoving against the front of his pants, and she arched into him. She wanted that thick length in her. Wanted to ride him and let go of everything else.

She didn't want to be a victim. Didn't want to be a monster. She just wanted...to be a woman, making love, going wild. Feeling pleasure.

Normal.

Maybe that had been her wish, after all. And he was giving her just what she'd asked for.

His hand slid under her shirt. Warm and strong, and when his fingers smoothed up her rib cage, when she felt him touch her breasts, pleasure pulsed through her. Mina tipped back her head, gasping, and he teased her nipples.

That was good...but... "Put your mouth on me."

His dark laugh rumbled. "I love a woman who tells me what she wants."

She didn't usually, though. Usually she had to be so careful with every word that she said. She was always afraid of pushing people to do what they didn't want to do...but she couldn't push him. And she couldn't hold back the truth of her need. She was just saying what she wanted.

He pulled the shirt over her head. Tossed it aside. She was wearing a thin scrap of lace as a bra, she'd hated it when she first put it on, thinking it was a cast-off from his previous lover but now, the bra felt sexy.

She felt sexy as he stared down at her. His eyes were shining with desire—literally, shining in a way that no mortal man's ever could. The darkness had given way to light, to a glow, the proof of his true nature. She'd only been with human lovers. And even then, she'd worried...

Had they wanted to truly be with her? Or had she influenced them with her voice? Said the wrong thing because she wasn't careful enough, took away their will or—

"You aren't with me." His voice was a fierce growl. "That won't work."

"Luke, I—"

But they were moving. He carried her back into his bedroom. Spread her out on the bed and stepped back. His gaze swept over her. "I fucking love the shoes, but they have to go." He caught her ankle and slipped one high heel off her foot. "Everything has to go." His fingers slid up the arch of her foot. She'd *never* thought that part of her body was an erogenous zone.

She'd been wrong.

She'd just never had Luke touch her there before.

"You are so gorgeous," he said.

Heat spread through her.

"I could just…" He slipped off her other high heel. It clattered to the floor. "Gobble you right up."

Yes, please.

His hands went to her waist. He unhooked the jeans, pulled them down her legs, taking her underwear with them. She was clad just in the bra and it was too much. She wanted it gone. Mina wanted him to see all of her. For the first time, she didn't want to hide even a single part of herself from a lover.

There were…marks on her body. Marks that she'd always been embarrassed about before. But Luke was touching her hips, sliding his fingers over the old scars. She didn't remember how she'd gotten them — they were thin and long, almost like the marks that would come from a knife, slicing against her skin.

For as long as she could remember, those scars had been there, on each hip, on the tops of her legs. A few along her stomach and sides.

Some lovers had frowned at them. They'd looked at her with worry.

Luke was bending his head. He was kissing them, his lips feathering over her. "Fucking gorgeous."

A smile slipped over her lips. Maybe she'd been wrong to choose human lovers before.

Maybe all along, she should have been looking for someone like him.

There was dark stubble on his jaw and it scraped lightly against her skin. She didn't mind that little burn, in fact, she liked it. Her hips arched toward him and his hand—those long, strong fingers delved between her thighs.

He touched her and she knew he'd find her already wet. She was. With him, it just took a kiss, a touch, and her body reacted. His fingers stroked her, then he was pushing into her core, and her hips jerked against him.

"Oh, sweetheart, I have to taste…"

He moved his body, sliding between her thighs. His dark head bent and then his mouth was on her. When he'd kissed her before, she'd thought…*The man knows how to use his tongue.*

The same thought flashed through her mind again. She didn't even try to hold back the moan that broke from her. She pushed her sex against him, wanting more, needing to feel the lick of his tongue and the thrust of his fingers. Luke gave her what she wanted—gave her that and so much more with that wicked, talented mouth of his. Her orgasm thundered over her, slamming through her body in a fast wave as she cried out his name.

And he kept tasting her. As she shuddered and her breath heaved, his mouth stayed on her. Aftershocks of pleasure had her sex contracting.

"Luke?"

His head lifted. The shine in his eyes was even brighter.

She was still wearing her bra. He still had on his shirt—unbuttoned, but on—and he was wearing his pants.

That wasn't going to do. "I want you naked. I want you *in* me."

As she watched, hunger flashed on his face. A wild, dark lust and she realized what she'd said. No, no, had she just influenced him? He'd said he would be safe, that he was—

He moved away from her. Stood at the edge of the bed. Stared down at her. "You need to let that fear go." His voice was so thick and dark. "I'm in control. Nothing bad will happen with me."

Her heartbeat was still racing too fast. "I thought you said you were the bad thing."

He dropped his shirt to the floor. His pants followed. He stood there, totally naked and her gaze drank him in. Those wide shoulders. Those rippling muscles. That thick, full cock.

She licked her lips.

"Maybe I'm bad so I can do good things to you." He moved back onto the bed, putting his knee on the mattress.

She parted her legs, wanting him to thrust deep, wanting that wild rush of pleasure again. She wasn't thinking about what would come *after.* After reality came back. After she left his bed. After she left him.

She just wanted this moment. This time.

This man.

He settled between her legs, spreading her thighs even wider. The head of his cock pushed against her, and she was so ready and wet that she knew he'd sink deep into her. But...

He didn't.

Luke's hand rose. Carefully, he pulled down the straps of her bra. She lifted up, arching toward him, and he undid the clasp in the back. He pushed the bra to the side of the bed and bent over her, his lips curling around one aching breast. When he licked her, when he sucked her, she bit her lip because it felt so good. She wanted to cry out, to shout his name but...

She knew two shifters were on the island. Shifters with extremely good hearing. This moment wasn't for them to overhear. It was just for her and Luke.

He kissed a path to her other breast. His cock was still lodged at the entrance to her body. Mina's legs rose and locked around his hips. She wanted him in. She wanted —

He sank into her, deep and full, thick and so hard. "Luke!" A whisper, a demand.

He pulled back, then drove deep. He licked her breast. Kissed her.

Her sex clamped greedily around him as she held him tight. In and out, deeper, harder, he kept thrusting into her. His head lifted. His gaze held hers. The bed jerked beneath his heavy thrusts. She loved it — loved the way his cock slid over her clit with each hard drive of his body. Her nails raked down his back and she lifted her head up, kissing his chest. His shoulder. When he moved closer to her, she licked the hot skin of his neck, then put her teeth on him, giving him a rough, primitive little nip.

He growled and thrust even harder.

His hands caught hers, and he pinned them to the bed. He was rougher now, slamming into her and her orgasm erupted. The pleasure seemed to go on and on, not a wave — a storm. Hard and strong, catching her and then sweeping right over her. And he was there, thrusting, pumping into her, claiming her, taking every single bit of her —

She felt his climax. The hot release jetted inside of her as his body shuddered and he gripped her even tighter. He was staring at her as the pleasure hit. Mina saw the ecstasy on his face and knew his climax was just as strong as hers.

It had *never* been that way for her before. Her body was still quaking, still holding so tight to his. Still wanting him.

Slowly, her heartbeat stopped thundering. Sweat slickened their bodies. Her breath didn't heave any longer and she wet her lips.

He kissed her. Soft. Tender. And —

"That was a nice start," Luke told her. "How about we go again?"

He was growing thicker within her. Readying again.

Mina smiled at him.

Yes, please.

***

"Why aren't the bugs working?" Garrick demanded.

Timothy Lang swallowed, his Adam's apple bobbing nervously. "I-I don't know."

"You *put* them in place, correct?"

"All five, yes, yes, I did."

But they weren't transmitting. Garrick was getting jack shit.

"They found the bugs," Madeline said as she paced nearby.

They were in a temporary base. Lucky for them, Uncle Sam had a Naval Air Station in the area, a place with plenty of room for their group and even a holding cell for their new friend, Eli. Plus some room for…extras.

"We need to be careful," Madeline continued doggedly. "Luke Thorne isn't just some playboy—the guy is trouble."

The guy was a pain in Garrick's ass.

"She wasn't there," Timothy said. He crossed his arms over his chest. "We searched that whole island and Mina *wasn't* there. Maybe he found the bugs and got rid of them because he was doing other things—running drugs or some shit. He may not have any connection to Mina at all."

"He knows her," Garrick said flatly. He'd seen the look in Luke's eyes. Jealousy. Possessiveness. Oh, hell, yes, the bastard knew Mina. "Maybe he stashed her somewhere else." The tricky SOB. "But he has her close. He wouldn't let a woman like her vanish."

He caught the look that Timothy and Madeline shared. Rage had him grinding his back teeth.

"Maybe you should back off this one," Madeline said softly, carefully. "You don't have the perspective you need to—"

His fist slammed into the desk near him. "I have the best fucking perspective! I *know* her, inside and out! I'm the one who made her work with us before. I'm the one who controlled *her*." His insides twisted. "She was our most successful weapon. The enemy never saw her coming—she could take out a whole base with just a few whispers. Getting her back is top priority. Not just for me...*for everyone* at our agency." The order to track Mina James had come down from the very top. But even if it hadn't, even if his boss hadn't wanted Mina back...

I would still be hunting her.

"Sorry," Madeline said, but she didn't sound particularly contrite. He'd have to watch her...and Timothy. That guy might be too soft. "What's our next move? You want us to bring in Luke Thorne?"

He'd love to toss that jerk into a cell. Garrick smiled. "We don't have to bring him in. We'll get him to come to us. *And* to bring us Mina."

"Good luck with that," Timothy muttered.

Garrick's eyes narrowed. "I don't need luck. I have something else." He smiled. "I have Luke's friend." A battered, but still alive Eli. "He's going to bring Luke to us. We just have to give Eli the right motivation."

Timothy swiped a hand over the back of his neck. "And what motivation would that be?"

"Oh, simple, if Eli doesn't cooperate, I'll kill him."

Anger flashed on Timothy's face as he dropped his hand. "When did we become the bad guys? I thought we were supposed to be the next wave of protection for our country. That we were trail blazers. Protectors, not—"

Garrick stood toe-to-toe with him. "In order to protect the humans, a few paranormals will have to die. It's an acceptable loss in my book."

Timothy glared at him.

"Is it acceptable in yours?" Garrick threw at him because he'd really started to wonder about the guy. "The lives of a few lost creatures who would as soon kill *you* as look at you? Because that's where you're getting confused, Agent Lang. You're thinking of them as people. They're not. Some of them are evil straight to their core. Some of them would love nothing more than to rip apart innocents. To spread bloodlust. Destruction."

"Isn't that what *we're* doing?" Timothy asked.

Garrick sighed. "This isn't what I wanted."

For a moment, Timothy looked hopeful. "Good, good, I knew you'd see reason, if you just stopped and cooled down. I knew—"

Garrick pulled out his gun and shot the other man. Timothy fell down, twitching, body jerking.

Madeline surged forward.

Garrick turned toward her, putting up a hand. "Don't worry, it was just a tranq."

Her eyes were wide, stunned. "You...knocked out a fellow agent?"

It wasn't as if this were the first time. "We need to put him in a cell and let the agency deal with him. If he isn't working with us..." Garrick shrugged and put his weapon back in the holster. "Then he's a threat. You realize that, don't you?"

Madeline's gaze flew between him and Timothy's slumped form.

"You *realize* that?" Garrick prompted. His fingers lingered near the holster.

She straightened her shoulders. "Yes, sir."

"Good." Because he'd been about to shoot her, too. And training new agents? Such a pain in the ass. His hand fell back to his side. "We'll take him to holding." Just where he'd left Eli. "And then we'll get Luke Thorne to come to us."

He'll bring Mina to me…or I will take away everything that man holds dear.

CHAPTER TEN

"I'm…sorry."

Mina forced her eyes to open. She really just wanted to sink into sleep and forget all the worries out in the real world, just for a while, but…Luke was apologizing. An event she was sure didn't happen often.

His fingers trailed over her arm. "I shouldn't have given you that drink."

"No," she agreed. "You're an asshole."

His lips twitched. "You need to stop doing that."

She settled deeper into the covers. "Then stop being an asshole."

His smile stretched. "I meant…stop making me like you."

He liked it when women called him names after sex? She'd make a mental note of that.

"It's…dangerous for me to trust the wrong people. I have to be very careful," he added. "Because if something happens and I were to ever lose my control…"

He hadn't lost his control, not even when things got all hot and heavy between them. "Can't imagine that," she whispered.

His smile faded. "That is a very good thing."

Was it?

"I wouldn't want you...hurt."

Nice, considering she didn't want to be hurt.

"So I needed the truth from you. And I still need it."

Uh, oh. Alarm bells went off in her head. He was *not* about to interrogate her while she was still naked in his bed. No way. No—

"The wine won't be in your system much longer. And I won't be giving it to you again."

"You'd better not," she rumbled. Some of that nice, after-sex languor had left her body.

He kept stroking her arm. "How did you get those marks on your body? Tell me who gave them to you."

"I don't know." Damn him, the wine *was* still making her talk. Her muscles tensed. "They were just there as long as I can remember." It was...scary, being the one who didn't have a choice, who had to speak when compelled. It made her hate her own power even more. She yanked the covers up to her chin, feeling far too vulnerable. *Don't look at my scars.*

"What about your parents?" Luke asked her. "Do they know what happened to you?"

"My father was a Navy man." And her heart twisted. "He was lost at sea before I was born."

He bent toward her and pressed a kiss to her cheek. "I'm sorry."

So was she.

"Your mother?" Luke prompted. "Tell me what happened to her."

Her heart wasn't just twisting now. It was being squeezed by an ice-cold fist. "You know...I would have told you all this, without the weird wine. Maybe you should have tried asking me." Her past wasn't exactly pretty but...*I would have told him.* "My mother stayed with me until I was six years old and then, one day...she walked into the water."

She felt him stiffen beside her.

"We lived along the California coast," Mina continued. "She left me with a friend..." The friend who would later turn Mina over to children's services. "And she just...she went straight into the water." That memory was one that had haunted her forever. Seeing her mother just walk away. The waves had beat at her, getting higher and rougher. And Mina had just been sitting on the beach, screaming.

Come back, mommy, come back!

"She left me." And the pain had never ended. "For years...I hated the water. I was terrified of it. Then one day, I decided I wasn't going to be afraid any longer." And, as if fate were playing with her, she'd realized that she had a natural gift for swimming. She could swim faster, harder, than anyone she'd ever met. She could hold her breath for almost five minutes. "I don't like being afraid," she said.

He pressed another kiss to her cheek. "No, I don't imagine that you do."

She sat up in bed, making sure to pull those covers with her. He backed up, but stayed close. Her gaze held his. "I can't make you tell me about your family."

Luke laughed. "Trust me, you don't want to know about them."

"Yes, I do. Isn't it *fair*," she stressed that word, "for you to tell me about them?"

He was silent a moment, and then… "The only family I have left is a brother. My twin."

Right. She knew about him. "The Lord of the Light."

His laugh was bitter. "Yeah, he calls his dumb ass that. We grew up…always knowing we were opposite, always being told that we were fated to destroy each other." He rubbed his jaw across her arm, the stubble rasping lightly. "How's that for a fun Christmas card greeting?"

"Do you…talk to him?"

"I try not to. Despite the shit that's been prophesized, I don't want to kill him." He went silent again, as if he'd shocked himself.

"Is it…true?" Mina asked. "Is he supposed to be good and you're evil?" Two twins — dark and light, good and evil, a balance in the world. So the stories went.

But stories could be wrong.

"You tell me," Luke said, his voice low. "Am I evil?"

Her hand lifted and her fingers smoothed over his cheek. His stubble rasped beneath her touch. He'd protected her, given her sanctuary. He'd also drugged her with some kind of truth serum. And locked her in a cell.

"You don't know, do you?" For an instant, she could have sworn that he sounded sad. "That's the problem, Mina. I don't know either."

"Luke —"

But…a phone was ringing. The sound was so incredibly normal that she was jarred. Luke swore and slid from the bed. He paced toward the heavy, wooden dresser and lifted his phone. She hadn't even seen it over there.

He frowned at the screen, then swiped his finger over it. Putting the phone to his ear, he said, "This is Thorne."

***

Garrick pressed the knife deeper into Eli's side.

The guy was bleeding all over the floor, twitching, but…at least the spiders weren't sliding off the fellow any longer.

"L-Luke?" Eli gasped out.

"Eli?" Luke Thorne's voice seemed to fill the cell. Garrick had turned the phone on speaker. He wanted to hear every single word of this conversation. "Where in the hell are you?"

Hell is right.

"M-Mina James…" Eli trembled. "She's…dangerous."

Garrick nodded. Those were exactly the words he'd told Eli to say.

"Don't…don't trust her," Eli added. "She h-hurt me."

Garrick pulled the knife back. It made a wet, gushy sound as it left Eli's side.

"Where are you?" Luke asked again, voice tight.

"I-I got out of the hospital," Eli's words tumbled out. "But I need help. Will you h-help me?"

Silence. Eli's ragged breathing seemed far too loud. Why wasn't Luke Thorne offering to help? Why wasn't he promising to rush to the rescue or —

"Agent McAdams," Luke drawled, "I'm guessing you're right there."

Eli's frantic gaze shot toward Garrick.

"If you're torturing Eli, I have to say...you're going to piss me off." Luke's tone was still mild. "And me pissed off? Not a good thing. Just ask Eli."

It's not. Eli mouthed those words.

Garrick's gaze narrowed to slits.

"I'm not the kind of man you can threaten," Luke continued. "I thought you'd learned that already."

The bastard was about to be a dead man. Garrick shoved Eli away. "I know you have her!"

"And I knew you were there...I could hear your desperate breaths."

Those breaths had been Eli's!

"If you don't bring Mina James to me," Garrick blasted at him, "I will slice your buddy Eli into pieces."

Eli was shuddering...and bleeding all over the damn place.

"Let's see if the spiders can still crawl out of him when I've got him cut open." Garrick's hand tightened on his knife. "Because I will do it, if you don't bring me Mina."

Silence. No, shit, the guy should be begging to make a deal! He should be—

"I'm coming for you, Agent McAdams," Luke said. The words were so dark. And...hushed? "You'll be the one cut open. You'll be the one begging. And you will *never*, ever touch Mina again."

The line ended. The bastard had hung up—on him.

A sigh came from behind Garrick.

"That didn't go so well," Madeline announced. Her high heels clicked on the floor.

Garrick turned toward her, smiling. "It went perfectly. He finally admitted that he has Mina. And he's coming to us."

"*Without* Mina."

Garrick just laughed. "No way. She'll be here. She'll be with him."

Madeline shook her head. "He just told you that you would never touch her—"

"I *know* Mina. She can't stand the thought of someone being hurt." The pool of blood on the floor was getting bigger. He might have cut Eli too deeply. Oh, well. "She'll find out what's happening. And Luke Thorne? He won't be able to keep her away. When Mina wants something bad enough…" His hand rose and pressed to the scar above his heart. "She gets it."

***

He wanted to crush the phone in his hand. Grind it to dust. Instead, Luke very carefully put the phone back down and he turned to face Mina.

A Mina who was already out of bed and frantically dressing.

Luke frowned at her. "What are you doing?"

"Going to the rescue…with you."

The fuck she was. He shook his head. "No, you're not."

She kept dressing. Jerking on those jeans, doing a little shimmy.

"Mina…"

She hooked the bra. Searched a few moments for her shirt then yanked it over her head.

He stalked toward her. Luke caught her arm and turned her to fully face him. "You aren't going anywhere."

But her face was determined. "I heard enough of that phone call to know what's happening, despite you trying to keep your voice all quiet." Her gaze was stark. "That bartender, your *friend*, Eli, he's being hurt…because of me."

"No, he's being hurt because Garrick McAdams is a dick." They should be clear on that point. This wasn't her fault.

Her jaw hardened. "If I return to Garrick, he'll let Eli go."

Luke cocked his head as he considered that. "Will he?"

She hesitated.

"Thought so," Luke murmured. "He'll just keep you *and* kill Eli. Time for me to stop the bastard. To *end* him."

Her eyes seemed so very big and stark. "It's my fight. I'm the one who brought him to you —

to Eli. I'm not just going to hide when you face off. I can help—"

So cute. "I don't need help." But he did need her to be safe. Her safety mattered far more to him than anything else. That realization was unsettling. He wasn't normally unsettled by anything.

"Everyone needs help, sometime." Her hand pressed to his chest. "I'm not staying behind. I'm not going to be locked up again. I'm stronger than I look, far stronger. I beat Garrick once, and I can do it again."

She was so determined. So desperate.

"I don't want him hurting you," Mina said, her husky voice seeming to slip right through Luke, "because of me."

He bent over her and pressed a kiss to her lips. "When will you see, sweetheart, that I don't hurt easily? I don't break, Mina." He broke others. Just as he was about to break Garrick. He'd warned the guy, but the agent hadn't listened.

Now he'd pay.

Luke turned from her and dressed quickly, quietly. He exhaled slowly then spun for the door. He found Mina in his path.

"I'm not a thing," Mina said. Her chin notched up. "Not some pet to be kept or some prize to be won. I don't stay where I'm put." Each word shook with anger. "You don't lock me up.

You don't *keep* me. I go where I choose. With whom I choose." Her eyes blazed at him. "A man's life is on the line. He's hurting, perhaps dying, just because I went into his bar. I'm not going to sit back. You *aren't* going to leave me. I'm coming with you, even if I have to swim every bit of the way."

He stared down at her.

"I'm not weak. I'm not going to slow you down. I can help." Her breath blew out in a low rush. "I *will* help."

Luke knew he could have forced her to stay on his island. There wasn't a dark creature that he couldn't control. He had absolute power over his dominion but...

He didn't want to control her.

Mina had spirit. She had fire. She wanted to fight. And, based on what he'd learned about her, she deserved her vengeance. He'd give her that gift. Perhaps she'd be grateful. He'd rather enjoy her gratitude.

He'd rather enjoy...her. *So be it.* Luke inclined his head and saw the surprise flash on her face.

"You...agree?"

"I agree, with conditions."

She nodded, fast. "Any conditions. Great, wonderful, you—"

"You don't get hurt." That was the condition that mattered. "If things go to hell..." When he was around, they tended to do just that. "Then you get behind me. I can take any fire, any damage, and still keep going." Immortality had its benefits. "You can't. So when bullets fly or fire rages, get that sweet ass behind me."

"You don't have to tell me that twice."

She seemed so fierce. So determined. But...

Afraid. He could see her fear, yet Mina wasn't letting that stop her. So very interesting. "You'll come back with me." Those words pushed from him. "When the battle is over, you come back here with me." He lifted his hand, and the Eye of Hell gleamed on his finger. "Then we'll work on the little...problem you have."

Her breath caught. "Luke?"

"You'll come back with me." For some reason, he needed to hear her say those words.

"I'll come back with you."

The weight on his heart—a weight that had never been there before—eased. He nodded. "Good. Now let's go find that bastard of an ex that you have..." He considered Garrick McAdams. "Because I might just finish cutting out his heart."

CHAPTER ELEVEN

The boat drifted into the dock close to midnight. Luke could easily hear voices and laughter floating on the wind. Key West was just getting the party started at that time.

"You want me to wait for you, boss?" Marcos asked.

Luke jumped onto the dock. He turned back, offering his hand to Mina. She followed him over, a quick, graceful little jump. "No need," Luke told him. "Go offshore." It would be safer for the man that way. "When I need you, I'll call."

Marcos nodded. A few moments later, he pulled away from the dock.

"He sort of reminds me of Charon," Mina said.

It was a name that Luke hadn't heard in a very, very long time.

"From mythology," she added. "Charon ferried the newly dead across Styx—"

"I know who Charon is." *Was.* She was hitting a bit too close to home for him, so he caught her elbow and steered her away from the dock. "I'm wagering your Garrick has eyes on the dock. They'll be reporting our arrival to him."

"He's not *my* anything," Mina snapped back with the bite he loved. "And if you think that Garrick's team is watching, then maybe we should have planned a more secretive entrance. Not a big, flashy Come-And-Get-Me deal."

He took his time strolling down the dock. There was an old pirate shop to the side, one that offered tourists real pirate's treasure, only the shop owners failed to mention those gold and silver bits were cursed. The tourists would learn that truth later. "Ah, now, sweetheart, haven't you realized yet? I am a flashy kind of guy."

"I am noticing."

They walked a few more feet...

And then the agents swarmed. At least half a dozen men and women in black — black clothes and black bullet proof vests — burst from the shadows and surrounded them. Mina stiffened, but Luke just smiled. "Right on time."

"This is a shitty plan," Mina said. "You really should have discussed it with me in much greater detail."

Yes, but she just would have argued. Tried to protect him. Been her charming self. So... "Just trust me."

Her head turned. Their eyes met.

"I won't let anyone hurt you," he promised her. As far as Luke was concerned, no one would *ever* be hurting Mina again. But during the boat ride over he'd realized a few important facts.

Garrick McAdams was a dick, yes. A bother. A pain to be eliminated. But he *wasn't* the boss of whatever little madness the humans currently had going. Someone else was giving the orders at the mysterious government agency that employed Garrick. And in order to truly protect Mina, well, Luke had to take out the man or woman at the top.

To do that, he had to get killing-close. What better way to do that than by offering himself up as bait?

A woman's voice shouted, "Drop any weapons that you have and put your hands up!"

"Madeline," Mina whispered as her hands rose. "I'd recognize that grating voice anywhere."

He could see Madeline perfectly in the darkness. Her red hair was pulled back, her body was stiff, and her gun was aimed not at his heart, but at Mina's.

That just won't do.

Luke stepped in front of Mina. From what he could tell, all of the human civilians had been cleared out of that area. Only the hunters remained. "Sorry. I don't have any weapons I can drop—" Luke began.

He didn't get to say anymore because Madeline opened fire. The shots thundered and he felt the impact in his chest. One, two, three.

Behind him, he could hear Mina screaming. He staggered and started to fall.

The agents pushed closer.

"*Stand back!*" Mina yelled. Her voice shook with a power that he could feel. "Drop your weapons and get the hell back!" Her hands grabbed for Luke's shoulders.

But the agents didn't fall back. Their weapons remained trained right on Luke and Mina.

"Ear plugs," Madeline shouted. "Can't hear a freaking word you're saying."

Mina trembled.

"You and your new boyfriend are both going down," Madeline yelled.

Mina was trying to push herself in front of Luke. A very noble gesture, but totally unnecessary.

He rose to his feet. Then he waved his hands.

The agents didn't know what hit them. They were so busy staring at him that they didn't see the threat coming from behind. A black panther lunged from the shadows. A snarling, white wolf leapt for their throats.

Six agents against two shifters? Those odds were hardly fair.

"Hurt them," Luke called out. "Don't kill them." *Yet.* Because he was sending a message, one that he'd make sure was loudly received.

Besides, he needed at least one agent left standing to lead him to his prey.

The agents fired wildly, but the shifters were moving too fast for them. One after the other, the agents hit the ground. And they didn't get up. When you were unconscious, it was difficult to move.

"You had back-up?" Mina punched his arm. "You should have told me they were here!" Before he could speak, she was pulling him closer. "And they *shot* you!" Now alarm raised her voice. "You're bleeding! I have to get you help, I need to —"

"I'm not bleeding any longer." The pain had lasted only for a moment. "No worries. It takes a whole lot more to knock me out than whatever they were firing." The bullets had actually just been pushed out of his body as he healed. He heard them hit the ground.

She stared up at him with fear heavy around her — he could feel it. "But they weren't trying to knock you out. They weren't firing tranqs at you. Those were…I think they were real bullets." She bent and picked up one bullet. "*Real,*" she whispered. Mina swallowed. "They wanted to kill you."

Lucky for him, they hadn't realized how impossible of a task that particular job was.

"One standing!" That was Rayce's voice. He glanced over to see the wolf shifter — naked now that he was in human form—holding Madeline in front of him. He'd yanked the plugs out of her ears and had tossed them to the ground. The redheaded agent was fighting fiercely. Too bad for her, a human could never hope to match a wolf shifter's strength.

Julian continued to pace in his panther form.

Mina whirled away from Luke and ran toward Madeline. She dropped the bullet she'd been holding. "You were trying to kill him!"

Madeline stopped her struggles.

Snarling, Mina pulled back her fist and drove it right at Madeline's face. "You don't get to just *kill* people!"

Blood trickled from Madeline's busted lip. "He's not a person." She spat blood on the ground. "Neither are you."

Mina's hand pulled back to punch again, but Luke caught her fist. He kissed her knuckles. "Easy, love."

Mina blinked at him, as if confused.

"I need her alive and awake." He rolled back his shoulders, straightened his bloody suit and said, "After all, she's going to take me to her buddy Garrick. She'll lead me right to him."

"The hell I will—"

He glided another step closer to Madeline. "Yes, yes, by hell, you *will*." He let his power flare, knowing it would show in the glow of his eyes. "Because you don't have a choice. You take me to Garrick or I will make every fear you have become a reality." He leaned toward her. "And believe me, I know all about the fears you hold inside. Fears are my specialty." They always had been. He leaned in even closer to her and searched her gaze. "Let's just see…what do you fear?" He reached out his hand and cupped his fingers around her chin. She tried to jerk away from him, but he held her tight and he saw.

"Uh, Luke?" Mina tapped his shoulder.

"Being different. Being like the paranormals your team *uses*. You fear becoming a monster?" He could see it all so clearly. Humans were often easy to read, especially the ones with weak minds. "Too late, you already *are* a monster."

When she tried to tear out of Rayce's arms, the shifter just held her tighter.

"I can change you," Luke said, not looking away from her. "You think I can't let my darkness take you over? Oh, I can. It can spread like a plague, from human to human, wiping you all out until nothing is left." Nothing but the dark. His dark.

Hadn't that always been his brother Leo's fear? That Luke wouldn't stop? That he'd let all of that evil out to taint the precious human world?

Her fear deepened.

"You will take me to Garrick. To him and to whoever is pulling the strings at your agency.

You've been playing with my paranormals and that shit is stopping. I will destroy your whole organization—"

Wind whipped against him. A deep, inhuman howl seemed to shake the night.

Luke's head jerked back. He stared above him, seeing the giant wings in the moonlight. "Oh, hell, no," he snarled. But it was too late. He was grabbed, yanked up, held fast and tight in an unbreakable hold. Below him, he could hear Mina screaming for him. He could hear Rayce's roar of rage.

But then in a flash, they were gone. No, *he* was gone, flying through the air, hurtling far and fast and leaving Mina behind. Mina, the woman he'd sworn to protect.

The woman he'd just left vulnerable.

Rage burst through him and Luke's careful control began to crack.

***

"Luke!" Mina screamed. She whirled around, searching the sky—the *empty* sky. "*Luke, where are you?*" Wind had whipped around them, like a mini-tornado. There had been a howl—no, more like the roar of a freight-train. Luke had been there one moment, and the next, she'd seen him surging up into the sky. Now he was just...*gone.*

"I'll track him," Rayce said, pushing Madeline toward Mina. "You and Julian take care of her. I'll get Luke."

He'd better get Luke back. "Who took him?"

But Rayce wasn't answering her. His bones were snapping—a terrible, stomach turning sound. He hit the ground on all fours and fur sprang over his body. She stared at him, stunned, because she'd never seen a shift up-close. His face changed, elongated. Wicked sharp teeth burst from his mouth. Claws sprouted from his fingers. That terrible bone-snapping continued and his muscles bulged. In minutes—seconds?—a beast was before her, and then the wolf bounded away, rushing toward the shadows.

And Mina was left there, surrounded by unconscious agents, a big, black panther at her side, and a stunned-looking Madeline in front of her. But then Madeline blinked, seeming to realize that she had a shot at freedom. She lunged away from Mina, rushing toward the building on the right.

The panther tackled her. He didn't slice her skin, but his big paw pushed between her shoulder blades, pinning her, face first, to that ground.

Mina raced toward them. "You aren't getting away, Madeline. You're taking us to Eli." Because Eli was the mission. Getting him to safety. She looked back up at the sky. *Where are you, Luke?*

Maybe they should try to hunt Luke first. Get Luke, then get Eli. Because she was afraid, terrified all the way to the pit of her soul.

Just what sort of creature was strong enough to carry off the Lord of the Dark?

Mina scooped up one of the guns that had been dropped on the ground. It felt oddly heavy in her hands. She pointed it at Madeline. "I don't know if this thing is loaded with real bullets or with tranqs, but if you try to run again, we'll be finding out."

The panther's shining eyes flashed toward Mina.

"What? I won't shoot her in the heart or anything. I know we need her alive to get Eli back." She braced her shoulders and tightened her grip on the gun. "You're going to get up, Madeline. Nice and slowly." She injected all of her power into the commands. "You *will* cooperate with us. You will take us to whatever base you're using."

Madeline wasn't struggling any longer.

The panther eased away from her. Madeline rose, nice and slow, and she turned toward Mina, her stare a bit cloudy.

Mina smiled at her. "Ready to cooperate?"

Madeline nodded.

"Good, then take us to your car." There had to be one stashed around there someplace. Mina frowned at the panther. "And maybe you can shift and borrow the clothes from one of the agents on the ground? Because you going in as a panther isn't exactly keeping things on the down low, now, is it?"

A rumble came from the beast.

Mina exhaled and, once more, her gaze lifted toward the sky. The fear in her belly hadn't lessened. She wanted to give chase, to run after Luke. He...needed her. "Tell me that Rayce will find him."

Again, the panther rumbled.

"That had better be a yes," Mina muttered.

***

Luke flew through the air and he twisted, his feet coming down hard just as he hit the rooftop. His knees didn't buckle, but his fists clenched in rage. He looked around, seeing the glittering high rises, hearing the rush of traffic far below. "Fucking Miami?" Luke shouted as he recognized some of those too-tall buildings. He hated the damn city — that was why he lived on an island.

There was a fast rush of wind, the beat of powerful wings and then...

His dumb ass of a brother appeared before him.

Luke didn't hesitate. He ran right at his twin and drove his fist into Leo's face. Leo's head snapped to the side. Luke drew back his hand, ready to hit again. "You had no right—"

Leo looked at him and his brother's eyes—as dark as Luke's own—gleamed. "You crossed the line. *You* broke the truce."

"We have no truce. We have you and we have me, and we have us both supposedly staying the hell out of each other's business!" Rage burned in him and smoke began to seep from his pores. Always a very, very bad sign.

But Leo ignored that obvious warning. "You attacked humans. I saw you. I was watching from above—"

"The way you always are," Luke growled. He was so tired of Leo's pompous bullshit.

"You hurt them. You were trying to *terrify* that human woman."

Luke smiled at him. "Trust me. She deserved that terror, and everything else I was going to give her."

Leo stepped closer to him. "You were threatening to let your darkness reign."

Luke looked down at his hands. Claws had torn from his fingertips. Long, black. Sharper than knives. "You shouldn't have interfered." Leo had taken him from Mina. If anything happened to her…

"Would you have let your darkness out?" Leo demanded. "Knowing what it would do the world? Would you have really done it?"

Luke turned away from his brother. He had already wasted enough time with him. Mina was waiting. Mina needed him. He felt his own wings pushing from his back, growing and cutting right through his shirt. His wings weren't soft. They were as sharp as the claws he now sported. He climbed onto the narrow ledge and looked at the city below.

"Luke!" His brother shouted his name.

Luke turned back.

Leo hadn't moved. He stood there, glaring. *Better watch it brother. All that rage…it will lead you straight to hell.*

"You're trying to take someone who belongs to me," Leo gritted, his words brittle. "I don't know what game you think you're playing, but it ends now."

"Those humans?" Luke knew his wings were stretching behind him. They were on a high-rise, far away from the prying eyes below. But even if someone had seen him right then, he didn't care. He was growing sick of the shadows. "The ones who've been using *my* paranormals? Torturing them? You're siding with them?"

Confusion flashed on Leo's face. "What?"

"Those treacherous humans — they were the ones you were so angry with me for…hurting. As if they weren't due some pain." He could give them plenty. He turned away once more, ready to leap off that roof —

"I mean Mina. I'm talking about Mina James. She's mine."

His control had been cracking. Little, tiny spider web-like cracks. But at Leo's words, something happened to Luke. He felt it, deep inside. Like a splintering. No, like an earthquake.

In a breath, he was in front of Leo. His claws were at his brother's throat. "Say that shit to me again."

Leo had gone statue-still.

"That's what I thought," Luke snarled. He'd always wondered…in the end, which of them would be stronger? Which would be left standing? He was ready to find out. "Mina is *mine.*"

He saw the understanding in his brother's eyes. The shock. "You…you had sex with her?"

He let his claws draw blood from Leo. "Mina is mine," he said again. Because there wasn't more to say. He didn't know what Leo *thought* he was doing, but—

"She isn't dark," Leo rasped, his lips barely moving. "You must have seen that. But…you ignored it? You're trying to…to change her? You can't. You can't take one of the light and make her your mate."

Mate. He tested the word in his mind. *Mina. Mate.* Why, yes, he rather liked that idea—

But in the next instant, Leo was shoving at him. Slashing at him because his twin had his own claws. His own wings. His own fire. Leo's claws swiped across Luke's stomach, and blood soaked his shirt-front.

"Her very name means *love*!" Now Leo was shouting. "You knew what she truly was — you didn't care! You're trying to taint her! To turn her — she is one of mine!"

"My Mina is a siren." He barely felt the slashes on his skin. "Sirens are dark creatures. They are — "

Leo let out a roar. He rushed at Luke, but Luke caught him, holding tight. They stared, eye-to-eye, fury burning from them both. "She's no siren," Leo denied. "And you *know* that. What kind of game are you playing with her? You recognize your own kind. You recognize the dark." He shoved Luke back. "You can lie to the rest of the world, but not to me."

They'd always seen through each other's lies.

"You knew from the beginning that she wasn't yours, but you tried to keep her at your side, didn't you? Always the selfish bastard."

Luke laughed. "You have no idea what I am." His wings beat behind him. "Or what I am capable of doing." He glared at his brother, the man who shared his face. The man who might wind up being his destruction. "Try to come between me and Mina, and you will find out."

Before Leo could speak again, Luke's wings flew out. They slammed into Leo's chest, cutting him deep and sending the guy spinning back across the roof. Luke didn't look at him again. He'd wasted too much time. He leapt into the air and let the full force of the shift sweep over him. It had been so long since he'd given into the call of his beast and his humanity — what small bit he fought to keep — vanished in that change. His beast was powerful. Deadly. Fire blasted into the night as he flew.

He was going to burn his enemies to ash. Anyone who got in his way, anyone who tried to stop him from taking what he wanted...

I will burn you all.

***

"Aw, hell," Leo muttered as he rose to his feet. Blood poured down his chest, but he ignored the pain. It would stop, soon enough. The injuries would heal. He'd recover, as he always did.

His gaze was on the sky, a sky that was lit every few moments by a blast of fire. His twin had transformed completely, losing the body of a man in favor of his dark beast. The beast's body blended perfectly with the night. Were it not for those flames...*no one would ever know he was there.*

But then, he knew that was what Luke wanted. To blend with the night.

I hope I didn't just screw us both even worse. He rolled back his shoulders. His wings scraped over the rooftop. He didn't transform fully — after all, Leo knew the danger in that, but he took to the sky, his wings beating at the air around him.

There had been such fury in Luke's voice when he spoke of Mina James. Such possession. Luke had always enjoyed owning things. Taking. He saw, he coveted, he owned. That was his brother's way.

But it wasn't the way things would work with Mina. They *couldn't* work that way.

She wasn't meant to be one of the dark ones, losing her soul bit by bit until there was no goodness left in her. She was meant for far more, and he would not let her fall for his brother.

No matter what battle he had to fight.

CHAPTER TWELVE

It was a fast, dangerous plan. It could also be a really, really shitty plan, but it was the best that Mina had been able to come up with on short notice — *and since Luke is gone.*

They didn't have his paranormal mojo to back them up, so they were winging things.

Julian stood to her right, wearing the clothes and gear and ID he'd taken from an unconscious agent back at their big fight scene. Madeline was to her left, her eyes glassy and her body tense. She was still under Mina's control, and they were going to use that fact to their advantage.

"You sure about this?" Julian whispered as they approached the gates that led to the Naval Air Station. Madeline had revealed that her team had been given a special wing in that facility for their work.

Work. More like torture.

Mina lifted her cuffed hands. She rather thought the handcuffs made a nice touch. Added a bit of authenticity. "I am not in the least bit sure." What she *did* know…well, it was that Eli was in that place. Luke had been determined to get him out and she…she was doing this. *And Rayce, you'd better be finding a certain Lord of the Dark, right away.*

The plan—such as it was—consisted of her playing the role of prisoner. Since the agency had been so determined to get her back, she figured they'd be jumping with joy when they saw her. So they'd all go inside, they'd be led to the prisoner holding section, and them, bam—Julian did his panther thing, Madeline attacked her fellow agents and, Mina got Eli out of there.

Simple. Desperate.

"Garrick is the one we have to worry about," Mina murmured. She didn't know why they hadn't seen him yet. She'd been surprised that he hadn't been lurking around the dock, waiting to pounce on them. He'd sent his goons and hadn't come to the scene himself, something that still bothered her. "Keep your eyes out for him."

"Looking for your ex, check." Julian's voice was barely a breath of sound.

Madeline wasn't making any sound at all. Mina elbowed her. "Call out to the agents in there. Tell them who you are and that you have me. Instruct them to let us inside immediately."

Madeline didn't hesitate. They were just a few feet away from the imposing gates that surrounded the station, and she called out, "I'm Agent Slate, and I've secured the prisoner we sought. Open the gates so that I can immediately confine her to the holding area." She lifted her ID and a bright light shone on them.

Mina's eyes watered in the face of that spotlight. *This has to work. It has to —*

There was a loud screeching as the gates opened. Uniformed men rushed out and surrounded them. Her breath eased out in a relieved sigh when she saw that Garrick wasn't among that group.

"She isn't gagged!" One of the men snapped. "She *isn't* secure! She can talk, she can—"

Julian slapped his hand around Mina's mouth, and he jerked her back against him in the same move. His body was tight, scarily muscled, and for a moment, she felt a flutter of fear. "I've got her," he stated coldly. "Satisfied?"

The guards exchanged uneasy glances, obviously not satisfied.

"Her throat was damaged during the fight," Julian added, voice rough. "A whole lot of agents were taken down and this lady—she didn't give up easily. So I had to punch her in the throat."

Hardly a good image. She squirmed against him, trying to make the scene look real.

"We need to get some back-up to the agents at the dock," Julian blasted when the others just stood there. "Agent Slate and I will take the prisoner inside. You guys get out there and help our team."

Finally, *finally,* the men nodded.

And a few moments later, with Julian's hand still covering her mouth, Mina walked back to the prisoner holding area.

There were cells back there, lots of them. And guards with big guns. She didn't know if those guns were loaded with tranqs or if they were sporting bullets—silver bullets, wooden bullets, or even your average shoot-to-kill human variety.

Madeline kept flashing her ID at people. Her movements were stiff and jerky, and Mina really wanted to give her another command, to reinforce her compulsion, but with eyes on them, she knew Julian wouldn't risk freeing her mouth, not right then. They had to wait just a bit longer...

They needed to find Eli.

"Maximum security," Julian snapped to the guard standing to the left—the guy clutching a really big gun. "Let's stop screwing around and get her contained."

The guy—a young fellow with pale blond hair—spun and quickly typed in a security code on the pad near a big, black door.

There was a beep, then a hiss, and that door opened.

"Excellent," Julian said. "Now keep any other guards back until I have her secure. I don't want to risk anyone falling under her control."

Because Mina was looking straight at Madeline when he spoke those words, she saw the flare of the other woman's lashes. Madeline's eyes went bright with emotions.

Uh, oh. We are running out of time. Mina needed to give that woman a new command, STAT. They crossed through the doorway, and a few seconds later, the door sealed closed behind them with another beep and a hiss. Cautiously, they walked forward. It was almost like being back in Luke's Chamber of Horrors again except that—

A low moan came from the right. Her gaze jerked that way. There were no cell bars, just glass. She could see right into that holding room and Eli was on the floor. A very bloody, battered Eli.

Julian shoved her away from him.

Madeline shook her head, opened her mouth to scream—

"*You stay silent,*" Mina ordered her.

Madeline's lips clamped closed.

A guard was rushing toward them—a man who'd been sitting behind a bank of screens in the middle of that space. "What in the hell is happening?" he shouted, lifting his gun.

Julian just snatched the gun from him and tossed it away. Then he drove his fist straight into the guard's face. The guy was unconscious before he hit the floor.

Mina ran toward the bank of screens. The screens showed different security feeds from the facility. She didn't see guards rushing toward them, so that meant they were still safe.

"Disengage his cell door," Julian ordered.

She looked up. He was in front of Eli's holding area. "I don't know how!"

His jaw locked. "I do." Then he lifted his hand and drove his fist into the cell door.

Alarms immediately began blasting. Heavy, deafening alarms. Mina jerked in shock and — and a door to her left opened.

Laughter came from that room — laughter that reached her even over that terrible, shrieking alarm. And it was laughter that she knew.

"Hello, Mina," Garrick greeted her. The jerk sounded…happy. Pleased. "I knew you'd make it this far. I was waiting for you."

Madeline slapped her hands over her ears and sank to the floor.

Six black-clad agents ran from behind Garrick. They didn't run to surround Mina, though. Instead, they went right for Julian. He swiped out at them with his claws, fighting them, punching. The guards lifted their guns.

"Stop!" Mina yelled as she surged toward Julian. "Don't hurt him—"

Hard arms grabbed her. Garrick yanked her back against his body. "They can't hear your voice. Not over that alarm. It was one of the safety precautions that I had in place. As soon as you entered this area, there was a thirty-second timer in place. It counted down…and then your time was up."

She'd thought the alarm had sounded because Julian hit the cell, but…it had all been part of Garrick's plan? She drove her elbow back into his ribs. He grunted at the impact, but didn't let her go. So she head-butted him. She kicked back with her heels. She clawed at him and—

Bam. Bam.

The bullets blasted into Julian. He stopped fighting.

His body fell.

"*No!*" Mina screamed. She twisted in Garrick's hold. "*No!*"

The agents came at her then. They swarmed her and she found herself being thrown into the cell right next to Eli's. They tossed her onto the floor, throwing her down hard, then running out. She leapt to her feet and raced toward the door, but Garrick shut that glass door in her face and, staring at her, he engaged the lock.

"*Let me out!*" Mina screamed. She could see Julian, still slumped on the floor. *Don't be dead. Don't be dead.*

Garrick cupped his hand around his ear. "What is that? Come again?' He smiled at her. "Sorry, my dear, but I can't hear a word you're saying. No one can."

She slammed her fist into the glass, again and again — but the glass didn't give.

Garrick laughed. "You can hear us — I've got the speaker feed going into the cell I prepared for you — but no one can hear your beautiful voice. And that means...you're helpless."

No, this couldn't be happening.

She kept pounding on the glass.

"It won't break," Garrick assured her. "It won't shatter. It is a special material the guys at NASA actually came up with to use in space but, hey, we recognized just how useful the material would be right here on earth. With people like...you." A faint smile still curved his lips. "I told you, Mina, you wouldn't get away again. I just had to use the right bait to pull you back in to me." His gaze slid to Eli. The guy hadn't moved from his position on the floor. A pool of congealed blood surrounded his prone form. "Though I don't think that bait will last much longer. He put up more of a fight than we expected and he seems very weak now."

She screamed — and the sound just echoed back to her.

"Don't worry. Eli's not dead...yet." Garrick motioned to the guards. They picked up Julian and his head sagged. "And neither is your new friend. I find I am quite curious about him. I do believe I saw claws spring from his fingertips."

Damn him. "You're going to regret this." But he couldn't hear her. He wasn't even *looking* at her. Garrick had turned away. He was following the guards who were carrying Julian out of there. They were leaving her in the cell. "No!"

Garrick glanced back at her. "Where's Thorne?"

I have no idea.

"Did you trade him in for the guy with the claws? Did you think that was the smarter choice?" He gave a sad shake of his head. "You just bring everyone down to hell with you, don't you, Mina? I guess it's a talent you have."

He walked out, taking Julian, leaving her there and —

Madeline stepped in front of Mina's cell. A Madeline who had a face contorted with rage. "You bitch," Madeline snarled.

Mina's chin lifted.

"I'm going to enjoy watching you suffer. We will break you, and I will make sure that it *hurts*."

Hardly the words of a kind, caring federal agent.

More like the words of a killer.

But then, Mina knew Garrick and Madeline were exactly that — cold-blooded killers. And they'd tried to make her into the same type of monster. She'd escaped from them before, stopping their plans.

This time…would she be so lucky?

***

Luke touched down at the dock. He landed as a man, fully dressed, as the old magic flowed easily through him. He wasn't like other shifters, after all. They bowed to him.

He looked around, but the agents who'd been there before were gone. There wasn't even blood on the ground any longer. Someone had done one hell of a fast clean-up job.

A growl rumbled in his throat. His head tilted back as he pulled in the scents around him.

You can run, but you can't hide. Not from me. Not ever from me. He inhaled again. *No blood on the ground, but I can still catch that coppery scent in the air.*

He heard the fast thud of footsteps, and Luke whirled.

Rayce was there, breathing heavily, glaring at him. "Do you know…" he panted, "how fucking hard it is…to track you…when you fly?"

The guy was naked, sweating, and obviously fresh from a shift. Luke waved his hand and clothes covered his friend.

"Thanks," Rayce muttered. "Forgot how…freaky it is…when you do that…"

When he worked his magic? Or when he shifted?

Luke stalked toward Rayce. "You had a job to do."

Rayce lifted his head. "Yeah…that job was to…protect my friend's back. *Your* back."

Luke shook his head. "You were to protect *her.*" And now Mina was gone. "You'd better know where she is…"

"Didn't you hear me?" Rayce's breathing had slowed. "*You* were my priority. For all I knew, your idiot brother was going to skin you."

As if that hadn't been done before. Good thing he regenerated so easily.

"Julian stayed with her," Rayce added quickly. "I went after you. Not my fault I can't fly."

Luke glared at him a moment longer.

"What is the deal?" Real shock was in Rayce's voice. "How are you so twisted up over her? Are you sure her voice isn't still messing with your head?"

It wasn't her voice. It was her.

Luke inhaled again, catching the scents around him. "They left us a blood trail to follow."

"Yeah, I noticed that." Rayce's mutter definitely wasn't thrilled. "Probably because it's a trap. This whole thing has been a trap from the word go and you know it."

Yes, he did. And he'd planned for the human's tricks. After all, he'd known that Garrick McAdams would play dirty. Luke just hadn't planned on his interfering ass of a brother. "They can't cage me." He rolled back his shoulders and felt the stretch of his wings. Why waste time? He'd fly and follow that blood scent.

"Oh, shit, here we go again…" Rayce swallowed. "Can you…*try* to slow down?"

He rose into the air. "No."

Death wasn't slow. Death was fast. He'd show the humans just what hell they'd unleashed. No one messed with his paranormals. No one touched those who belonged to him.

No one.

***

Julian groaned as he opened his eyes. His chest *hurt* but considering his last memory was of bullets blasting into him, that pain was hardly surprising.

The fact that he was still alive? That was a bit of good news.

But the fact that he was chained to a wall in a pitch black room? *Not so much fun.*

"Sonofabitch." The curse slipped from him. Luke was going to kick his ass over this. He'd gotten caught. Worse, he'd let Mina get caught. And Luke didn't exactly act all sane where she was concerned.

Julian rose, testing the length of the chains. They were thick, hard, and made of silver, but he wasn't a freaking werewolf, so that silver didn't burn him. *Good thing they caught me and not Rayce.*

He'd get out. Eventually. He just might have to cut off his own hand first, not the most ideal of options but—

A faint rustle reached him.

His head turned and he stared into the darkness. A cat could see well into the dark. He knew his eyes would be glowing, shining with the power of his beast, as he gazed at—

His cell-mate?

Hell. He wasn't even alone in there. His nose twitched. Blood. Dirt. Someone had been in that cell for a very, very long time. "Come on out," he growled. "I won't bite."

Footsteps shuffled forward. He saw the tangle of long, blonde hair. Fragile shoulders. A small body. And—

Her head tipped back. Her fangs gleamed, even in the dark. "I might." Then she flew at him, her fangs going right for his throat.

Shit. It just wasn't his night.

CHAPTER THIRTEEN

Mina inched closer to the cell beside hers. She put her hand on the glass. Eli was looking up at her, and the poor man barely seemed to breathe. "I wish I could help you." His face was battered, bruised. Dark circles surrounded his eyes. "It's my fault this happened to you." Her fault he was lying there, dying.

It wasn't an easy death, either. Every breath was a struggle. And she hated it so much. No one should be in such agony.

Eli's eyes began to close. The air around her seemed to get colder. Tears trickled down her cheeks. She'd come to save him, not to watch him breathe his last breath. Not to —

"I'm back, Mina." Garrick's cocky voice blasted through her speakers. Her shoulders jerked. "And I have a present for you."

He could shove any presents right up his —

"It's a necklace. One that I think you'll like."

She didn't want to look away from Eli so she didn't. If he was dying, she wanted him to know he wasn't alone.

"Or actually…" Garrick mused. "You might hate the necklace. But I'll love it. Because you see, it will allow me to control that wonderful voice of yours."

Her hand moved to her throat. Fear slithered through her.

"I'm going to slide this necklace in the cell to you. Then you're going to put it on. You'll secure it, and when it's in place, I'll let you out of there."

Because he thought he'd have control of her. Just because she was wearing some dumb necklace?

"If you cooperate, if you put on the necklace for me…I'll see to it that Eli gets medical attention."

Her heart lurched in her chest.

Eli shook his head. Such a faint movement.

"I want you to put the necklace on, Mina." Garrick's voice had hardened. "I want you to show me that you *can* work with me after all this time. We need to rebuild our trust."

He was insane. He could take their trust and shove it up his—

She heard a series of beeps. Then a grating behind her.

"Put on the necklace," Garrick ordered her. "Or…well, I guess you could just keep standing there, watching that guy struggle for breath."

Damn him. Mina whirled away from Eli and saw that a small tray had been opened near the bottom of her cell. The tray came from some kind of compartment that she hadn't noticed before. She ran to it and inside — it wasn't a necklace. It was a choker. Almost…a collar.

Still on her knees next to that tray, she looked up at Garrick.

He smiled — the charming smile that had tricked her so long ago. "Put it on," he urged.

Her fingers were trembling as she lifted it up to her throat. Her hands slid beneath her hair as she brought the clasp to the back of her neck. It hooked together easily and was tight against her skin. Black, but with a heavy emerald stone in the middle that—

Something stabbed into her throat, a quick piercing that felt like a knife. She grabbed for the choker, but it wouldn't come off. It seemed to have banded to her skin. She clawed at it because that pain was excruciating. It hurt so much and —

Garrick lifted his hand and revealed a small device cradled in his fingers. "If you stop fighting, it won't hurt as much."

She stilled.

"Good. See…that's what I'm talking about…rebuilding our relationship, one painful step at a time."

He might not be able to hear her, but she could still rage at him. "You fucking —"

Mina felt shock rush through her. She'd just *tried* to speak, but no sound had escaped her lips.

And he seemed to delight in her shock. "That was perfect." He waved his hand and her cell door immediately opened. "Worked like a charm."

She tried to speak again. *"You're a sick sonofa –"*

No sound. Her lips were moving. She was mouthing the words, but no sound would emerge.

He grabbed her arms and pulled her close. He pressed a wild kiss to her lips and she clawed her nails down the side of his face. But Garrick just *laughed*. "It really was a charm, my Mina." He tapped the emerald in the middle of her choker. "Other paranormals chose to cooperate with my team. You should have done the same." His fingers stroked her skin, right above the choker, lingering near her rapid pulse. "A witch gave me this. Said she knew just how to reign in your power. Of course, I had our techs tweak things a bit. When science and magic work together, the results are quite spectacular."

No, they were terrifying.

"I control you now." His fingers curled around her neck. "Only I can remove the collar."

Collar. Now he wasn't pretending. She wouldn't, either. Mina let him see the hate in her eyes.

"You will speak when I allow you to speak. You will follow the orders that my agency gives to you. You will do *exactly* as you are told…or I will see to it that you *never* speak again. I can take your voice from you. Take it completely, and you will be helpless for the rest of your days."

No, she wouldn't be helpless. She wouldn't have the power to compel others, but she'd still be able to fight. He didn't understand her, he never had. She'd gone to Luke because she'd wanted that terrible power taken away.

But losing her voice wouldn't destroy her. Just as Garrick *wouldn't* destroy her. She wouldn't let him.

"Guards!" Garrick called, raising his voice. "Get Eli to the med ward! Patch up the guy before we start swimming in his blood!"

He was…he was really going to help Eli?

Garrick's hand slid away from her. "See…it's that trust I spoke about. We'll fix the rift between us. Soon enough, things will return to the way they were before. You'll want me again."

Insane. No doubt.

He caught her hand and lifted it to his shirt-front, putting it right above his heart—and the scar there. "And I'll forgive you," Garrick said.

She waited until the guards had removed Eli. Waited until he was out of there and on his way to get help. Then she smiled up at Garrick, and, moving her mouth slowly so that he'd be able to read her lips she told him, "*Screw you.*"

He just laughed. "Doesn't work, baby. Not without the voice."

He turned away. Sauntered out of the cell. Shut the door and *left* her there.

"We are going to be great together," he said, his words drifting back to her. "Just you wait and see."

She grabbed for the necklace and began to claw it, but the choker — the collar — just tightened, threatening to cut off her breath.

"Oh, don't do that." His voice had sharpened.

Her head jerked back and she stared at him through the glass.

Garrick wiggled the remote in his fingers. "Only I can get that off. Try to cut it, try to pry it loose, and it will just keep tightening. It will tighten until you can't breathe. You'll die long before it comes off." Then he smiled. "God, I have missed you. Welcome back, baby."

Her hands fell to her sides and fisted.

***

The scent of blood led to the Naval Air Station on the island. Luke hovered above the facility, his gaze on the humans he could see moving below. Like desperate bees, buzzing around.

Wind whipped against him and he knew just who'd appeared to ruin his fun. But then, he'd smelled Leo coming this time. Righteousness could reek.

"You can't kill those humans."

Luke just stared at him. "After all these centuries, after all of the wars we've seen, you should know by now that humans aren't innocent. Sometimes, they are the monsters."

"It's not our place—"

"Then who should be punishing them? Who should be stopping them? They took what was mine, and that crime *will* have a cost."

Leo gave a grim shake of his head. "You are to stay just with the paranormals. I handle the humans. You *know* — "

Luke grabbed his brother's shoulders. "I know that you're a pain in my ass. I know that you've stood back and just *watched* for far too long. Well, guess what, brother? The time for watching is over. Now, you're about to get down and dirty in *my* hell." Then he didn't hesitate. Using all of his considerable strength, Luke shoved his brother straight down, sending him barreling for the building below. He kept up the force on his brother's shoulders, flying down with him as they got closer and closer to impact.

He wanted to get in that facility. So...why not just bust his way inside?

Right before impact, Luke let his brother go and he watched as Leo slammed straight through the roof of the facility, leaving a big, gaping hole in his wake.

How absolutely perfect.

***

When the ceiling caved in on her, Mina screamed. Or, well, she tried to scream. But the collar made sure that no sound slipped from her lips.

Something big — with giant, black wings — had just broken its way into her cell. The wings were huge — easily six feet long but they were…sharp. Gleaming. She backed up against the wall, trying to flatten herself because she had no idea what fresh hell this was and —

The wings vanished. In a blink, they were gone. A man knelt in the middle of the rubble, his dark head was bent and what looked like dust and plaster covered his broad shoulders.

His *familiar* shoulders.

He tilted back his head and his dark gaze met hers.

Relief swept through Mina, almost making her dizzy. She'd known that Luke would come for her. Okay, maybe she hadn't known, but she'd really, really hoped. Mina ran to him, feeling a wide smile stretch her lips.

He blinked at her, as if in surprise, and he rose to his feet.

She threw herself against him, holding him tightly. She shot onto her toes and her mouth pressed to his as she pulled his head toward her.

It took her only about two seconds to realize…something was wrong. *Very* wrong.

The body against hers was hard, strong. Sexy. The mouth against hers was sensual and skilled but…

No fire ignited in her blood. That wild, reckless need didn't flare within her. Maybe it was because she was in prison, her voice was gone, and danger was everywhere or maybe…maybe…

She pulled her lips from his. Mina searched his eyes. Her lips parted and she mouthed the words she couldn't speak. *"Who. Are. You?"*

But then the air around her seemed to heat. There was a rush of hot wind and —

Luke stood a few feet away from her. He wore the fancy suit that he'd had on when they dined on his balcony. He looked sexy, polished, and utterly…furious. The Eye of Hell gleamed on his hand.

Her gaze jerked from him to the man before her. A man who looked exactly like her Lord of the Dark. *Exactly.*

She tried to retreat, but the man holding her just tightened his grip.

"Thanks, Luke," he said, his deep voice so similar to Luke's that Mina ached. "You sent me straight to the person I needed."

Luke's head turned to the side as he cracked his neck. Then he rolled back his shoulders. She wanted to tell Luke that this was all a mistake, that she'd gotten confused, but Mina couldn't say a word.

His twin. This is Luke's twin.

And the really, really bad situation that she'd been in? It had just gotten about a hundred times worse.

But then an alarm started shrieking. The same alarm that had heralded the arrival of Garrick and his goons before. Sure enough, doors flew open and armed men rushed toward her cell. Garrick was leading the pack, and his eyes seemed to double in size when he saw that there appeared to be two Lukes in her cell.

"I should get her to safety, don't you think?" the man holding her murmured.

Before Luke could reply, the guy had scooped Mina into his arms and flown straight up—flying right through the gaping hole he'd left in the ceiling.

CHAPTER FOURTEEN

"What in the hell?" Garrick blasted.

"Exactly," Luke snarled right back, enraged. "Just hold that thought for one fucking moment." His knees bent and he shot into the air, flying right after Leo. His brother dared, *dared* to take Mina? No, it would not happen.

His skin heated. Burned. Smoke filled the air around him. His body stretched and his bones snapped. The shift rolled through him and when he looked down, when he saw the humans running out of the station and firing up at him...

His control broke. Luke opened his mouth and he breathed his fire onto them.

***

"Look at him."

Mina hated that his voice was just like Luke's. She hated that his body was the same. His face the same. *Leo.* The twin.

"Look at the man you took for a lover and see him for just how evil he truly is."

Her head turned. She saw a cloud of smoke rising from the Naval Air Station. Her breath rushed out as flames burst into the air — bright orange and red flames. And in the middle of all that fire…someone was moving.

Some*thing* was moving.

The creature burst out of the flames — big, dark, its mouth bursting with razor sharp teeth. Its massive wings cut through the air and its tail whipped behind the beast.

Not just a beast…

Scales were on its body. Big, heavy-looking scales that gleamed in the moonlight. Its eyes were huge but…serpentine in shape. Just like its head. Only it wasn't a snake coming at her. It was a dragon. *A freaking dragon!* Breathing got very, very hard for Mina.

"That's his true form. That's what he is beneath the mask of a man. Evil and darkness. He burns and he destroys and he doesn't care who he hurts." Leo's grip on her tightened. "I will take you away from him. You'll be safe, I guarantee it. You were never meant to be with him. You aren't one of his creatures. You aren't—"

Gunshots cut through the night. She saw the bullets hit the dragon flying toward them. Luke wasn't just hit once. Not twice. But again and again. The dragon's giant body jerked and blood burst from his wounds. The gunshots hit his wings, ripping through them and…

It fell. The dragon fell.

No, *he* fell. *Luke.* His body crashed back to earth, falling right toward the shooting agents.

She opened her mouth, screaming for him, but no sound emerged. Nothing came out, not even a whimper as terror nearly choked her. *Luke!*

"Well, that was…unexpected." The air fluttered around her. "I'll get you to safety. You'll be free. You'll—"

She wasn't leaving. She grabbed for the collar at her neck, yanking it with all of her strength. She could feel it tightening, biting into her skin, sinking deeper and cutting her air supply off as she struggled.

"What are you doing? What's happening?" Alarm had entered Leo's voice. "How can I help you?"

Get me down. Get me to Luke.

Her throat was being pierced—a sharp slice right from that cursed emerald. It was cutting into her and dizziness swam through her head. She just had to get the collar *off.*

"Why are you fighting this way? For him?"

She nodded even as she kept clawing at her throat.

"Dammit." Leo's arms tightened around her. "And here I thought we'd get away clean." But then he turned his body and instead of flying up, they were suddenly hurtling straight toward the ground. She sucked in a deep breath and choked on the smoke as they went through that black cloud that the dragon—Luke—had created. Mina felt the lance of heat around her skin and then...

She was standing on the ground, right in the middle of the smoke and the flames. The man who'd held her moments before seemed to have vanished, but Luke...

He was a few feet in front of her, on the ground, his body naked, bleeding.

Mina ran to him. He was face down on ground that had been blackened, and she rolled him over. Her heart was about to burst from her chest. He was covered in blood. His arms were twisted, the bones seemingly shattered. His face—his handsome face had been smashed. His nose was broken, a bone poking from his cheek. She felt tears raining down her own cheeks because he didn't seem to be moving—not moving, not breathing.

One of her tears fell onto his face. She smoothed her fingers over his neck, searching desperately for a pulse. *Don't do this to me, Luke. You're supposed to be all powerful. Bullets can't take you out. That's not the way this works.*

"Get away from him, Mina!" It was a familiar voice roaring at her. The voice she heard in her nightmares. Her head lifted and she saw that armed men now surrounded her. Garrick and his men. Garrick had a pistol in one hand and that hated remote for her collar in the other. He was glaring at her. Seething with his fury. "I don't know *what* that bastard is," Garrick shouted. "But our scientists will figure him out. They'll cut him apart and piece him back together. He'll be a weapon no one else can beat. *Our* weapon."

She still hadn't felt Luke's pulse. She didn't think he could be anyone's weapon. Not when he was…gone.

No, no, don't be gone. Please. I don't want to lose you. More tears tracked down her cheeks and fell onto him. The flames raged around her. Flames he'd created before plunging back down to earth.

"Mina…" A warning edge thickened Garrick's voice. "Step away from him, *now*."

Then she felt the jerk beneath her fingers — Luke's pulse, starting again. Oh, dear God, he *had* been dead. But he'd come back. His eyes were still closed, his body far too battered and bloody, but Luke was alive.

She had to keep him that way.

If Garrick and his men got hold of him, they *would* cut him open. They'd keep him captive. She had once thought nothing could stop Luke, but that had been before she saw him fall from the sky.

She would keep him safe. Her fingers lingered against his skin for just a moment more. Then Mina rose. She eyed the men around her, all men who were armed and ready to attack. Men who were staring at her as if she were some sort of monster. But *they* were the ones planning to cut up Luke.

"Come to me, Mina," Garrick ordered her.

Garrick. The man who thought he had her under such control. He'd been her lover once, back when she'd foolishly believed his lies. Before she'd realized he wasn't actually working for the FBI. He was working for some covert group within the government, a group that specialized in unusual warfare techniques. Off the books, secretive.

Deadly.

Garrick had wanted to use her. He'd tried to force her to use her powers to kill.

That wasn't who she was.

Or, rather, it wasn't who she'd *been*.

She started walking toward Garrick, making sure to keep her head bowed, making sure her steps seemed uncertain and that she let shudders wrack her body. Not hard, really, because she was terrified.

Mina was also furious. And if she looked up, if she made eye contact with Garrick, he'd see that rage. He'd attack. She couldn't let him do that.

Mina intended to attack first.

"Good, Mina." The bastard sounded so satisfied. Then, raising his voice, he said to the men there, "Once she's clear, shoot that bastard again. I want to make absolutely certain he's out before we take him to containment."

Her jaw ached because her teeth were clenched so tightly. She just had a few more feet to go…Almost there…*yes.*

Mina stumbled when she was near Garrick. He lunged to grab her and she grabbed *him.* Mina snatched the gun from him, just yanked it right out of his grip, and then she pushed it against his head. Her reflexes had always been fast — far faster than a human's — and the whole switch took less than two seconds.

He blinked at her, stunned. "Mina?"

She just stared back at him. Thanks to that bastard, she couldn't speak, but she thought he could get the message from her eyes well enough.

I will kill you.

"There is no out for you here, Mina," he said, his words thick. "No way you get to walk away."

She could kill him right then. Just squeeze the trigger and…*bam.* One of her biggest problems would be gone, but then she'd still have to deal with his guards.

Keeping the gun pressed to his forehead, she looked at the others, needing them to understand — everyone had to back the hell away. They needed to get away from Luke. Luke…who was now rising to his feet. He blinked, his expression confused, groggy, and then he seemed to realize where he was and exactly what the hell was happening.

She kept her right hand tight around the weapon. With her left, Mina pointed to the sky. This time, her message was for Luke. *Get your ass up there. Fly away. Be safe.* She'd hold off Garrick. His men weren't going to move, not with that gun jammed against their leader's head.

She only counted four armed men. Normally, she would have thought Luke could take them out, no problem but...

They took him out. Brought him straight out of the sky. Now she was terrified.

"Mina, I think you miscalculated." Garrick didn't sound afraid. Or angry. Just amused and that made her tense even more. "You have the gun, yes, but I still have this..." He lifted the remote. And he pushed it.

Excruciating pain sliced into her throat. Her mouth opened in a scream, but no sound came out.

"Mina?" Luke still seemed dazed. "What's happening to you?"

She wanted to fall to her knees, to claw at the collar, but instead, she just pointed to the air again. He had to go. He had to go *right then.*

"If you don't move the gun," Garrick said, giving her his smile. "I'll take that voice of yours away permanently."

No, he was lying. Bluffing. He wanted her power. Why destroy it?

"You can't get out of here," Garrick continued, damn near gloating. "Your...*hero* is too damaged. We weren't packing tranq or even normal bullets when we hit him. I guess you could say we got an upgrade."

Her gaze dipped to the gun.

"You're outnumbered, Mina." The pain kept cutting into her. "And...really...do you want to die for that freak?"

Helpless, her stare flew to Luke and that was when Garrick lunged forward. His body slammed into hers. They hit the ground with an impact that had her shaking. He grabbed her wrist, twisted it, nearly shattering the bones and she screamed—

No sound.

At least, no sound from her.

A deep, guttural bellow seemed to shake the very earth itself. And suddenly, Garrick was flying through the air—being *thrown* through the air. Luke was there. He scooped Mina into his arms. Held her. His gaze searched her face, so desperate. So worried.

"Fire at him!" Garrick yelled. "*Shoot* him until he's down again!"

She looked over Luke's shoulder. Saw the agents aiming. She squeezed her eyes shut, an instinctive reaction as—

Howls. Growls. A gunshot blasted, and her eyes flew open. A giant white wolf was in the middle of the smoke and the flames and he'd just taken down one of the agents in black. As she watched, the wolf leapt at another agent, going for his throat. There were screams and yells as the agents tried to figure out where the hell the beast had come from—

Wind blew against her body. The fast whip of wind that she now knew signaled wings. *Wings batting at the air.* Her stare snapped back to Luke, but he hadn't shifted. He was holding her, cradling her in his arms, and his body was still that of a man.

Leo appeared behind him. "You *owe* me for this." He locked one arm around Luke and lifted him into the air. Since Luke was holding Mina, she rose, too. Leo hoisted them with one hand, as if their weight were nothing to him.

Below her, the wolf was still attacking, dodging bullets. Fighting fiercely.

"Get the hell out of there, Rayce!" Luke roared.

The wolf stilled, only for an instant, then he turned and disappeared into the smoke.

They were getting away. Alive. Safe…able to come back and fight another day. They were going to make it.

"Mina!"

Garrick was in the middle of the smoke, glaring up at her. "Come back to me...*now!*"

He had something in his hand—the gun? No...the remote.

"Come back...*now.*"

The pain blinded her that time. She could feel the slice in her neck, but it was worse, as if something were burrowing beneath her skin.

"Come back or die!" His thundering threats were following her.

Mina closed her eyes. *Closing your eyes doesn't make the bad things disappear.* No, she knew that truth. She also knew she wouldn't try to get Luke to take her back down. If she did, if they went back, he'd suffer, too. Their grand rescue mission had gone to shit.

So she let the pain sweep over her. She tightened her hold on Luke. And she knew that...whatever happened...

It was her choice. And her choice...it was Luke.

CHAPTER FIFTEEN

They landed on the island — or rather, Leo dropped Luke on the dock. Luke held tight to Mina. She'd been so silent, so still, during that flight. The flight itself had only taken a short time — his brother had used his enhanced speed to get them out of there once that soon-to-be-dead jerk Garrick had begun screaming his threats.

"We're safe," Luke told Mina.

She didn't stir in his arms. Her body was slumped against his.

He looked up, glaring at Leo. "You will pay."

Leo's eyes widened. "What? Are you serious? I just saved your ass — and *her* sweet ass, too." He waved his hand and clothes appeared on Luke's body. "And I hate talking to you when you're naked. It's like looking into one really twisted-ass mirror."

A growl rumbled from Luke's throat. Did his brother think he was a fool? "Don't you think I don't know what they did? What *you* gave to them? There's only one weapon that could have cut through my wings that way. Only one item that could have made me bleed." A near-fatal attack. "Did you think you weren't strong enough to end me yourself? So you started working with the humans? Was that your fucking plan all along? To get them to do your dirty work?" He'd wanted to find the head of the snake at Garrick's government agency. Luke was very much afraid he might be facing that snake right then.

Leo took a step back. "That's not…it didn't happen that way — "

"I am going to end you." He made that promise easily. "And I don't care what hell that brings." But his gaze darted down to Mina. Why hadn't she stirred?

"No, I guess you don't care. That's your problem, *brother.* You never care. You don't care about the destruction you leave in your wake. You don't care about the lives you wreck. You don't even care about the woman in your arms! Not really. She's just another possession to you, nothing more."

Mina was everything to him. And she wasn't moving.

Come back or die! That fool Garrick had screamed those words at her. Luke had thought the human was threatening to shoot her. His brother had obviously thought the same thing because that had been the moment that Leo flew faster, rushing them out of that area.

But now…

Carefully, Luke lowered Mina to the dock. Her dark hair spread behind her. There were dry tear tracks on her cheeks. Just the sight of them made his heart ache. "Mina?" His fingers slid over her, moving carefully and then…pausing as he stared at the emerald on her throat.

"Are you even listening to me?" Leo blasted him. "Selfish bastard! You would destroy the delicate balance on this world because you *think* I betrayed you. You won't listen to reason, even though I truly did just save your sorry ass—"

"Mina didn't speak to me." He remembered that now. He'd woken in the smoke and fire and Mina had been there, but she'd been pointing up in the air, obviously trying to get him to fly away. As if he would have left without her.

His fingers slid around the emerald. There was something about it that nagged at him.

"She didn't speak to me, either." Leo edged closer.

Luke's fingers slid against the collar on her neck. "Someone put this on her." He couldn't get his fingers beneath it. When he touched the strange fabric, it actually seemed to tighten around her skin. "Mina?" He needed her to open her eyes. Those too bright eyes that had always seemed to bewitch him.

But she didn't stir.

"That...emerald looks familiar to me," Leo muttered.

Luke's gaze focused on the emerald. It was familiar to him, too. But where had he seen it...*When?* And...

Oh, the fuck, no. "Mina!" he roared her name.

Her gaze flew open. For just an instant, she stared at him, happiness flashing in her eyes and then — then she started clawing at the collar, trying to pry it off her neck even as her face went first red, then purple.

"She's choking!" Now Leo sounded worried. "Get that thing off her!"

Garrick did this to her. "It's not an emerald." It had been so very long since he'd seen a creature like that one. And it *was* a creature. A very distant cousin to the scarabs that had been so popular in Egypt with a long ago queen.

Leo let out a low hiss. "Not those buggers. Hate them. They're made from — "

"Dark magic," Luke finished as he curled his fingers around the creature's back. Yes, the Ori was a dark beast, and that was why he could pull it away from Mina's delicate neck. Normally, once an Ori latched onto its prey, it never let go, not even after death. But when he touched the emerald green back, the beast shivered. The Ori's body trembled and Luke pulled it back. As he did, he saw the long needle that the Ori had discharged into Mina's neck—a stinger, really, and he heard Leo muttering in disgust behind him.

By the time he'd pulled the Ori off Mina, the needle was easily three inches long. And it had been embedded in her throat. *Oh, Mina, sweetheart, I am so sorry.* The sting of an Ori was a hundred times worse than the bite of a snake. The beast was small, but so very vicious, one of Luke's creations from a long time ago.

Several life-times ago. But he'd never, *never* meant for it to be used against someone like Mina.

When the needle finally slid free of Mina's neck, the collar that had been wrapped so tightly around her throat snapped. The collar was a new invention—he was sure Garrick's team had come up with that contraption so that it fitted into the Ori's body.

"Get rid of that thing," Leo snapped at him.

Luke crushed the Ori to dust in his hand.

Then he looked back at Mina's face. Her eyes were on him. He realized they'd been on him the whole time he'd been moving that Ori out of her. *How had Garrick gotten hold of that thing?* "You're going to be all right," Luke assured her. "It's gone now. It can't hurt you anymore."

Her lips moved.

But he heard no sound. "Mina?"

Again, her lips moved, but no sound emerged and as his heart seemed to constrict in his chest, Luke realized just what had been done to his beautiful Mina.

Garrick had learned how to steal her voice.

His gaze flew to his brother, then back to Mina. Did she know? Did she realize? Did she—

Mina smiled at him. That beautiful, warm smile. Then, very slowly, he saw her lips form the words. *It's okay.*

No, no, it wasn't okay. Mina was hurt. She'd lost her voice. She'd—

Leo grabbed him, hauling Luke to his feet. "She traded her voice for *you*."

Luke shook his head. No, no, Mina hadn't—

"That jerk—the one she called Garrick—he had some kind of device in his hand—must have been a remote for the collar."

Luke's head was pounding.

"I didn't realize what it was at the time, but now it all makes sense! She could have taken it from him, but instead, she took his gun because she was trying to buy time for *you*."

Luke's hands flew to lock around his brother's shoulders. "You were there...*watching?*" Just watching and not helping Mina? His rage turned even darker.

"I'd never seen you fall! I thought you were going to leap up at any moment and attack!" Leo yelled back. "But you didn't. When I realized that…I got both of you out of there."

Just not before Mina's voice had been taken.

Mina. Beautiful Mina. She had—

She was on her feet. Shoving between him and Leo. She stood there, her hair tangled around her shoulders, a line of blood dripping from her throat. One of her hands was on his chest, one on his brother's. And, again, her lips moved slowly.

Worth it.

"No, I'm not." He wanted to fall to his knees right then and there. He was the Lord of the Dark. He could control all beasts of the dark— that was how he had removed the Ori. "But I'll fix this, you'll see." He put his hand on her throat and focused all of the dark energy within him. He ruled the dark. That meant he could heal the dark creatures who'd been hurt. He'd brought others back from the brink of death, mending their bodies and their minds. He would give Mina back her voice. He would fix her. He *would.*

But her blood kept dripping down through his fingers. His hands were glowing, power bursting through him. He even felt the stretch of his wings behind him.

Yet her wound didn't heal.

"I told you," Leo spoke softly. "She isn't one of yours. Maybe you can finally see that now."

Mina was just staring at Luke, a faint line between her delicate brows.

Luke's gaze jerked toward his brother. "Heal her."

Leo hesitated. "If I do, then she *will* be mine, you know that, right?"

Mina frowned at them. Then she stared at Leo and shook her head. Immediately, her gaze returned to Luke. It almost hurt to look into her eyes. *There is no almost about it. This woman has gotten to me. And I will do anything for her.*

Anything…even lose her.

Leo's voice was flat as he warned, "If I do this, the traits that were dormant in her will be pushed out by the healing. She will leave you."

Mina grabbed Luke's hand. Again, she shook her head.

She wanted to stay with him. He could see that. Even though Leo could give her back her voice, she was still…*Choosing me. What have I done?* He swallowed, shoving down the lump in his throat. "There's a story, love," he told her, his words tender, "I think it may be one you heard before."

The line between her eyes deepened just a bit.

"There was once this beautiful mermaid who fell in love with a man she saw while swimming one morning. She wanted to be with him so she traded her voice for days with him."

Her lips parted.

"It was a foolish trade," Luke said, hating the growing rasp of his words. "Because that man wasn't worth it. He was not worth *any* of her pain. He carried too many sins on his back. He would never be worthy of her." No matter what he fucking did. Luke put his forehead against hers, knowing this was it. The end.

For them.

For him.

"You won't lose anything for me," Luke vowed. "I won't let you." Then he moved fast, turning her in his arms. She was struggling and he *hated* it because she should never know fear or pain. "Heal her," he said to his brother. "*Now.*"

Leo reached for her throat. His fingertips just touched her and a cascade of light seemed to explode. The light swallowed Mina's body, surrounding her, enveloping her. Luke felt the warmth slide over his skin.

And when the light faded…

Leo was gone.

Mina stood before him, her body trembling. His hands were still wrapped around her shoulders, holding her far too tightly. Carefully, he turned her back to face him.

"What in the hell was that?" Mina demanded.

Not hell, not even close.

He yanked her close, holding her in a hug that was no doubt crushing her, but Mina's beautiful voice was back. She was safe.

Her hand shoved against him. "Don't ever pull that crap with me again!" Mina snapped at him. "And I don't know what you and your weirdo twin were talking about, but I don't belong to anyone but myself! I'm not yours and I'm not his! So forget that freak train right now."

He loved her voice. Loved her passion. Her fire.

I love her. That knowledge was there, pushing up deep inside of him. He wasn't supposed to love. Everyone thought he *couldn't* love. And certainly, not love someone like Mina. Someone who was good and pure of heart. Someone straight from the light. But he stood before her, and the truth was undeniable. He looked into her bright eyes and he knew that he would do anything she wanted. Face any fight. Battle any foe. Give up all of his power...

For her.

His hand curled around her delicate jaw. He pressed his lips to hers. Need burst within him. The wild, fierce desire he only felt for her. He knew their time was limited. His brother was gone, but Leo would be back. And Mina would vanish.

I need her once more.

Not just once. He wanted her a thousand more times. A million. He wanted her forever, but the devil didn't get a happy ending. That had never been in the cards for him.

She would be happy.

She would also be far away from him.

"There it is," Mina murmured against his mouth. "That's what I missed. That's how I know it's *you*."

He didn't know what that meant, Luke just understood that the woman in his arms was the most important person in his world, and he was about to lose her. He scooped her into his arms and carried her back to his home. The home that had always felt more like a prison until she'd arrived.

He kissed her as they walked up the stairs inside. Her body was soft and warm, ever so perfect. When he touched her, he felt good.

They reached the landing. His head lifted and he just fucking feasted his eyes on her for a moment. He wanted to remember her, needed to remember her. Because he'd be living for centuries without her.

"Why do you look so sad?" Mina asked him.

He knew her voice would haunt him. The voice that had first enraptured him. Then bewitched him.

"Because I want you too much," he said.

She smiled at him. "There isn't such a thing. You can never want me too much."

She didn't understand. He would have to tell her, but...*after*. After he had one last time with Mina. After he felt her body against his. After he touched the only heaven he'd ever found — with her.

But her smile slipped. "Wh-what about Rayce?"

"He made it out." He'd seen the wolf flee.

Her eyes seemed to darken. "They took Julian away. And Eli — he was hurt so badly." She pushed against his arms and he put her down on her feet. Her body had gone tight with tension. "We have to get them back."

"I will." He was far from done with Garrick McAdams and his *agency*. "Don't worry, Mina. I don't lose those who are mine."

"There's that word again. You and your brother sure like to throw it around a lot."

He'd thought she was his. No, he'd hoped. And he'd ignored every sign to the contrary. "I swear, I will get them out."

"We should go back now," Mina argued. "We need to get there —"

He pressed a kiss to her lips. "We left the place in chaos. They will have called in every bit of back-up that they had. Dawn is here, and the time to attack isn't now. I will hit them at night, and I won't leave without my men." *At night, when my strength is always greatest.*

"*We* will attack," Mina said, giving a hard nod. "You and I. Look, okay, I get that the last big rescue plan didn't go over so well."

No, it hadn't. Because he'd underestimated his prey. He hadn't realized that the humans had been given extra help in their battle.

Someone gave them Ori. And…someone had given them the bullets they'd used to rip through his wings. Normal bullets would never be able to pierce him. His brother had denied the betrayal, but…"You told me that they kept other paranormals."

Mina nodded.

Those paranormals had given up his secrets. The dark paranormals had turned on their leader.

But was it possible that Leo's brethren had also fallen captive?

It would explain a lot. If Leo had spoken truthfully and truly not betrayed Luke, then maybe he'd been involved because he was trying to help his own kind, too. Maybe…

"You have that look again," Mina whispered. "Like you're sad." Her fingers pressed against his cheek. "I don't want you to be sad, Luke. Not ever."

Soon, he'd lose the only reason he ever had to be happy. "I'm going to make love to you, Mina."

She flashed him the smile that made his heart ache. "I was rather hoping you would. Especially after that ever-so-sexy way you carried me up the stairs."

He blinked at her and the ache he felt turned warm. Mina did that. Still surprised him. Still enthralled him. He would never quite figure out the way her mind worked.

But he would mourn her loss forever.

I've only known her for days. How did this happen? How?

"I don't understand the power that you and your brother have."

Few did.

"He…healed me, right? Is that something he can do, because he's…from the light?"

No, it's something he did because you are of the light, sweet Mina.

"And you were a dragon." She gave a quick, nervous laugh. But she kept touching him. "You are the fiercest thing that I've ever seen." She sounded admiring, not scared.

And Luke realized the truth. "*You* are the fiercest thing I've ever seen."

Her smile notched up, its beauty nearly blinding him. *How will I live without her?*

He turned his head, caught her hand, and pressed a kiss to her palm. She'd been through so much, and blood still lingered on her clothes. That just wouldn't do. He wanted to take away her pain. To wash it all away…

He took Mina to his bathroom. Soon the shower was on, blasting water down. He stripped Mina, taking his time, using gentleness and all the care he possessed. He wanted her to know how much she meant to him.

If he could, he would have traded everything he had for her.

Steam filled the shower. He slipped inside first, and Mina followed, their hands linked. She seemed so delicate and fragile. He wanted to protect her, to damn near worship her. Instead, he was going to lose her.

Fate was a cruel bitch.

He took soap in his hand and slid it over her body. Over her shoulders. Down her arms. On her stomach and up to the curves of her breasts. Her nipples were tight, pink, and he lifted her up against him, putting his mouth on her breast because he loved her taste so much.

She arched into him, moaning, as the water poured down her body.

His cock was hard, aching, and he wanted to drive deep and hard into her.

But he needed to make this memory, for both of them. Mina in the water. Him with her. Maybe…maybe she'd remember.

But perhaps not. Her kind had such short memories. Especially when they returned to the water.

He kissed his way to her other breast, laving the nipple, biting her lightly. Her nails sank into his shoulders and he loved that small flash of pain. He wished that she would mark him, that he would always carry her mark.

And I will, deep inside.

His hand slid down her body. Pushed between her legs. She was so soft and silky. He thrust two fingers inside of her and her sex clamped tightly around him. He kissed her neck, licked her skin. Pressed a tender kiss to her throat.

She'd offered her life for him. Did Mina realize that she was the first to make such a sacrifice? "I didn't deserve it," he rasped. He thrust his fingers into her again and loved the ragged gasp that she gave. That quick breath of pleasure.

His fingers slid from her and she moaned, protesting. Mina was so sensual. The water beading on her skin made her seem to glow with beauty. The blood was gone. Her pain—seemingly erased.

His hands moved to her hips. He lifted her against him, holding her easily and Mina locked her legs around his waist. She stared into his eyes, a sensual smile on her lips. His cock was wedged at the entrance to her body. One push, and he'd be inside. The pleasure would overwhelm them both. Make them forget everything else.

But he hesitated. He wanted this moment to last—Mina, clinging tightly to him. Mina, holding him, trusting him. Loving him?

A guy could hope. Even a guy like him.

"Inside, Luke," Mina ordered, her voice the sexiest of demands. "You're driving me crazy! I need you!"

And he would never deny her, not anything. He drove into her and sank deep. Her heels pushed against his ass as she let out another moan. The sound of her pleasure drove him wild. He eased back, then thrust into her, deeper, harder, pounding into her again and again.

Every glide sent his cock pushing over her clit, and he knew the pleasure was surging through her. He needed her to break. Luke wanted her control to splinter as she surrendered to him and to the fierce desire that raged between them.

He pushed her back against the marble wall of his shower. He put his mouth against hers, thrusting his tongue past her lips even as his hips surged against her. Her inner muscles clenched around him, her whole body went tight—

And Luke swore he could taste her pleasure. Mina erupted around him, her sex rippling around his cock, her body jerking and he let himself go. Luke emptied into her, the beast that he kept inside roaring his release. Mina's hands were sweeping over his back, she was holding him as if she never wanted to let him go…

But soon enough, she'd walk away. The ocean would call to Mina, and she'd leave him. She'd go, and his world would rip apart.

CHAPTER SIXTEEN

Julian's neck ached. He could feel the blood slowly dripping down his throat.

"I'm so sorry," she whispered. "I-I never wanted this."

Because she was turned away from him, the vampiress didn't see his sudden flinch. "Rose..."

She looked back at him. He could see the tear tracks on her face. Her beautiful face — one that had been burned in his memory long ago.

"I deserve one hell of a lot more than just a bite from you," he said. His voice gruff. She should want to rip him apart. After all, it was his fault that she — *no, stop. Take it one step at a time.* "How did you get here? How did these goons catch you?"

"I'd gone too long without eating." She swallowed and he heard the delicate click of that movement. "Agent McAdams found me in Chicago. He said that he could help me. That he could...he could change me back."

Julian took a step toward her. He'd ripped the chains right from the wall when she'd first come toward him. Apparently, he'd just needed the right motivation to break free. Now the battered remnants of those chains dangled from his wrists.

Rose threw up her hand. "No, stop it! Don't come closer! I-I'll attack if you do!" Her voice was sharp and desperate. "*They've starved me.* That's how McAdams has *helped.* He lied to me. He promised that he'd help but he just wanted to use me."

What McAdams wanted was a swift trip to hell. Julian would be happy to oblige the man.

"He's starving me because he wants me weak. Weak means controllable in his mind. He's going to use me, try to get me to turn into some kind of weapon." Her laughter was bitter, wild. "I thought the FBI was supposed to be good! They're just as bad as—" But she broke off, clamping her lips together.

As bad as I am? He eased out a careful breath and took a step toward her. His nostrils flared, pulling in the acrid scent of smoke that was drifting through the air. Before, he'd heard gun shots, distant screams, but all of that noise had died away.

Only the smoke remained.

"We need to get out of here," he told Rose. His Rose. Holy fucking hell, what were the odds that he'd find her like this? He'd tried to find her before, searching desperately, even going to her asshole brother Michael, but the guy had turned him away.

And I thought she was better off without me.

He'd been wrong. Rose had been hurting, and he hadn't known. With an effort, Julian kept his voice steady as he said, "In order to escape, you have to be strong. So if you need more blood, baby, drink up."

Her shoulders stiffened. "Don't call me that." Her eyes—dark green and glittering—locked on him.

Julian lifted his hands in front of him. The chains dangled. "My mistake. A slip of the tongue."

She growled.

"Rose?" It had been so long since he'd seen her. So long since he'd gone to Luke, desperate, and made the deal to save her life.

Or rather...the deal to bring her back from the dead.

"I never wanted this," Rose whispered.

His heart slammed into his chest. "What did you think I was going to do? It was *on* me. My fault. I'm the one who—"

"You're here because McAdams and his twisted group of agents have given me my first assignment." Her brittle voice cut right through his words. Her face was as he remembered it—a soft oval, big, deep eyes, and full, sexy lips. Her skin was too pale though, and he could see the dark shadows that lined her eyes. "You're that assignment."

The scent of smoke deepened. It sure seemed as if that whole place was going down in flames. He could hear the shriek of an alarm now. One that seemed to be growing louder with every moment that passed.

"Agent McAdams told me that I was supposed to attack whoever was placed in the cell with me." Her shoulders straightened. "He said…he said I was to kill that person."

Shit.

"If I didn't…" Her head tilted forward and the dark curtain of her hair — dirty and tangled because she'd been kept prisoner for who the fuck knew how long — swept down to cover her face. "Then McAdams said I'd be the one to suffer."

He intended to make certain that McAdams suffered — a painful, excruciating anguish.

"I'm sorry," Rose told him. Her breath rushed out on a sad sigh. That was the thing about vampires — they still breathed. They still felt. They still *lived*, just in a different way. A way that required blood and fangs. "But I don't have a choice."

She might not, but he did. Julian's gaze flew around the cell. He ran to the wall and drove his fist into it, again and again, but the strange glass didn't break. His hands bloodied as he punched, but the glass wouldn't give.

Then he felt her touch on his shoulder. Soft, light, and sending heat flooding right through his whole body. He tensed, his bloody fist still raised.

That was always the way it had been between them. She touched him, and he wanted. He craved. He lost his sanity.

"I'm sorry," she said again.

And, through that glass, he saw Garrick McAdams and his men—armed men who appeared a bit singed and ash-covered—running toward the cell.

Julian's jaw locked.

"I really hate," Rose added, voice almost…wistful. "For you to have to watch me die again."

What?

Garrick opened the cell door.

Rose locked her hand around Julian's shoulder and she heaved him back—far away from the agents. His shoulders thudded into the back wall.

Too late, the words finally registered for him. Rose wasn't going to kill him. She was going to sacrifice herself. *No, no, no!* He opened his mouth and the roar of his beast erupted, seeming to shake the cell.

"She should have drained the guy by now!" It was the redheaded woman behind Garrick who spoke first. *Madeline.* Yeah, he recognized her easily enough. She lifted her weapon, aiming it right at Rose. "You knew the assignment."

Rose ran at her.

Julian lunged for them.

The agents fired at Rose — a barrage of bullets that slammed into her body and she jerked like a marionette on a string.

The change hit Julian right then, white-hot and burning. His beast literally clawed to the surface and shoved the man back. He hit the floor on all fours, his paws and claws scraping over the surface. Fur erupted from his body as he watched Rose fall.

Not again. It can't happen again.

"Fascinating," he heard Garrick say. "But I don't have time for this shit now. The big boss is coming to meet us, and we have to *move.*"

Garrick aimed his gun at Julian. Julian saw him through the panther's eyes. His prey. He surged toward the bastard even as Garrick fired, again and again.

The bullets thudded into him. Other agents were screaming. Shooting.

Julian didn't stop. He slammed into Garrick, taking that bastard down.

"Shoot him!" Garrick yelled. "Keep shooting him! *Stop him!*"

Julian locked his teeth around the man's throat. *You're done.* His teeth sank into the bastard and—

"Time for my payback," Madeline said, voice nearly purring with satisfaction. He felt the muzzle of a gun press between his eyes. "You and that little bitch should have left me alone. No one messes with my mind." Then she fired.

His teeth shoved down hard in a last, desperate bite. *If I'm going out, I want to take him with—*

Darkness closed around Julian. A cold, final darkness.

And he wondered, if, in the next world, he'd ever see Rose again.

***

"You're a dragon." Mina was still trying to wrap her mind around that fact. Meanwhile, though, her body was currently wrapped around his. Her arm was curled around Luke's stomach. Her leg was draped over his thighs. They were in his bed, their bodies twined so closely together. She felt safe. Warm.

Protected.

Almost…loved?

"I did *not* see that one coming," she confessed to him and Mina pressed a quick kiss to his shoulder.

His hand slid over her hip, seeming to linger a moment on one of her scars. "There were things I didn't want to see, either."

His voice was thick with what she could have sworn was sadness. But why would the Lord of the Dark be sad?

She licked lips that had gone suddenly dry. A deep sense of foreboding swept over her. "What haven't you told me?" She looked at his hand, the hand that was tenderly stroking her scar. The Eye of Hell still gleamed on his finger. "Luke?" Mina prompted when he remained silent.

His hand lifted. He, too, stared at the Eye. "You never needed this."

Yes, she had. "Garrick has more resources than you realize. You saw that—that collar he put on me." She didn't want to remember the pain and terror that collar had brought to her. "We can't underestimate him again. I *do* need the Eye. You can use it to take away my dark power and—"

"There is nothing dark about you." His gaze slid to hold hers. "There never was. You are the most generous woman I've ever met. You're brave and you're strong and your heart isn't tainted by anything."

The heart in question seemed to warm.

"You were willing to trade your life for mine," he continued and he—held his breath? *How very unlike him.* Then Luke asked, "Why?"

Why? "Because it was right," she spoke, slowly, feeling her way. Her emotions were tangled. She didn't even clearly understand why herself. She'd just known that she couldn't let Luke suffer. That his death would not happen.

"Of course." His hand slid away from her hip. He rolled from the bed. Stood there, naked, staring down at her. "I forgot that was the way Leo's kind acted. Right and wrong. Good and evil. All that jazz."

She wasn't feeling so warm and safe any longer. Mina pulled the covers up to her chin. "Luke?"

"I lied to you, Mina."

No. Automatically, she shook her head. She and Luke had a bond, she knew it. She might not be able to explain it, but Mina felt it. He cared about her. And she was completely tangled up in him.

"I'm not planning to wait for nightfall before I go after Garrick and the others. I just wanted to fuck you one more time, and then I'm walking away."

Wait—*what?* Mina jumped to her feet, yanking the sheet with her and wrapping it clumsily around her body.

He waved his hand and clothes covered him. Pity he hadn't used that same trick to cover *her*.

"We didn't *fuck*." Those were the angry words that jumped from her mouth. "Don't you dare say that to me, got it?"

"Then what did we do?" His head cocked as he studied her. His face was a cold, hard mask.

"We made love!" Mina nearly yelled those words at him. "It was more than just physical. You *know* it was."

"But you don't love me."

Silence.

Her lips were still parted and her breath heaved out. "I—" Mina stopped. She didn't know what she felt. Was it love? She needed him, she wanted to protect him, she was so eager for those rare moments when he smiled or laughed and…

He's the Lord of the Dark. He turned into a dragon and burned half of Key West. But his flames had never so much as singed her skin.

"Can you love?" Mina asked him, and she was desperate to know the truth.

He turned his back to her. "The beast that I became…that's who I really am. The man is just the mask I wear. Inside, my heart is black. I yearn to let my fire out. To rage and destroy everyone in my path." He paced toward the balcony. Opened the doors and stepped outside.

She rushed to follow him, the sheet trailing behind her like a wedding dress train. When she stepped onto the balcony, the wind whipped at her, bringing the crisp, salty air of the ocean.

The ocean.

Her gaze was pulled toward that glistening water and she found that she couldn't look away.

"Beautiful, isn't it?" Luke mused. "I always enjoy coming up here and staring at the water. Pity I never realized it would be the thing I'd grow to hate the most."

What? Mina tried to drag her gaze off those waves but they actually seemed to be calling to her. *So beautiful.*

"I have to always watch myself." His voice was low, but it carried over the pounding surf. "Always be careful to contain my darkness. Because if I do let my control break, I can destroy the humans out there. All of them. My power will spread like a sickness, infecting them. Wiping out humanity until only my paranormals are left. And those who are mine? They are dark. They battle inner demons every moment. They don't…they don't love easily."

Her eyes closed. It was the only way she could stop staring at the water. What was happening? The waves had seemed to mesmerize her.

"You asked if I could love."

She focused on his voice. The deepness. The roughness. *Luke.*

Then she felt his touch. His hands were on her shoulders, holding her tight.

"I can."

Her eyes opened.

But…

She and Luke weren't standing on the balcony any longer. He'd moved them—used his power—and now they were on the edge of the beach. The waves came forward, tickling her toes, and a spark of pure joy slid through her.

"I'm letting you go," he said and his smile broke her heart. "That should show just how fucking much I *can* love." He pressed a kiss to her lips. "See? My brother was wrong about that. Even in the dark, a little light can shine."

Then he—he guided her toward the waves.

But he kept her sheet. She was standing there, naked, while the waves pushed against her body. No, they weren't pushing against her. They were almost, wrapping around her. Hugging her?

Welcoming me.

And she found herself turning away from Luke and wading deeper into the water. She didn't want to leave him, but she felt strangely helpless in that moment. *The water is calling to me.*

"Your mother didn't go to the water to die, Mina!" His shout followed her as she went out even deeper. "She went because she had no choice. Her kind never does!"

Her kind?

"The fact that she stayed six years with you is amazing. Mermaids aren't supposed to be able to resist the ocean's call for that long. The ocean is a mermaid's true love. Her heart. But when she had a half-mortal daughter, your mother fought the call. She fought it for six long years, and she stayed with you."

The water was up to Mina's waist now and her legs...they were feeling so funny.

"But a mermaid can't stay out of the ocean forever. If she'd kept trying, she *would* have died. She had to go back. Just as you...have to go."

Her head turned. She looked over her shoulder at him. He was on the beach, his legs braced apart, his gaze focused totally on her.

"You're not a siren, love. You're a mermaid. When Leo healed you, he brought forth all of your dormant powers. Your human side is gone, and the ocean is calling to you." His arms crossed over his chest.

"I'm scared." The words slipped from her, so low but...

Luke heard her.

"You don't need to be." His gaze became bright, a sign of his power. "You never need to fear. Those scars on your body? Those are just there to help you transform. They actually aren't scars at all. You'll get gills. Your legs will become a beautiful mermaid's tail."

She could...she could almost see the gleam of scales on her legs, just beneath the waves.

"And when you go beneath the water…" His voice was strong, but rough. "The life you'd known before will be gone, just as it was gone for your mother. The ocean doesn't come in second place, not to anyone. You will know only it—a mermaid's obsession. There will be no other life. There will be no other love."

She stretched out her hands in the water. It just felt…so good. So right. But she kept looking back at Luke.

"You won't remember me."

What? Of course, she would always remember him. He was unforgettable, her Lord of the Dark. And they had to go and fight Garrick. They had to get Julian back. Had to rescue Eli. They had to—

Her legs had become a tail. She flicked it in the water and a laugh of wonder escaped her.

"I will never forget you, Mina."

The waves crashed over her, pulling her in deep, and Mina sank into a new world.

***

An hour later, Luke was in the same spot, staring at the pounding surf. Looking for the flash of a mermaid's tail.

"She's not going to come back."

His dumb ass of a brother had just appeared at his side. Luke didn't even glance his way. His focus was on the spot he'd last seen Mina.

"You know her kind don't have a choice. The ocean is their joy. She didn't leave you to…to hurt you." Leo seemed to stumble over those words, as if unsure how to comfort his twin. Mostly because they'd never comforted one another before. "She left because she had to go home."

"Fuck off." Before he turned his growing rage on his brother.

"Figured you'd say that," Leo muttered. "Look, I healed her, okay? That was what you wanted. You wanted—"

I wanted her. He'd wanted to keep her with him, forever. But even more than that… "I wanted her alive. Happy." The Eye of Hell seemed to heat on his hand. That damn Eye was part of him. Mina hadn't realized that. No one ever did. He wielded it because he owned the darkness inside of it. The Eye only did what he *wished.*

And right then, he was trying so very, very hard not to be a selfish bastard. Trying so hard…

Not to wish her back to me. But a mermaid couldn't stay with someone like him. In order to stay, the Eye would have to change her.

She'd lose the new life that she'd just found.

His hands fisted. *I will not wish it. For once –
for fucking once – I will let the choice be Mina's.* The
ring kept heating on his hand. *It will be Mina's
choice.*

Leo the dumb ass stepped closer. "Mermaids
experience only joy in the ocean. You know that.
They command every creature beneath the
surface. Even great whites will thrill to a touch
from her fingertips."

But Mina was afraid of sharks. He
remembered how she'd frozen that first night. He
took a step forward. The water hit his shoe. What
if she was afraid right then? What if she saw a
shark and it terrified her? What if –

"I didn't think you had it in you," Leo
continued, the words bemused. "To sacrifice your
happiness for someone else."

The waves kept breaking against the shore.
"You ever think the damn stories about us are
wrong? Maybe I'm not evil to my core." His lips
twisted. "And maybe you aren't so freaking
good."

"I'm not."

A surprising admission.

"I've made mistakes, too. Mistakes
like…Garrick McAdams."

Very slowly, Luke turned his head to look at
Leo.

"I didn't pay enough attention to what the
humans were doing. I didn't realize just how

powerful that group was becoming." Leo heaved out a breath. "You think I gave them my arrows, don't you? That I gave them my arrows because only their tips can pierce the hide of a dragon."

Luke just stared at him. Leo's arrows were very special and very ancient. They were made of material no longer found on earth. The only material that could truly hurt his kind. *Not just hurt me, but kill me.*

"If you think that, why am I still alive?" Leo asked.

Luke looked back at the water. "Because even if you betrayed me, you still saved *her.*"

He heard Leo's sharp inhalation. "You…love her, don't you?"

I will always love her. "My good will toward you is ebbing. I have humans to go destroy. You probably don't want to watch that part. Being the squeamish sort that you are." He waved dismissively toward him. "I'll get back your arrows. Try not to lose them again."

"I *haven't* lost them."

And once more, Luke studied his brother.

"I did not betray you that way, I swear." Leo didn't even blink. "But I want to find out what is happening. I *have* to find out." A grim smile curved his lips. "After all, brother…what wounds you, well, it also wounds *me.*"

True. They did have the same weaknesses, but their strengths were very, very different.

"I think they've taken some of my kind, too," Leo continued. "There have been some troubling disappearances of late. I can't let that keep happening. I protect what belongs to me."

Something else they had in common.

"They've vacated the Naval Air Station." Leo rolled back his shoulders. For just an instant, Luke saw the shadow of wings behind his brother's body. "But we can track them."

The dragon could track anyone, anywhere.

"Are you ready to hunt, brother?" Leo asked.

He hadn't hunted with his brother in centuries. "I don't plan to play nicely with these humans. Are you ready for that?"

Leo's lips pressed together, but he didn't argue.

Interesting.

Luke smiled at him. "Then I'm ready." He motioned to the sky. "By all means, you first."

Leo erupted, heading straight up, and he shed the body of a man. A great, hulking dragon shot toward the sky.

You try to act as if you're civilized, but I know the truth. Inside, you're just like me.

Luke didn't immediately fly off after his brother. He stood on the beach a moment, waiting...

Then he sighed. "Are you going to keep lurking back there forever?" Finally, he heard the quick rush of footsteps approaching him. He turned around and saw Rayce closing in. "I was wondering how long you were going to eavesdrop."

Rayce lifted his brows and appeared vaguely insulted. "Eavesdrop? No way, man. I was just hanging back to make sure the world didn't explode because you and your twin were so close together." A little pause. "I figured you'd go for each other's throats."

They hadn't. "You know the old saying...*the enemy of my enemy is my for-the-moment friend.*"

Rayce shook his head. "That isn't the way the saying goes."

Almost helplessly, Luke glanced back at the water. "It's not?"

"No. But I get what you mean. You and Leo are teaming up to take out Garrick McAdams and his goons because you're both scared those humans are causing too much trouble."

The waves were churning. The sky starting to darken. A storm was coming. His storm. "Those humans hurt Mina. They will pay for that."

"Uh, yeah, about Mina...did I see her very nice ass walking into the water?"

Luke's shoulders tensed. "Mina is gone." *And I feel her absence like a hole in my soul.* Only he wasn't supposed to have a soul. No soul, no heart.

Pity he had both. Or rather, he'd had them.

He was pretty sure the ocean had taken both away.

"You can get her back, right?"

Mermaids didn't come back, not as a rule. They often had dalliances with humans, brief affairs sparked by curiosity. All mermaids were given one chance to walk on land, a chance to taste human love and compare that love to the joy they felt in the sea.

Nothing could ever compete with the sea. The freedom. The power.

A mermaid's life.

"Mermaids and sirens are very similar," Luke murmured. "Both have captivating voices. Power that can compel. Sirens lured sailors to their doom long ago, but mermaids, I think they were even worse." He put a hand to his chest. "Mermaids got sailors to love them, and just when those foolish sailors thought they held paradise, the mermaids would turn away. They'd choose the ocean."

"I didn't think there *was* really a choice for mermaids."

There was something in Rayce's voice...*Sonofabitch.* Luke scowled at his friend. "You knew, didn't you?"

"That Mina wasn't a siren?" Rayce came a bit closer, his voice growing stronger. "I suspected. She didn't seem to have that cold touch, if you know what I mean. A bit too soft on the inside."

He looked down at his ring. "She wanted me to use the Eye to take her dark power away. She didn't understand that she wasn't dark at all." Right then, he hated the Eye. He hated the whole fucking world. "Why didn't you warn me to stay away from her?"

"Because I thought you deserved a chance to be happy, too."

His head whipped up.

"Tell me the truth, O' Great Lord of the Dark." The title was mocking but Rayce's gaze was dead serious. "Weren't you happy with her?"

"*Yes.*"

Rayce's hands flew up into the air. "Then why aren't you fighting for her? Why aren't you using your power, using that freaking Eye, using everything that you have to keep her with you?"

Rayce had wanted the truth. So Luke would give it to him. "Because I love her. And I find that, more than my own happiness...I want hers. I want her to have the choice. I want her to have whatever she desires most."

Rayce's mouth dropped open in shock.

"So I'm going to kill some people." Luke nodded decisively. "I'm going to spread terror and hell, and I'm going to spend the rest of my exceedingly long life missing a mermaid who won't even remember me. That happens, you see. Did you know that?"

Rayce shook his head. "No, Luke…"

"It's why her mother never came back for her," Luke continued grimly, the words just not stopping. "When a mermaid returns to the ocean, she forgets her human life. It's as if that time never was. The longer you stay in the water, the more those memories vanish." He gave a bitter laugh. "How is this for my own private hell? I'll never forget her, but Mina won't even remember my name."

The cruelest twist of fate.

"Luke, fuck…I'm *sorry.* I didn't know—"

Luke exhaled and a puff of smoke blew from his lungs. Time for his beast to come out. "Stay on the island. Things are about to get ugly in the Keys."

"Luke—"

He flew straight up into the air, traveling fast, shifting easily and the beast started hunting its prey.

Maybe I should just stay this way. No longer even pretend to be a man. I've lost her, so what is the fucking point? What is the point of trying to keep my control? She's gone.

And I…hurt.

CHAPTER SEVENTEEN

The water was beautiful, so clear and warm. She swam deep, then shot to the surface, moving so fast. Far faster than she'd ever dreamed.

Her tail was powerful, propelling her forward. She was racing with a dolphin and laughing because she was beating him. She broke through the surface and did a roll in the air, pushed again by her magnificent tail.

She splashed into the water. Sank deep. She was moving so quickly, swimming right past coral reefs and sunken ships. Her hands touched the fish that rushed eagerly toward her. They surrounded her and danced for her.

It was amazing.

It was...home. She felt it, all the way in her bones. This was where she was meant to be. Happiness beat in her heart. Such pure joy and —

A shark was up ahead.

For a moment, she stilled and a shiver of fear slipped through her. The shark's eyes were so dark, and its mouth open as it swam toward her. She could see those deadly rows of teeth. *I'm*

*afraid of the shark. It's just like before, when I was
trying to get away from Luke, and the shark was there.
I froze and —*

The memory vanished when the shark
bumped her.

But the shark didn't attack after that bump. It
just…stayed beside her. Her shaking fingers
reached out and she touched its side.

The shark seemed to vibrate against her, as if
enjoying her touch. In that moment, she knew
there was nothing to fear. Not in the ocean. The
certainty was soul deep. She didn't have to be
afraid. Not any longer. She never had to fear
again.

She should tell Luke. She should —
Luke.
The name was in her mind, lingering.
But…
Who was Luke?

She spun beneath the water. The shark had
disappeared. The school of fish was gone. She
was all alone right then, just a few feet from the
wreckage of an old plane.

Who is Luke? The question battered at her. She
stared at her fluttering hands. At her beautiful
tail, and another chilling thought sliced through
her…

Who am I?

Because she couldn't remember…she
couldn't even remember her own name.

She looked up, seeing a streak of lightning flash just beyond the water's surface. Her tail snapped down, propelling her once again as she rushed upward to follow that lightning. Rushing—

Her head broke the surface. She started to suck in a desperate breath of air because she'd been down below so long but...*I don't need to hold my breath underwater.*

Lightning flashed again. Thunder rolled through the air. Her head tilted back and she stared above her. Too late, she realized that the sound hadn't been thunder.

It had been a roar. Her eyes widened as the lightning came once more and, this time, she saw just what had made that terrible roar. A big, hulking beast was flying through the air. A beast with giant, black wings. A long, serpentine tail. Sharp teeth and fire flying from its mouth.

She dove beneath the waves, fear beating at her. That creature was horrifying.

She sank deep beneath the water. The ocean soothed her. Comforted her. Joy pulsed in her veins once more.

The school of brightly colored fish swam toward her and—

Who is Luke? Her gaze darted upward once more.

***

Luke touched down at the remains of the Naval Air Station. The place appeared deserted, the buildings now black and singed. A wave of his hand had clothes on his body as he stormed for the broken front gate.

Leo appeared in his path. "They *aren't* here. I've tracked them to a boat that departed about thirty minutes ago—"

"They left someone behind." He could smell the blood. Judging from that heavy scent, they'd actually left more than a few *someones*. He shoved Leo out of his path and, moments later, he was in the bowels of that place. No guards rushed out to meet him. No one came at all.

But the scent of blood just grew stronger.

He hurried down a flight of stairs. Luke turned to the right and there—through a thick pane of glass, he saw the two men who'd been left behind.

Agent Timothy Lang sat in the middle of the room. His arms were tied behind his back. His feet were tied to the legs of a chair.

And sprawled at his side, a deep pool of blood around him…*Julian.*

"Keep calm, Luke," Leo warned. The guy had followed him. "Stay in control, stay—"

Luke lifted his hand and shattered that glass. Then he stepped through the now-broken wall and the shards of glass crunched beneath his feet.

"OhmyGod," Timothy stared up at him with wide eyes. "Garrick said you'd come back. I wanted him to be wrong. I *needed* him to be wrong."

Luke bent next to Julian. He turned his friend over and a low hiss escaped him when he saw the damage that had been done. *They shot you in the head.* Fucking bastards. He put his hand to Julian's throat.

"I didn't do it!" Timothy cried out. "I swear, I didn't! Garrick said you'd be pissed as all hell when you found your dead friend and that you'd kill me, too. He wanted you to do that, to get rid of me because I know what a twisted SOB he is. That bastard turned on *me.* He's trying to get you to do his dirty work and kill me so I can't report him to the higher-ups at the agency, but—"

"Shut up." Luke glared at him. "Or I will kill you."

Timothy gulped and immediately shut up.

Luke glanced back at Julian. "My friend isn't dead yet. That's why you're still breathing, Agent Lang. If I'd found his dead body, you *would* be in pieces right now."

"Luke…" Leo said, a warning in his voice.

What? He'd spoken the truth. He was getting damn sick of Leo always *warning* him and *cautioning* him. He didn't need that crap. Luke put his hand on Julian's chest. He focused all of his power on the shifter. *You don't get to cut out of this world so easily.* It was much easier to heal a dark creature than it was to bring someone back from the dead, but he would have brought Julian back, no matter the cost.

He had few enough friends as it was.

The bullet slid from Julian's head. The terrible wounds to his head and face closed. Julian's lips parted and he sucked in a deep breath. Then his eyes flew open — his gaze full of fear and desperation and he roared —

"Rose!"

Rose? Luke pulled back his hand. "It's rather customary to say thank you."

Julian jerked upright. His frantic gaze shot around the cell. "*Rose!*" Then he was grabbing Luke's shirt, his hands fisting in the material. "Where is she? What did you do with her?"

Rose. It was a name from Julian's rather bloody past. And, while — once upon a time, Luke had done *something* to her — this time, he had no clue about the woman. Luke turned his head and stared at a profusely sweating Timothy Lang. "Ask the agent here. I think he may know."

Instantly, Julian was on his feet. Claws burst from his fingertips as he shoved his hand against Timothy's throat. "*What happened to my vampire?*"

A gurgle was the only sound Timothy made.

Luke rolled his eyes. "Speak, man. Prove to us that it's better to keep you alive."

Timothy's breath whooshed out. "Garrick took her. He wants to—I heard him say he wants to use her. He's never had a vampire in his program before. Said she was…special."

Julian's claws were drawing blood. "She is."

Luke put his hand on his friend's shoulder. "Ease back."

He saw the look of surprise that Leo threw his way. What? Did the guy really think they were just mindless killing machines?

Agent Lang is the one that Mina liked. She said he was kind to her. Luke would repay that kindness. "Cut the ropes off him, Julian."

Julian sliced through the ropes.

Then Luke bent forward until he was eye-to-eye with the human. "Did you enjoy watching the paranormals suffer?"

His brother moved to stand at the man's back. Leo put one hand on the guy's shoulder. When it came to his precious humans, Leo had a special gift. He could always tell when they spoke the truth, as long as he touched them when they spoke.

"I-I didn't," Timothy answered. "Made me…sick."

Leo nodded.

"Then why did you stay?" Luke demanded.

Timothy's eye lashes fluttered. "We were supposed to be the good guys. I thought…I thought we were helping the weak." He licked his lips. "Too late, I saw what we really were."

And, once more, Leo nodded.

"If I let you go," Luke said, "what will you do?"

"Run as fast as I can," the guy blurted.

He didn't need Leo's confirmation of that truth.

"And will you try to rejoin Garrick's merry crew?" Disdain dripped from Luke's voice.

"No." Timothy's voice had gone hoarse. "I never want to see them again."

Leo nodded. Another truth.

"Do you know what atonement means?" Luke tilted his head to the side.

"Y-yes…"

"Good." He nodded. "Because you're going to fucking atone for your crimes. You're going to tell me everything that you know about Garrick and his men. You're going to help me make sure that any paranormals they have are freed. You are going to help me put all of this *right* again."

Timothy nodded. "You…aren't killing me?"

"Not right now."

Leo's hand remained clamped around the agent's shoulder.

"Who is Garrick's boss?" Luke asked.

"I-I don't know."

His gaze snapped toward Leo. And, dammit, his brother nodded.

Snarling, Luke stepped back.

"But-but I know the guy is connected to the vampire!"

That desperate outburst had Julian snarling once more.

"Connected?" Luke asked, attention caught. "How?"

Timothy's wide eyes were on Julian. Or rather, on Julian's claws. "I don't know for certain—I swear, I don't. I just know that Garrick said his boss is the one who told him about Rose Kinley. The boss is the one who said we had to bring her into the program."

"Your boss is a dead man," Julian promised. "You bastards *starved* her!"

"I didn't!" Timothy cried out. He lifted his wrist to reveal an old bite mark—two small circles. "I gave her my blood when the others weren't looking. I wanted to help her!"

And that small act was helping to save his ass right then. "What else do you know?" Luke asked him. This guy was their lead. He'd pry all the information out of Timothy's head.

Timothy's hand dropped. "I-I know where the other paranormals are being held." He licked his lips. "I can give you a list of the locations."

Good. Luke intended to free all of the others. He turned to Julian. "Take Timothy back to the island. Once I've dealt with Garrick, we'll need those locations." Then he headed for the door.

There was another blood trail to follow in that hell-hole. He had to get to—

"No." Julian's voice was flat. Hard.

And it was the first time the guy had *ever* refused an order from the Lord of the Dark.

Luke stilled. He didn't look back. "Excuse me?"

"Rose is out there. I saw them *hurt* her. I have to find her. I have to go after her, right the fuck *now*."

Luke's shoulders were tight with tension and fury. Carefully, he turned to face Julian. "I just pulled your ungrateful ass from the jaws of death."

"*She is out there. They starved her. Kept her prisoner. My Rose.*" His hands were clenched at his sides. "You don't know what it's like to care about a woman this way. You don't understand and I can't make you, but I *have* to help her. She needs me, and I won't let her down again."

I understand plenty. He was walking around without his heart. Trying to do one job. Eliminate Garrick McAdams and the threat that his "agency" posed because Luke could never allow them to go after Mina again. She had to be safe.

Always.

Luke blew out a slow breath. "I will bring your Rose back."

"She needs *me*! She—"

"She's on the boat with Garrick," Leo interrupted.

Luke fired a glance his way.

Leo shrugged. "I trailed them earlier. I *told* you this already. Remember? The boat that left thirty minutes ago? I saw them and it would have been rather hard to miss a vampire being carried around in a coffin."

Julian flinched.

"She's on the boat, traveling far and fast." His twin was just the helpful one with information. "And, unless I've missed something in the last bit, panther, you can't sprout wings to find her so you're going to be grounded on this one."

Julian took an aggressive step toward Luke. "I need her. I will trade *anything* to make sure she's safe. Get me on that boat. Help me, and I'll make any deal."

That wasn't the way this situation would work. He whirled away and rushed out of the cell. He followed the lingering scent of blood into what looked like a small medical ward.

A man's still body lay on one of the makeshift beds. Long, thin, pale. Tubes and machines were hooked to the man. They beeped steadily.

"I don't see your spiders, Eli," Luke said as he approached the bed. He put his hand on the other man's chest, much like he'd done with Julian. Only this time, Eli was actually much better off. He looked like shit, but it appeared as if the humans had tried to patch him up before they'd hauled ass out of there.

Eli's eyes opened as the machines beeped louder.

"*Luke.*" Leo's voice was sharp. "We really need to get out of here. You know they left these men here for a reason."

Yes, he knew. He wasn't an idiot. They were all bait.

"And the fact that no guards are around?" Leo pressed. The guy had followed him— everyone had followed him in there, even a nervous, foot-shuffling Timothy Lang. "Doesn't that give off warning signs in your head?"

Luke lifted his hand off Eli's chest. "You aren't done yet."

Eli gave him a tired smile. "Didn't...think I was."

Luke helped him to sit up.

"Wh-what will I owe you?" Eli asked.

He gave that a moment's thought. "I could use some new whiskey. Seems some fool agent destroyed my last shipment."

Eli laughed. A spider tattoo had appeared on his throat. It seemed to move, just a bit.

"We need to get *out* of here!" Leo thundered.

Luke sighed. "Yes, you're right. The building is probably going to blow up any moment."

"What?" That terrified cry came from Timothy.

Luke hoisted Eli over his shoulder, despite the man's protests. "You were all left behind for two reasons." He motioned toward Timothy. "Leo, he's human and since that makes him yours, you carry his ass out."

Leo gave a curt nod.

Luke let his wings spread behind him. "Where was I?" he muttered. "Ah, yes. My reasons. One...bait. Garrick knew I'd come looking for you. He left a nice blood trail for me to follow so I would come deep into this building and get you all. I'm betting he had sensors and cameras and all sorts of things rigged to watch me. So he knew the minute I arrived. That was the minute that he probably gave the order for this place to blow."

Julian sidled closer. "Uh, to blow?"

Luke nodded. "Reason two, you see. You were all loose ends. *I* was a loose end, too. If we all die in the explosion that's about to happen, then Garrick walks away scot free." He now had Eli over his shoulder, and one hand clamped on Julian's arm. "Not happening, by the way."

Leo was already hurtling straight up, going through the ceiling, making a nice exit hole as he dragged Timothy up and out with him. Luke's wings fluttered and he shot into the air, following fast.

The explosion rocked beneath him seconds later. One explosion, another, then another…The rush of flames raced after them as the building itself seemed to erupt. The heat surrounded him but he just flew faster. Harder.

And Garrick's grand plan? Not very effective. *Try harder next time, you sonofabitch. And don't ever use fire against a dragon.*

Luke flew back to his island. He dropped off Eli right next to a stunned looking Rayce.

"As many whiskeys as you want," Eli promised him quickly. "*Forever.*"

Leo lowered Timothy onto the ground. The guy looked queasy. Humans never seemed to adjust well to paranormal speed.

Luke pointed at the agent. "Rayce, don't let him out of your sight. We'll need this one later."

"Right." The wolf nodded quickly. Then he cast a nervous glance at Leo.

"Are we fucking ready now?" Leo asked. "Or do we have a few more dozen pit stops you want to make while McAdams gets away?"

My, my. Someone was getting pissy.

Luke still had a strong grip on Julian. Ignoring his brother's fury, Luke said, "I'll take you to your vampire." Someone should get a fucking happy ending.

It sure wasn't going to be him.

But then, it wouldn't be Garrick, either. That man wasn't going to ever get a happy ending.

Instead, he'd just get a slow death. Luke's wings spread wide and —

"Wait!" Timothy yelled.

Luke glanced at him.

"He's…he's on the boat because he's going after *her*."

Luke felt his blood begin to ice.

"Garrick McAdams has always been obsessed with Mina James. He can't let her go." Timothy was speaking fast, the words coming out rapid-fire. "When he had that collar designed, he made it to include a tracking device because he never wanted to lose her again."

Luke's jaw had locked. He forced it to unclench as he gritted, "I destroyed the collar."

"But not until *after* the Ori had already deployed its stinger. The tracker was attached to the stinger. The tracker is *in* her. I heard Garrick talking to Madeline when they tied me up…he had Mina's signal. He was going out on the boat because he was getting her. He isn't going to stop, not until he has her again. I don't…I don't think he *can* stop."

Luke's gaze jerked to the ocean. Mina was out there and she was being…*hunted?* No. *No.*

"The boss you're after—the man in charge of all the agents—he was the one bringing the boat." Timothy's shoulders sagged. "Now I know why they were saying all that stuff in front of me.

They were sure I'd be dead and you'd never learn about any of this..."

But he knew everything now. *Garrick and the mysterious boss are together. Time to end them both.*

He flew into the air and the shift swept over him again. Soon it wasn't a man's hand holding tightly to Julian. Instead, a dragon's talons curled around his friend. Fast, faster he flew and the ocean blurred beneath him.

If Garrick hurt Mina again...if that bastard dared to touch her...

I will pry the flesh from his body.

CHAPTER EIGHTEEN

A boat was approaching her, moving so fast and leaving a giant wake in its trail. She stared at it, her eyes narrowing. So strange...she could recognize a boat but she couldn't remember her own name. When she tried to see her past, her head ached. A fog seemed to settle around her mind, and the ocean would pull her in deeper as if saying...*Don't worry about that. It doesn't matter. Only the moment matters.*

But when she'd heard the growl of that boat's engine, curiosity had pulled her up. She almost felt as if she were looking for...

Something.

Someone?

Now her eyes raked over the boat. A large vessel but...

Not the one.

The name of this boat was *Seaman's Journey.* That...didn't seem right to her. *It's not the boat I was looking for. It's the wrong one.* Not a prize at all.

But...why would she be looking for a boat?

She started to ease beneath the water.

"Mina!"

The cry carried easily over the water.

"Mina, I know you're here! *Mina!*" There was so much desperation in the man's voice and…

That's my name. My name is Mina. Certainty filled her. It should have made her feel good to at least have that — a name — but she was suddenly very afraid.

That big boat was closer to her now. She didn't want the man calling out to find her. Every instinct she possessed screamed at her that he wasn't the right man.

Then who is?

Mina turned away and her tail splashed the water as she headed beneath the sea.

***

"There is no way Mina James is out here." Madeline stood with her hands on her hips, glaring at the water. "We're sixty miles from shore. Yeah, I get that the woman is a good swimmer and all…" She lifted a brow as she turned to Garrick. "But no one is this good."

"The signal is tracking right here." Frustration seethed through his blood. He was staring at his control panel and the damn thing showed Mina. She was — "Moving," he snapped out. "Fast." Exceptionally fast. Too fast. "Turn this boat around!" Garrick bellowed, but then…

No, I have a better idea.

"Stop!" His voice thundered out.

"Turn the boat around, stop — why don't you try making up your mind?" Madeline muttered.

His gaze raked over her. She was increasingly getting on his nerves. Maybe she wouldn't be making it back to the mainland. If the boss weren't on board, he would go ahead and just shoot the woman. But since the fellow *was* there, Garrick had to play things a bit more carefully.

Later, he'd kill her.

The captain stopped the boat.

"Shut off the engine," Garrick ordered. He rubbed his throat. That damn panther had bit him, but luckily, the freak had been stopped before he did any permanent damage. Excitement had Garrick's heart drumming in his chest. He could still see Mina's signal, moving fast away from them. But soon enough, she'd be turning around. She'd be coming straight to him. "And bring up the coffin."

Two men on his right — newer agents — turned and hurried to obey.

Madeline tilted her head. "What are you planning?"

He smiled at her. "I know Mina's weakness." And he'd use it against her. "She didn't have the heart for killing." That was why she'd run from him. She hadn't liked doing what needed to be done. She'd been too soft on the inside. "She can't watch others suffer."

Understanding lit Madeline's eyes. "Bait."

"I do enjoy using it." His chest puffed out a bit. He was ninety-nine percent sure that his last baited plan had gone off without a hitch. He'd seen Luke Thorne in the security feeds right before that Naval Air Station had been blown to bits. *Try to come back from that one, you bastard.* His boss was on the radio right then, talking down below as he got his contacts to spread the word that there had just been a training accident at the station. No terrorist attack or anything like that. Nothing for the public to fear. His boss was very good at PR cover-ups.

And I'm good at making traps. This time, he'd use the perfect bait to lure Mina to him.

"Aren't you a bit curious about how she can swim so fast?" Madeline asked.

He was. He'd learn that secret, once he had her on the boat. But first, he had to get sweet Mina to turn around and swim *toward* him.

The two agents were returning, a coffin in their hands. It wasn't a wooden coffin because that would have been too easy for the vamp to break. Like the cell that had housed her in Key West, this coffin was made of very special glass. He could see the battered vamp inside. She was weak, and wounded, but still alive.

For the moment, anyway. He figured it was a good thing that his boss had seemed to lose interest in her of late. This way, the guy wouldn't mind if she had to endure just a bit more pain.

"Put her down right here." Garrick pointed to the edge of the boat.

The agents complied, and they held the coffin upright so that he could stare at the vampire's face. A fairly attractive face, though she was far too thin. Starvation would do that to a woman.

"I need your help," he said, knowing she could hear him perfectly.

Her eyes narrowed with hate. She was out in the sunlight, but she wasn't burning or anything, and it wasn't because of the glass. Since acquiring Rose, he'd learned that old story about sunlight burning vamps? Total myth. And it was actually fairly easy to *kill* a vamp. The only problem was that they had a tendency to come back from death.

"There's someone in the water that I need, and you're going to bring her to me." He thought it was kind to explain what was happening.

But Rose closed her eyes, effectively trying to shut him out.

He tapped on the glass. "These holes let air in to you." Because she needed to breathe. He'd learned that when he accidentally suffocated her one day. But then, she'd come back hours later. At first, the boss had been furious about her death. But when the guy had realized that she just came back, he'd stared at her differently. "These same holes will let water in, too," Garrick added. "Sorry, Rose, but you're about to drown."

Her eyes flew open. Terror was in those depths.

"Relax. It's not as if you won't wake up again, eventually." He nodded toward the agents. "Toss her overboard."

Her mouth opened in a scream.

The coffin flew toward the water.

***

Mina stilled when she heard the splash. She heard it and actually felt the vibration in the water. She turned back and saw that something had fallen over the side of that boat. Something that was slowly sinking down into the water.

She started to swim away but...

She turned back. She had to see what was happening. Curiosity compelled her.

As she neared, Mina saw a woman, struggling frantically, pushing her hands out against—*wait, she's trapped in some kind of box.* Mina hadn't even noticed the box at first because it was clear, like glass. But now she could see that the big box was filling with the water and the woman inside was utterly terrified. Mina's eyes widened in shock and she surged forward, whipping her tail against the water. She reached that box in seconds and her hands slapped against the glass. She stared into the woman's frightened gaze. The woman was shouting, but there was no way to make out her words. Mina couldn't understand her, but she could see the flash of—of fangs? Yes, fangs as the woman's mouth opened and her face contorted with fear.

She should conserve her energy and air. She won't have long.

Mina pounded against that glass again. It wouldn't break beneath her fists so she swam down and tried to lift up the big box. Her tail shoved hard against the water but the box was so heavy she couldn't lift it.

Why is she in the box? What's happening?

There were more splashes in the water. Mina looked around, startled, and saw that men in scuba suits were coming toward her. Maybe they could help the woman in the box.

But they had...guns. No, not guns, not exactly. The shape was wrong. Spear guns? *Yes.* They were staring at her in shock and they weren't helping the terrified woman. Mina motioned desperately toward that odd, glass box.

One of the men fired. His spear came right at Mina. It sank into the side of her tail and her lips parted as agony pierced her. Another man threw a net around her and he started hauling her away from the box.

They didn't seem to care about the trapped woman. They were focused just on...*catching me.*

Mina struggled desperately, but she couldn't get out of the net. And the woman in the box was sinking ever deeper. The divers didn't even look back at her. They just left the woman, and they took Mina toward the surface.

She broke the surface of the water, screaming, "Help her! *Help her!*" But no one paid her any attention. She was hauled out of the water — still bound in that net — and tossed onto the boat. She sprawled hard on the old wooden deck, her body shaking and her tail bleeding.

A woman's voice cried out, "Dear God, what *is* she?"

Mina's head turned to the right. A redhead stared at her in horrified fascination. *I should know her.* The knowledge whispered through her, but the woman's identity was just beyond Mina's grasp.

Another man came forward, the sun glinting off his blond hair. He reached for her, and Mina flinched, but he was just removing the net. He stared at her with wide hazel eyes, and then he smiled. "You are so perfect."

He was staring at her as if he'd just been given the best prize in the world. And he utterly terrified her.

"There's a woman in the water," Mina whispered. "You need to help her."

He just waved that away. "Mina, I am never letting you go."

Her tail...it was feeling funny, and not just because of the spear still in the side of it. She looked down and saw that her scales weren't shining quite as brightly. "What's happening?" She looked back up at the man. "Who are you?"

Surprise flashed on his face then. "You don't know?"

She knew her instincts were screaming he was someone bad. But—

"I'm the man you love, Mina." His smile was incredibly tender. "And the man you'd do anything for."

He was a liar. "Help the woman in the box."

He knelt next to Mina. "Will your legs come back, the longer you're out of the water?"

Her legs?

"I can't believe you held this wonderful secret from me." His hand curled under her chin. "Mina, Mina, Mina...what else have you been holding back?"

Her lips trembled. "H-help the woman in the box."

"Forget her. If she's not already dead, she will be."

Monster. The word burst into her head. *He's a monster.* She shoved at his hand and tried to flee, but she couldn't move with her tail. She could only flop there, trapped, while they all stared at her. The monster — he stared at her with lust in his eyes. The others stared at her as if she were some sort of freak. And the redheaded woman was even touching the gun at her side, as if she were thinking about shooting Mina.

"Help me," Mina begged.

The monster smiled. "We'll help each other, Mina. You'll come back with me and together we will do amazing things."

No. They wouldn't. *"Help me!"* Mina screamed because she was trapped. Helpless. Afraid.

The monster laughed. "What? Do you think Luke Thorne is going to magically appear? Do you think he'll hear your screams? He's dead, Mina. I killed him. There's no one left to care about what happens to you. No one, but me."

Luke Thorne.

That one name pierced through her, driving far deeper than the spear had.

Who is Luke?

Luke.

Luke…

The sky seemed to darken overhead.

Her heart was hurting. Tears were streaming down her cheeks. *I killed him.* Mina shook her head and suddenly, some of the heavy fog that had seemed to fill her head — suddenly, it lifted.

In her mind, Mina saw a man sitting at an old, faded bar. He had dark hair and a face built for sin. He was drinking a dark amber liquid. His head turned toward her and a faint smile lifted his lips.

Luke.

She saw him again, only he was in the middle of some kind of cell. His face was furious as he yelled for her to run.

Luke.

And she saw him again. Dark hair mussed. Eyes bright with passion as he stared down at her. In that memory, they were in his bed. He was making love to her and she—

She'd been so happy. With Luke.

"He's not dead," Mina whispered. *Luke.* She kept repeating his name in her head like a mantra and every single time that she thought of him, the fog that had shrouded her memories dissipated a bit more.

I'm Mina and he's Luke.

"Luke got blasted to bits, darling. Trust me. He's gone."

Mina looked up. She saw the shadows above them. Not shadows, though, not really. Just big, dark dragon wings. "You can't kill the Lord of the Dark." She glanced back at the monster. *Garrick. I remember you now, too.* "But he will kill you."

Fear flashed on Garrick's face. He looked up, too, and then she saw the terror race across his face.

That was good. He *should* be terrified. Because Luke was going to kick his ass.

"Fire at him!" Garrick bellowed at the agents around him. "Shoot that bastard out of the sky!"

They grabbed for their guns and started firing. Mina screamed, loud, lost, desperate—

And time seemed to freeze.

Glass burst all around her—every bit of glass on the ship just shattered. The men—and even the redheaded woman—screamed. They dropped their guns and immediately covered their ears.

Mina heard her own scream echoing around her. It seemed to linger in the air, hanging there as the others dropped to their knees in apparent suffering.

"Stop...her..." The redhead—*Madeline. I remember you now.* "Stop her from...screaming...her screams...*hurt!*"

Garrick put his hands around Mina's throat. He started squeezing. Her screams were cut off as she choked. Her hands flew up, punching at him, but he just tightened his grip. "When you...pass out..." he rasped. "I'll stop."

What?

But then there were more screams. Only they weren't coming from her this time. Over Garrick's shoulder, she saw that the dragon had landed. In a flash, the beast vanished and Luke was in the form of a man. Julian was with him, and the shifter's frantic gaze shot around the ship.

"Rose!" Julian bellowed. "Rose, where are you?"

Luke's twin was behind them, and he was causing the humans to scream as he punched them and tossed them overboard.

Dark spots danced before Mina's eyes.

"Welcome to hell." Luke's voice. Cold, brutal and —

Garrick was ripped away from her. In the same instant, a soft cloth wrapped around Mina's body. She'd been naked, but now she was covered with some sort of shirt that dipped over her shoulders and fell to her — well, to mid-way down her tail.

Her breath heaved in and out of her lungs as she slapped her hands against the ship's deck to steady herself. She looked up and saw that Luke held Garrick, only Luke's hand wasn't that of a man. His fingers were the talons of a dragon, and those talons were drawing blood as they tightened on Garrick's throat.

"What did I hear you say to *my* Mina?" Luke asked, tilting his head, his eyes glowing with power. "Right. *When you pass out, I'll stop.*" Blood flowed down Garrick's neck. "Guess what? I won't stop, not until you're dead."

She wanted to stand up and run to Luke, but tails weren't made for standing. She could only drag herself forward with her hands as she fought to get closer to him.

"I'll kill *her*," Madeline shrieked. "If you don't let him go, *now*, she's dead!"

Mina felt the barrel of the gun press to her temple.

Very slowly, Luke turned to look at Madeline. He didn't ease his grip on Garrick. Blood kept flowing from the struggling agent's neck. Mina realized that all of the other goons under Garrick's command were gone. Leo had tossed them all overboard. He'd even thrown the boat captain into the water. The only people on the deck were her, Luke, Leo, Garrick, Madeline, and Julian.

"*Where the fuck is Rose?*" Julian bellowed.

Madeline laughed. "That vamp is at the bottom of the ocean."

Julian didn't hesitate. He ran to the side of the boat and dove over the edge.

So then it was just Mina, Luke, Leo, Garrick and Madeline.

In a stand-off.

"You don't want her to die," Madeline said to Luke. "Because you're as freakishly obsessed with her as Garrick. So how about you don't play with me, hmmm? Let Garrick go. Then you—and your twin over there—you two get the hell away from me!"

Luke didn't let go of Garrick. "I'm not obsessed."

"Bullshit." Madeline jammed the barrel harder against Mina's temple. "Talk about men being led around by their cocks. She's a freaking *fish,* can you not see that? She's—"

"Mermaids have incredible power," Leo said softly. "That power draws others to them. Garrick is like the lost sailors of old. He saw her, wanted to possess a fantasy, and he decided that he would do anything to have her. He was driven by his own greed and lust. Mina did nothing to *make* him this way." He paused. "He's just a fucking screwed-up bastard, that's all."

And he was a bastard still held prisoner in Luke's grasp.

"I *will* blow her head open," Madeline yelled.

Slowly, Luke released Garrick. As soon as he was free, Garrick ran to Madeline's side. He put his hand to his throat, trying to stop the blood flow.

"I'm not obsessed," Luke said again. He straightened his shoulders and stared right at Mina. "I'm in love. There's a difference."

She couldn't breathe. He was...he loved her?

Luke. My Luke. How had she forgotten him, even for an instant? She could *never* allow that to happen again.

"Give me the gun," Garrick snapped. "*Now, Madeline.*"

Madeline hesitated.

"He'll kill you if you do," Leo called out. "That's his plan, you know. To kill me, to kill Luke. Then to kill you. At that point, he thinks he'll be left with the lovely Mina."

"But we're not easy to kill," Luke growled the words.

The boat rocked in the water. Mina's tail seemed to burn.

"Who is your boss?" Luke asked. He was staring at Madeline. "Who gives the orders? And where the hell is the bastard? Because I was told he should be on this boat. Is he hiding? Like a coward?"

"Tell him *nothing*," Garrick ordered in the next breath. "Give me the gun — or just shoot the bastards yourself! You're still using the bullets I gave you, right? You still have them?"

"Yes," Madeline said. But she didn't give him the gun. She didn't aim at Luke or Leo. She kept the gun shoved to Mina's head.

"Who do you work for?" Luke's voice was low, deep.

Madeline laughed. "I work for the U.S. government. We know all about the paranormals, and we're going to use them to make sure we have the best weapons in the world."

"We aren't weapons," Mina whispered because a broken whisper was all she could manage then, thanks to Garrick's strangulation of her. "We're people."

"No, you're not. Even the vampire's brother knows that. Rose's brother was the one to create our unit. *Operation Night Switch.* ONS. He's the one who found out about the beasts out there. He's the one who organized us. He's the one who told us your weaknesses."

Vampire's brother. Rose. The woman in the box. Mina had seen the flash of her fangs.

"Madeline, quiet!" Garrick grabbed for her, yanking the gun right out of her hand.

Finally, Mina was free. Madeline and Garrick were fighting over the weapon so she used that moment to her advantage. Her tail flashed out and slammed into their legs. Both Madeline and Garrick fell hard, tumbling onto the deck. The gun flew from their fingers and skittered across the bow.

Take that, assholes.

"Get her back in the water!" Leo bellowed. "Her tail is burning—she needs to go back in! You get her and I'll take care of the humans!"

Yes, Leo was right. Her tail was burning. It *hurt* as if she were drying out or something.

Luke scooped her into his arms and rushed with her to the side of the vessel.

"Stop." Mina stared up at him. Luke. His face was so hard and handsome. His eyes—*I could get lost in them.* "I don't want to leave you."

He was on the edge of that ship, his arms tight around her.

"I couldn't even remember you moments before." Fear flashed through her. "Why? What happened to me?"

His expression was tender as he stared down at her. "That's the way it is for your kind, love. You know only joy. That's why you are one of Leo's creatures. There is no pain or darkness in your world. Mermaids know happiness so the ocean takes away all other memories. No more flashes of pain or regret. The ocean comforts you by only letting you live in the moment."

Her arms tightened around him. She didn't like the sound of that. "I don't mind my pain." She needed him to understand this. "I would take any pain to stay with you."

Torment flashed on his face. "Mina…"

"You are joy for me." As impossible as it sounded, her words were true. The Lord of the Dark made her happy. "I don't want to forget again. I *can't* forget."

"You're meant for more than me. I will destroy you if you stay with me."

Mina shook her head. He was wrong.

"Your kind can't live without the ocean. It's your breath. Your life's blood. Look at your own mother. She couldn't survive without it. She had to leave *you*. If I try to keep you with me, the same thing will happen. The water will keep calling to you. It will drive you mad." He bent and pressed a kiss to her lips. "That can't happen. I can't *let* it happen. You will be happy. I swear, you will be." He lowered her until she was in front of him. "Good-bye, Mina."

No, no, he *couldn't* do this.

She grabbed his hand, held tight. "*I love you.*"

His eyes widened. Her fingers were around his, and she felt heat lance her from the Eye of Hell.

And then a gunshot blasted. She saw shock register on his face...shock and pain and then...

He let her go. She scrambled, her fingers sliding over his, reaching frantically for him, but it was too late. She clawed at him, trying to stay—

I don't want to forget! I want to be with you!

And right before she fell into the water, Mina yanked the burning-hot Eye of Hell right off his hand.

CHAPTER NINETEEN

He'd been shot in the back.

Only a coward shot another man in the back. A bastard attacked when another's back was turned.

For an instant, Luke wondered if he'd truly been duped by Leo. Had his brother been working with the humans all along, waiting for this one moment when Luke had been distracted? Because it wasn't an ordinary bullet that had burrowed near Luke's spine. He didn't think it had been a bullet at all.

There had been a blast when it fired but…

He reached around and yanked the arrow from his back. *An arrow, not a bullet.* Slowly, he turned to face the threat.

He saw Leo, eyes wide with shock. Leo had one of his hands on Garrick's throat and his other hand was around Madeline's shoulder.

He didn't fire. Leo had been too busy with the humans.

Luke looked to the left, to the little stairway that led below deck. A man stood there, a man with dark hair and bright green eyes. A man holding a crossbow. *A loaded crossbow.*

"Do you remember me?" the man asked.

No, Luke had no fucking clue who the guy was. He was about to reply, but the poison in that arrow had seeped into his spine. Luke's legs gave way and he fell to his knees.

Leo didn't fire, but the arrows are his. They are poison itself, death to dragons.

As Luke slumped, the mysterious man turned the crossbow on Leo. "I came to you," the stranger continued, voice almost wooden. "Begging for your help. You were supposed to give my sister back to me, but you said there was *nothing* you could do."

Leo stared at him in shock. "Michael? Michael Kinley? Y-you're Rose's brother. She was a vampire. Dark, so I had no dominion over what happened to—"

"I *begged* you, but you wouldn't help her. And soon I realized what had to be done. You were right. She was no longer the woman I'd known. She was dark, a weapon to be used."

Fucking hell. Luke clenched his teeth against the agony rolling through him. He had to push the poison from his system. Unfortunately, that wasn't the fastest process. It literally had to bleed out from his pores.

"I'll use her, I'll use Mina James, I'll use every paranormal that I find. They will be my weapons." The dark-haired man smiled. *Michael. Leo had called him Michael.* "I will be the one to rule. You and your twisted twin? You're both done. Hope you enjoy hell."

And he sent an arrow hurtling toward Leo.

Leo shoved Madeline aside and he yanked Garrick in front of him.

Luke roared his fury as the arrow sank into Garrick's chest. *That kill should have been mine!*

Garrick sucked in a deep breath, then his body stiffened. He was dead instantly. No human could ever last against that paranormal poison.

In the next moment, Michael had another arrow cocked and ready to go. He fired even as Leo lunged toward him. This time, the arrow hit Leo in the shoulder.

But it didn't stop him.

He lurched forward.

Michael sent another arrow straight at him. At the last moment, Leo dodged and that arrow sank into his side.

His brother fell then, slamming into the deck, taken down as the poison seeped through his body.

Michael laughed. "I know your weakness." His gaze slid to Luke. "Same weakness for both of you. When I was begging Leo for help, I took the liberty of stealing some arrows from him. Since he wouldn't help me, I knew I'd be paying him back." He shrugged one shoulder. "It took some time to get my group of agents up and running. Took some time to get all of my game pieces in place, but I found I could be patient." He aimed another arrow at Luke.

Luke was still kneeling on the deck. The poison held him immobile. He would stay that way for a few more moments, until his body pushed the nasty brew out of his system.

Provided I don't take an arrow to the heart in the meantime, I'll survive.

Leo hadn't even noticed a human had stolen the most powerful weapons imaginable from him. Why? Because the guy was too damn trusting where they were concerned. He'd always been so convinced that Luke and his kind were the darkest threats out there. *How does it feel to be wrong, brother?*

A glance at his slumped brother provided Luke with the answer. *Not very good.*

Luke huffed out a breath and tried to keep Michael's attention focused on him. "You…used your own sister…"

"Don't look at me like that. You're the one who made Rose into a monster. She was a human before. You should *never* have touched her."

Luke remembered Rose all too well. She'd been a human once before, that was true. But she'd been a human loved by a very powerful supernatural.

Julian had loved her. And even then, Julian was beneath the waves, searching desperately for her. He was—

"*You fucking bastard.*" Julian's voice. He'd just climbed onto the boat and water poured off him. He held Rose in his arms, but she didn't seem to be moving. "*Michael.* You did this?"

Michael jerked the crossbow toward Julian. "No, *you* did this. By taking something that never should have belonged to you!" He fired. Julian held Rose in his arms so he twisted his body, turning to protect her.

The arrow sank into his shoulder. He bellowed in pain.

"Time to kill you all," Michael shouted. "Good thing I have the perfect weapon." He smiled. "Patience is truly its own reward." He advanced toward Leo.

***

Mina sank beneath the waves. The water surrounded her, comforted her. Her tail swayed beneath her and a slow joy began to seep through her veins.

She should swim, fast and far away.

She should…

She had something in her hand.

Mina's fingers unfurled, just a bit, and she saw the ring.

Big and heavy and oddly warm.
Luke.

His name flashed through her. She saw his
image in her mind. She looked back up, seeing
the bottom of a boat above her head. Luke was
up there. He'd been hurt right before she sank
beneath the waves.

Mina shoved the Eye of Hell onto her ring
finger, and, strangely, it seemed to fit. The band
tightened around her finger and Mina swam
straight up, heading for that boat. She wasn't
leaving Luke. The Lord of the Dark needed her,
and she was going to be there for him. She would
always be there for him.

She broke through the surface. "*Luke!*" She
grabbed the edge of the boat and hauled herself
up. Her tail was dragging her back down.
Dammit. "I need legs." She pressed the Eye to her
tail. "*I need legs. Take away the tail. I don't want to be
this way.*" Luke had said the Eye wouldn't work
for her, but a desperate woman would try
anything and—

Her tail vanished. Pain lanced through her,
white-hot and electrifying as her scales seemed to
melt away. The agony was excruciating and tears
poured down her cheeks.

But...

Then the pain turned into only a throb. Her
legs were back. *I'm back.* Mina laughed, even as

she cried, and she heaved herself up over the side of the boat. "Luke, Luke, I'm back—"

And she was apparently in the middle of a stand-off.

Mina froze. She still had on the long shirt that she figured Luke had conjured for her before, a shirt that fell to the middle of her thighs. Luke was on his knees, his gaze desperate as he stared at her. Quickly, her eyes swept the scene, taking in everyone and everything.

Garrick was on the deck, not moving. Dead?

Madeline was huddled near the ship's wheel, her eyes massive and her face frozen in a mask of fear.

Julian was slumped near an unmoving woman. *The woman who'd been in the glass box. The box that had sank in the ocean.*

And Leo—Leo was on his back. Some guy with a cross-bow stood over him, ready to fire.

"Stop!" Mina yelled.

The guy's head turned toward her. He blinked. "You should be gone."

She had no idea who he was.

"Mina James." He smirked at her. "Failed experiment. Too weak. Too soft." His head cocked. "Guess what, Mina? I'm the man who gave the order for your capture. I'm the man who ordered all of that wonderful pain inflicted on you. I'm Michael Kinley, and I'm the man who created Operation Night Switch. I'm the man who—"

"You're the man who is going to die." Mina sucked in a quick breath. Her voice wasn't hoarse any longer. Her throat didn't ache from Garrick's hands. She felt powerful. Stronger than ever before. Because of the Eye? Maybe. Right then, she didn't really care why. "Listen to me, and listen well…"

He blinked. His gaze seemed to go hazy. "What…? Stop!" He was raising the cross bow and trying to aim it at her.

Mina wasn't going to let that happen. "You won't fire the weapon."

He froze.

"You won't shoot at me. You won't shoot at Luke." She braced her feet. "You'll surrender to us. Then you will *never* hurt any paranormal again."

He was sweating. "You…*bitch.*"

"Drop the cross-bow."

She saw the strain on his face, but he was helpless. She was injecting every bit of power that she had into her voice. Every single bit and for once, she wasn't afraid of her magic. She gloried in it.

This man had hurt Luke. He'd hurt her. He'd hurt *countless* others. But he wouldn't do it any longer. He'd stop.

She'd stop him.

He dropped the cross bow, but then he laughed. "You think I'm the only one? There are others out there, others who are helping me. You might stop me, but they'll keep going. We have dozens of paranormals imprisoned right now. Shifters, muses, witches…we will use them all. It's bigger than me now. Bigger than anything. It won't be stopped. *I won't be stopped.*"

"Yes, you will." Mina eased out a slow breath. "Jump into the water." She pointed to her side. "Come here and jump in."

He walked toward her. She saw the sweat on his brow. He was right at her side, almost at the edge of the boat, when he yanked a knife from the holster at his hip. He swiped it right over her throat. Her eyes widened in shock because—no, she hadn't seen that coming.

She'd never expected…

Blood flew and Mina's hands shot up, trying to cover the terrible wound.

"I'm not Garrick," the man snapped. "I'm not obsessed with you. And I'm not that dumb ass over there…" He jerked his thumb toward Luke. "I don't love you. As far as I'm concerned, you're a waste of space."

Her gaze flew to Luke. She needed to see him, just one more time. Her Luke. Her—

He was changing. Shifting right before her eyes. The boat rocked and swayed beneath his weight because the dragon was immense. He opened his mouth—

"Hell is hot, Michael." The dragon spoke with Luke's deep, dark voice. "Ready to feel the flames?"

And he let his fire loose, sending it right over Michael. The human screamed and Mina closed her eyes, not able to bear that terrible sight as he burned.

Her throat hurt. Her body shook, and Mina knew her end was coming, too. Strange, but she wasn't afraid.

She was sad, though.

There were so many things that she wished she could have done. A whole life that she wished she'd been able to lead.

She heard a terrible crack. The boat shuddered beneath her. She tried to open her eyes, to glance around her. She saw that fire was everywhere and the vessel seemed to literally be breaking apart beneath the weight of her massive dragon.

Boats weren't made for beasts that size.

Her lips curled. He'd be her last sight, right before death. Because she was drowning right then, no, choking on her own blood.

"Get her!" Leo bellowed. "I'll get the others! *Hurry!*"

Why hurry? There was no time left. Mina knew that.

But the dragon lunged toward her. Its talons reached out for her, but it was Luke's hand that touched her. "You will not die."

There were some things that even the Lord of the Dark could not control.

"You will *not*, Mina." He scooped her into his arms and then they were flying, going high above the sea. She looked back and saw the boat sink beneath the churning waves. Smoke drifted up in the air.

The monsters were gone.

And she was dead.

***

"Heal her!" Luke roared.

Mina was in his bed, her beautiful throat sliced open and her blood soaking his sheets. His useless dumb ass of a brother just stood beside him, a lost expression on his face.

"Don't just stand there!" Luke snarled at him. "Heal her! She can't hold on forever!" It was a miracle that he'd gotten home with her.

But then...Mina was a miracle. His miracle. His life. His everything.

And she won't die. I won't watch her die.

"I *tried* to heal her." Leo put his hands on Mina's throat. "I'm trying again now, but it's not working. Something has changed. I *can't* fix her."

"She's a mermaid! That makes her one of yours—you have to be able to heal her!" Shit, shit, shit! She was too pale. She was ice cold to the touch. And in moments, she'd be *gone.*

Leo pulled back his blood-stained hand. "There is nothing I can do."

No, that wasn't true. "You hold dominion over all the creatures of the light."

Leo's mouth thinned. "Perhaps she isn't light, not any longer."

"What?"

Leo pointed to Mina's slender hand. "I thought you were the only one who could wield the Eye."

He…was. But the Eye was on Mina's delicate ring finger. When had she gotten it? He struggled to remember. He'd been putting her back into the sea. She'd grabbed his hand. *Tricky Mina, did you finally steal my Eye?*

"You used the Eye on her?" Leo asked, shaking his head. "If you did, you know that changes things. It will change *her.*"

He hadn't used it on her. But…

Luke shoved Leo out of his way. Luke put his hand to Mina's throat and he poured every single bit of his power into that touch. "You will heal."

And he felt it. The transfer of power, of magic, from him to her. A dark shadow hovered over his hand and then sank down into Mina's neck. Her eyes flew open as she gave a desperate gasp.

"Holy fucking hell," Leo said, stunned. "That worked."

Mina stared at Luke with — with love in her eyes. Not fear. Not pain. Not shock.

"I've been…looking for you," she said, her voice husky and weak. "For a long time."

And I've been searching forever for you, love.

Carefully, he lifted his hand from her throat. The wound had closed. His head sagged forward and his eyes squeezed closed as relief swept through him. He felt wetness on his cheeks. Dammit, *dammit.* "You will *not* come that close to death ever again." He grabbed her hand and pressed it to his wet cheek. That was when he felt the Eye of Hell, hot with power against him.

Stunned, he eased back. His eyes opened and he stared down at the ring. It grew hotter only when it was wielded.

"Mina, did you use the Eye?" Afraid again, he looked up at her.

"I had to get to you." She smiled at him. His beautiful Mina. His every waking dream. "I know…you said it wouldn't work…but I had to try…"

"What did you try? What did you do?"

"I couldn't get on the boat with my tail." She frowned, a faint furrow between her brows. "So I wished that I wouldn't be that way. I wished the tail would go away."

He felt Leo's hand clamp down on his shoulder. The guy squeezed him, hard. "She traded her tail for you."

Just like the mermaid from legend. She'd traded for a man who didn't deserve her. And the damn Eye of Hell, it had greedily accepted her trade.

But why? Only Luke should have been able to control the Eye. It did what *he* wanted, and only him and—

And the Eye knows what I want. It's part of me.

He wanted Mina. He wanted her with him, always. And when he'd been putting her back into the water, hadn't he thought that? That he wanted her to stay?

I wanted it to be her choice.

"What did I do?" Luke whispered, nearly hating himself in that moment. He'd tried to do the right thing, but deep down, he was just a selfish bastard. He'd wanted Mina with him, forever, and now she'd lost her chance to be free. If her tail was gone, then she would never be able to transform again. She would be trapped forever as a...

As what?

On the boat, her voice had still compelled. She'd made Michael do just as she'd bid. And Luke had just been able to heal her.

Only two beings could control with their voices. Mermaids and sirens.

Mermaids were of the light. But sirens...

His eyes opened. He stared into Mina's eyes. *She is mine.*

He was the Lord of the Dark. He ruled all within his dominion, but Mina...He bent to his knees beside the bed. He would bow to her. He would do *anything* for her.

Even spend eternity making up for his selfishness. His dark powers had turned her into the one thing she'd feared being.

"Luke, what's wrong?" Mina asked him, her words tight with worry. "Tell me what's happening."

And he told her, not because of any power or compulsion but just because there was nothing he would not give her. "The ring is tuned to me, Mina. I told you that before. It's a ring of darkness. You couldn't have wielded it, not on your own, but selfish bastard that I am...my deepest desire was for you to stay with me." He stared into her eyes and knew she'd see him for the monster that he was. "The ring knew that. So when you made your wish, when you said you wanted the tail gone...it transformed you."

"Into what?" Her voice was a whisper.

"I think you know."

Her long lashes lowered. "A siren."

"Yes." Pain knifed through him.

"I won't be able to go back to the water."

He shook his head. "I'm…sorry." It would have been easier to just cut out his own heart because—

"I'm glad." Her lashes lifted. She smiled at him. *Smiled.* "The water made me forget who I was. The way it felt down there—that wasn't real. That wasn't what I wanted." Her smile dimmed. "If being a mermaid means the only joy you really know is in the ocean, then I don't want to live that way. My mother forgot her own daughter—how is that joy? That…that's hell to me." Her hand lifted and her fingers smoothed over his cheek. "Want to know what heaven is?"

He was staring at heaven.

"It's being with you. I knew something big was missing from my world even when my mind was trapped in that fog. *You* were missing, Luke. I need you." She caught his hand in hers and brought his fingers to her lips. Carefully, she pressed a kiss to his hand as he knelt by the bed. "I love you."

His whole body tensed. "Say it again."

Leo cleared his throat. "Uh, yeah, this scene is getting a little, um, personal. I think I'll just step outside. There's a vamp and a panther that I need to speak with anyway so I'll just be seeing myself out." His footsteps shuffled toward the door.

Luke didn't look at him. There would be time — later — to deal with his brother. To deal with the prophecy of destruction that was foretold for them both.

There would be time to change fate.

My fate is changing already. The Lord of the Dark wasn't supposed to have a soul. He wasn't supposed to love.

But he did. He loved completely. Deeply. Eternally.

"I love you," Mina said even as the door clicked closed behind Leo.

Luke stayed on his knees. "I will give my world to you, if you just stay with me. I know you don't want to be a siren, I know —"

"Being a siren means I *can* stay with you." Her smile came again. "Being a siren means I can have the man who makes me happy. You're what I want. Together, I know we'll control my power. I won't hurt anyone."

Because even though she had powers born of darkness, his Mina was still good. *She* was his soul. His balance.

"When you swam away from me before," Luke said, needing her to know this, "I wanted to give you a better life. A life not tied to someone like me —"

But she shook her head. "The only life I want is with you. How many times do I have to say it? I love you."

He was supposed to be *unlovable.* Without redemption. Without hope. But Mina...

Mina saw past his monster. She didn't fear his beast. She was the one woman who didn't care about the sins around him. She looked deeper.

And she gave him a reason to *be* better. "And I love you." He pitied any fool who *ever* tried to take her from him again.

The last man who'd tried was nothing more than ash. Luke knew the tale of exactly what had transpired on that ship would spread. Any enemies he had would know what fate waited for them...*If they ever so much as think of hurting her.*

He leaned forward and his lips pressed to hers. A careful, delicate kiss.

But she put her hand to his chest.

Instantly, he stopped. "Mina?"

"I'm covered in blood. Most of it is mine and that just isn't sexy."

He stared at her a moment, frowning, and then...Luke laughed. "You did it again."

Her brows rose.

He stood and hoisted her into his arms.

"Did what?"

"Surprised me. Charmed me. I warned you about that." He pressed another kiss to her lips as he carried her into the bathroom. "When you do that, it just makes me want you more."

He turned on the shower. Stripped them both with his magic and soon had her — naked — under the warm stream of water. With tender care, he cleaned her body. He touched her skin so gently.

And he kept kissing her. Luke tried to show her that he could have restraint. He could hold back.

"Oh, Luke, I want *you.*" Her voice was silken with temptation now. "I want you rough, I want you wild, and I want you dark."

He stilled.

Her smile — the one that was purest sin — flashed. And her delectable dimples winked. "What makes you think I'd ever settle for anything less?"

You're doing it again, love. Enslaving me.

But he gave her what they both wanted. He pinned her wrists to the shower wall with one hand, hoisting them high above her head. He lifted her hips with the other, positioned his full and aching cock at the entrance to her body, then Luke drove deep, sinking into her with one fierce thrust and loving the moan that he dragged from her.

He didn't go slowly. He wasn't tender. He was desperate. He was wild. He was *frantic* for her. Mina wasn't gone. She wasn't dead. She wasn't beyond his reach.

His Mina was just where he wanted her to be. In his arms. His cock buried deep in her body.

Their hearts pounding together in a furious rhythm. She was with him.

Mine.

Just as he would always be hers.

Each hard thrust raked over her clit. He knew she loved that. Her head tipped back and she arched against him. He bent and took her breast into his mouth, laving the nipple and lightly biting her. Her sex squeezed around him, so tight.

He thrust again. *Again*.

She came. He felt the pleasure rip through her as she cried out his name.

He was with her, tumbling over into that maelstrom of release, surging hard toward his climax. A climax that nearly gutted him with its power.

His breath heaved out of him as he held her. The water battered down on him and slowly, his head lifted. He stared into Mina's eyes.

I'll have her forever.

His heartbeat stuttered.

Mina tilted her head. "Luke, is everything all right?"

"No." He swallowed down the lump in his throat. "It's better." Truly, his heaven…she was right there. And he would *never* let her go again.

He freed her bound hands. The Eye of Hell glinted on her ring finger.

He pressed a kiss to Mina's lips as her hands pressed to his chest, and then Luke began to thrust again.

EPILOGUE

Leo walked down to the beach. The island was quite beautiful as the sun set. He could certainly see why Luke had sought refuge at that place. Far away from prying eyes. Quiet, peaceful.

He hadn't realized just how much peace had been missing from his life until that moment.

He heard the crunch of footsteps behind him and Leo squared his shoulders. Time for another battle. Why were there always so many battles to face?

But when he spun around, he didn't see a fragile vampire standing there. Rose wasn't waiting to face him. Instead, the panther shifter was there...and Julian Craig appeared quite pissed. Not particularly surprising, considering the things that had transpired.

"Her own *brother* was the one gunning for the paranormals?"

Leo lifted his chin. "Michael Kinley didn't take well to Rose's transformation."

Julian surged forward and his hands fisted on the shirt that Leo wore. "*I* was behind her transformation. I'm the one who begged Luke to bring her back—and making her into a vampire was the only way he could do it."

A boat's motor roared in the distance.

"It was my fault." A muscle jerked along Julian's jaw. "I did this. I hurt her. All I ever do is hurt her."

Frowning, Leo looked to the right. He saw Luke's boat racing through the water. Racing *away* from the island. "Tell me that Rose isn't on that boat."

"I can't be near her without causing Rose more pain."

Shit. The shifter was trying to be noble. Dark creatures weren't supposed to play that card. "Very bad mistake, panther." He rolled back his shoulders. He'd have to go and stop Rose. Or at least, try to stop her. He had a rule about not interfering with free will. He stepped away from Julian, intending to fly off—

But razor sharp claws sank into his shoulder. "You're not going anywhere. You're not hurting her, either. We've both done e-fucking-nough to Rose."

"On the contrary…" His gaze was still on the boat. "We'd both better haul ass. The danger to Rose isn't over."

Those claws dug deeper. "*What?*"

"Michael wasn't the only one after Rose. On the ship, he clearly said there were others at play. And…" This was going to be the tricky part. The part that just might cause the panther to slice him open. Leo braced for the pain. "I know of one very dangerous man in particular who would love nothing more than to add Rose to his collection."

Julian growled. A deep, inhuman sound. Only fitting, since he wasn't human.

Leo turned his head until he was staring into the shifter's glowing eyes. "I think we need to talk a bit more…" he murmured.

And then…they did.

THE END

###

Want to read Julian and Rose's story? Look for ON THE PROWL available September 13, 2016.

A NOTE FROM THE AUTHOR

Thank you so much for taking the time to read THE DEVIL IN DISGUISE. I hope that you enjoyed the story. I had an absolute blast writing Luke's tale. He was a very fun guy. I love starting a new series, and I think there will be lots of great paranormal characters to explore in the "Bad Things" world.

If you'd like to stay updated on my releases and sales, please join my newsletter list www.cynthiaeden.com/newsletter/. You can also check out my Facebook page www.facebook.com/cynthiaedenfanpage. I love to post giveaways over at Facebook!

Again, thank you for reading THE DEVIL IN DISGUISE. Stay tuned for the next book!

Best,

Cynthia Eden
www.cynthiaeden.com

ABOUT THE AUTHOR

Award-winning author Cynthia Eden writes dark tales of paranormal romance and romantic suspense. She is a *New York Times, USA Today, Digital Book World,* and *IndieReader* bestseller. Cynthia is also a three-time finalist for the RITA® award. Since she began writing full-time in 2005, Cynthia has written over fifty novels and novellas.

Cynthia is a southern girl who loves horror movies, chocolate, and happy endings. More information about Cynthia and her books may be found at: http://www.cynthiaeden.com or on her Facebook page at: http://www.facebook.com/cynthiaedenfanpage. Cynthia is also on Twitter at http://www.twitter.com/cynthiaeden.

HER WORKS

Paranormal Romance

Bad Things
- The Devil In Disguise (Bad Things, Book 1)
- Blood and Moonlight Series
- Bite The Dust (Blood and Moonlight, Book 1)
- Better Off Undead (Blood and Moonlight, Book 2)
- Bitter Blood (Blood and Moonlight, Book 3)

Purgatory Series
- The Wolf Within (Purgatory, Book 1)
- Marked By The Vampire (Purgatory, Book 2)
- Charming The Beast (Purgatory, Book 3)
- Deal with the Devil (Purgatory, Book 4)
- The Beasts Inside (Purgatory, Books 1-4)

Bound (Vampires/Werewolves) Series
- Bound By Blood (Bound Book 1)

- Bound In Darkness (Bound Book 2)
- Bound In Sin (Bound Book 3)
- Bound By The Night (Bound Book 4)
- Forever Bound (Bound Books 1-4)
- Bound in Death (Bound Book 5)

Night Watch Series
- Eternal Hunter (Night Watch Book 1)
- I'll Be Slaying You (Night Watch Book 2)
- Eternal Flame (Night Watch Book 3)

Phoenix Fire Series
- Burn For Me (Phoenix Fire, Book 1)
- Once Bitten, Twice Burned (Phoenix Fire, Book 2)
- Playing With Fire (Phoenix Fire, Book 3)

The Fallen Series
- Angel of Darkness (The Fallen Book 1)
- Angel Betrayed (The Fallen Book 2)
- Angel In Chains (The Fallen Book 3)
- Avenging Angel (The Fallen Book 4)

Midnight Trilogy
- Hotter After Midnight (Book One in the Midnight Trilogy)
- Midnight Sins (Book Two in the Midnight Trilogy)
- Midnight's Master (Book Three in the Midnight Trilogy)

Paranormal Anthologies
- A Vampire's Christmas Carol

Loved By Gods Series
- Bleed For Me

ImaJinn
- The Vampire's Kiss
- The Wizard's Spell

Other Paranormal
- Immortal Danger
- Never Cry Wolf
- A Bit of Bite
- Dark Nights, Dangerous Men

Romantic Suspense

LOST Series
- Broken (LOST, Book 1)
- Twisted (LOST, Book 2)
- Shattered (LOST, Book 3)
- Torn (LOST, Book 4)
- Taken (LOST, Book 5) - Available 11/29/2016

Dark Obsession Series
- Watch Me (Dark Obsession, Book 1)
- Want Me (Dark Obsession, Book 2)
- Need Me (Dark Obsession, Book 3)
- Beware Of Me (Dark Obsession, Book 4)

- Only For Me (Dark Obsession, Books 1 to 4)

Mine Series
- Mine To Take (Mine, Book 1)
- Mine To Keep (Mine, Book 2)
- Mine To Hold (Mine, Book 3)
- Mine To Crave (Mine, Book 4)
- Mine To Have (Mine, Book 5)
- Mine To Protect (Mine, Book 6)

Montlake - For Me Series
- Die For Me (For Me, Book 1)
- Fear For Me (For Me, Book 2)
- Scream For Me (For Me, Book 3)

Harlequin Intrigue - The Battling McGuire Boys
- Confessions (Battling McGuire Boys...Book 1)
- Secrets (Battling McGuire Boys...Book 2)
- Suspicions (Battling McGuire Boys...Book 3)
- Reckonings (Battling McGuire Boys...Book 4)
- Deceptions (Battling McGuire Boys...Book 5)
- Allegiances (Battling McGuire Boys...Book 6)

Harlequin Intrigue - Shadow Agents Series
- Alpha One (Shadow Agents, Book 1)

- Guardian Ranger (Shadow Agents, Book 2)
- Sharpshooter (Shadow Agents, Book 3)
- Glitter And Gunfire (Shadow Agents, Book 4)
- Undercover Captor (Shadow Agents, Book 5)
- The Girl Next Door (Shadow Agents, Book 6)
- Evidence of Passion (Shadow Agents, Book 7)
- Way of the Shadows (Shadow Agents, Book 8)

Deadly Series
- Deadly Fear (Book One of the Deadly Series)
- Deadly Heat (Book Two of the Deadly Series)
- Deadly Lies (Book Three of the Deadly Series)

Contemporary Anthologies
- Wicked Firsts
- Sinful Seconds
- First Taste of Darkness
- Sinful Secrets

Other Romantic Suspense
- Until Death
- Femme Fatale

Young Adult Paranormal

Other Young Adult Paranormal
- The Better To Bite (A Young Adult Paranormal Romance)

Anthologies

Contemporary Anthologies
- "All I Want for Christmas" in The Naughty List
- Sinful Seconds
- All He Wants For Christmas

Paranormal Anthologies
- "New Year's Bites" in A Red Hot New Year
- "Wicked Ways" in When He Was Bad
- "Spellbound" in Everlasting Bad Boys
- "In the Dark" in Belong to the Night
- Howl For It

48268668R00190

Made in the USA
Middletown, DE
14 September 2017